Reserved Indefinitely

Rhea Morrigan

Published by CleverQuill Publishing, Fiction Division

Printed in the United States of America.

EBOOK ISBN: 978-1-969012-05-1

PAPERBACK ISBN: 978-1-969012-06-8

The characters and events portrayed in this book are fictitious. Any similarity to real persons, living or dead, is coincidental and not intended by the author.

Adults Only Content Warning

This book contains explicit language, sexual content and adult situations that may be unsuitable for some readers.

Editor: EpochWriter
Cover Art: Rhea Morrigan

Dedication

To every deliciously curious reader holding this book right now: this is for you.

You could have picked a calm book. Maybe one with polite kisses, a cake recipe, and absolutely no scenes that make you blush in public. But no… You chose this. A story where the doors are not just open, they're practically flung off the hinges, and every chapter comes with a pulse-pounding combination of desire, danger and the occasional plot twist that makes you gasp loud enough to alarm your pets.

I dedicate this book to the part of you that loves trouble.

The part that says "one more chapter" and suddenly it's three in the morning, and you're emotionally involved with fictional people who do not, in fact, exist.

The part that secretly hopes the door will not fade to black at the good parts.

The part that wants banter like knives, kisses like confessions, and hands that do not know the meaning of "appropriate distance."

Consider this your official survival kit:

- A fan, for obvious reasons
- A snack, because nothing kills tension like hunger
- A reminder that it's totally fine to make questionable dating decisions… Well, maybe in fiction only.

To those who thrive on late-night reading binges, who whisper "just one more chapter" while it's three in the morning—this one's for you. You understand that a mystery is twice as intriguing when the clues come with undeniable chemistry.

Thanks for trusting me to make your heart race and your eyebrows rise. I won't waste a single beat. Or button. Stay hydrated, keep guessing and enjoy the ride.

With love, laughter and a touch of danger ~

Rhea Morrigan

Table of Contents

Acknowledgements

To **Raeann Blake**, creator of *The Seven Brothers of Elko* and enough standalone titles to fully stock a book-boyfriend harem: Thank you for encouraging me to keep writing by cheering me on when I nearly quit after the first book in the Buck Hole Hollow series. I have somehow ended up here at my eighth book, the first book in the Watauga Lake series. This is partly your fault. May you forever regret encouraging me, in the best possible way.

And, more importantly, for sharing your words. Readers, you may adopt as many of her cowboys as you like, but you still can't have mine. That would be Jake. Just don't tell Brinley. I don't think that Texas sass would mix with this Tennessee sass without bloodshed—or at least some bruised knuckles.

To **Michelle Romao**, beta reader and author of *Finding Faith*, *Theo's Heart*, and *Heaven Sent*—thank you for poking holes in my plot, my logic, and occasionally my sanity, all in the name of better books. Your faith in my stories has outlasted my faith in my first drafts, which is saying something.

To my amazing **ARC Readers**: Thank you for reading this book before it had its makeup on, its hair done, or its typos fully banished. You showed up early, stayed late, and dove into these pages when they were still nervously chewing their nails about release day.

Your excitement, messages, and reviews mean more than algorithms, ads, or any perfectly curated aesthetic ever could. You turned a lonely writing cave into a crowded cheering section, and this book goes into the world braver because you were here first.

So this is for you—

For every highlight, gasp, DM, and "I stayed up way too late for this." Thank you for loving these characters loudly and helping them find their way into other readers' hands.

Chapter 1

Josh groped for the phone as its harsh tone jarred him awake. "Hello," he mumbled, his soft voice barely audible to the caller.

"Josh!"
"Hmm."
"Josh! Wake up!"

He sat up and swung his legs over the edge of the bed, rubbing the sand out of his eyes. "Who's this?"

"Chief Townsend. Josh, the studio is on fire!"

"Wha-what? Shit. I'll be right there."

He ended the call, checking the time as he threw the phone on the bed. The display showed that it was just after six in the morning. He'd been up all night working on a special project and hadn't gotten home until just about four in the morning. He stood to get dressed, and then sat back on the bed, shaking his head as if it would make what he'd just heard go away. When it didn't, he pinched himself to make sure he wasn't dreaming.

"Ow," he mumbled as he reached for his jeans that were on the floor. As he pulled them on, his hands brushed against the dried clay and paint left from his marathon work session from the day and night before.

Still perched on the side of the bed, he wiped the sleep from his eyes. "Damn, I'm tired." His mind wandered to the reason for his late nights. "Ain't got time for this mess."

Suddenly, his mind clicked on what the Chief said. "What does he mean my building is on fire?" That thought caused Josh to hurry. He grabbed a fresh T-shirt, shoved his arms into the sleeves, and ran down the hall and out the front door, snatching his keys and jacket on the way past the hall tree in the entryway.

He slid into his jacket as he rushed to his truck. He didn't have far to go—Gann Studio & Gallery was only a couple of miles down the road, right at the end of Watauga Lake's Main Street. Four blocks away, a sheriff's deputy stopped him. Josh rolled down his window and pointed toward the store. "Chief said my studio—"

"Go!" the deputy yelled, pointing. "Chief's waiting for you."

Chief Townsend flagged him down about a block away. "Park in Novah's driveway."

He pulled into the wide parking area in front of her house and home office, keeping as far to one side as possible so that he wouldn't block the reclusive writer. "Not that she can leave in any case," he muttered as he slammed the truck door shut and jogged past several sheriff cars and other emergency vehicles toward his studio. Hank and his deputies had the entire road blocked so traffic couldn't get through.

He and Novah had never really gotten along, though they tried to act civil if they met in public. *Figures, the one place I decided I liked and found a studio would be the same place she lives. If I had known that—*

His reserved demeanor didn't stop a string of choice words from leaving his mouth as he caught sight of his burning studio, the firefighters drenching it with water from the lake.

Chief Townsend raised his eyebrows. "Bad night?"

Josh turned toward the Chief as he rubbed his hand through his uncombed hair. “Uh, yeah. I was working on a sculpture all night.”

“You know, that woman isn’t worth the shit you’re putting yourself through. Most women aren’t interested in the amount of time you dedicate to your business, and they’ll eventually break it off. You need another artist who understands dedication to her craft. When’s the last time you got a good night’s sleep?”

He shrugged. “I don’t know. Few days, maybe.” Josh ignored the rest of the Chief’s comments about women.

“By the looks of that scraggly mess on your face, I’d say at least that,” Chief Townsend mumbled.

For most of his thirty years, Josh had wanted to be a potter. This long-standing ambition shaped much of his life and decisions from an early age. Ever since his parents bought him Play-Doh at three or four years old, just to keep him out of their hair, he became fascinated with clay.

He didn’t get into relationships. He was too busy doing what he loved best—creating art for others to enjoy. But this woman...Laura. She’d gotten under his skin.

He’d started to catch feelings for her, but when she realized it, she wasn’t willing to give in to it. She didn’t want to compete with his business. And this is why he seldom saw anyone more than a date or two.

Most people thought he was being shallow, but not only were none of the women he met so far "the one," they didn't understand his need to work the clay at all hours of the day. It was a way to earn a living, but more importantly, it calmed him in ways that nothing else ever could.

He got into working with the medium when he was just a kid. He grew out of the Play-Doh and asked his mother for real clay by the time he turned six. He couldn't remember when he wasn't able to form it into whatever shape he wanted.

His parents worked opposing shifts, so they wouldn't have to pay for a sitter. As a result, he never knew what it was like to be a real family, but he had plenty of time to practice with clay. Sure, they spent holidays together, at least when his mother didn't have to work a shift at the nursing home or his father's job didn't call him in because someone was out sick from the restaurant on a holiday.

Josh had kept some of the first pieces he created with fast-drying clay. He didn't need to fire that type of clay, and never did, so he kept them protected. If they got wet, they'd eventually disintegrate.

He thanked his lucky stars that he had decided to leave them in storage in a humidity-controlled room in the cellar of his house. It was specially built with heating and air conditioning to protect items sensitive to extreme temperatures and humidity, including the bulk of his stash of clay and extra paints.

When Josh turned twenty-two, he'd saved enough from selling his pottery and sculptures to put a down payment on a storefront in Watauga Lake, a small town he'd found while driving around one day. It was only a little over an hour from his hometown, but he didn't have anything holding him in Adams Mill, Tennessee, since he didn't have siblings. *Thank dog*.

The very reason he spent so much time with his art was the same one he worked so hard for during school. Throughout high school, he'd read everything he could get his hands on about business administration. He never went to college because he planned to get his pottery business off the ground as quickly as possible.

He'd worked out a construction loan for the purchase of the building and gutted it, turning it into a storefront and a studio. The spacious, open attic was perfect for a gallery.

Josh stared at the darkened area that was once his first-floor retail shop and hoped the hallway at the back of the store had been able to protect that area from the flames. It led to the public bathrooms, a small private kitchen, and his studio, which took up the whole width of the rear of the building.

If the door was closed, there was a chance. A slim chance, but a chance.

His pride and joy. He couldn't see whether the fire affected the back of the building—only the retail section on the first floor and at least part of the gallery on the second floor.

He built the studio to hold everything he needed for his creations. He would be devastated to lose the long work table and potter's wheel, which faced a giant picture window that looked out onto the lake.

The kiln was against the side wall near the middle of the room. He closed his eyes when he pictured the wall of shelves that held pieces in various stages of completion, including those waiting to go into the kiln, hoping the fire and water hadn't destroyed them.

The opposite wall held a floor-to-ceiling storage area that included a wide shelf, drawers underneath and specifically designed cabinets to keep everything he needed to create his pottery and statues.

He hoped the set of spiral stairs that led upstairs into the refurbished attic was safe enough to climb. It was one room with shelves lining the two sides. The rear featured a picture window, just like the one in his studio. The center of the room held several display units for his special projects. He decorated the walls with vibrant-colored pottery—some he made to display, and some made by other artists he looked up to.

"It's all ruined. I just know it," Josh thought. Gann Studio & Gallery was still emitting acrid black smoke, and firefighters continued hosing it down. At least he no longer saw the flames. Not that it made much of a difference.

He shook his head, turned away from the building, and leaned against the quaint stone wall in front of Cassidy Accounting Services. He sighed as he stroked his moustache, his eyes fixed on the firefighters wrestling the final, hissing tongues of flame.

This disaster was going to set him back. He could recreate his one-of-a-kind pieces, but they'd never be the same as the originals. Clay was too malleable for that. Nothing ever came out the same, no matter how hard he tried.

People grabbed onto the rusticness of his designs, especially those with more noticeable characteristics. He even painted them with slight differences to capitalize on the fad of obviously handmade goods. Though he wouldn't go so far as to call it a fad—not like others did—since in all the years he'd been creating, people preferred the variation instead of the cookie-cutter pottery churned out by machines.

Josh started his truck, but sat there for a few minutes—until he saw a flash of color pass by the front window of Novah's house. "Shit. That's all I need is for her to come out here and harass me for parking in her driveway," he muttered.

Yep. That's just what I need. Another woman who complains about me working too much. Laura was bad enough.

Although Josh had broken it off with Laura, it hit him harder than the others did. He thought she understood what it meant for him to feel the slippery clay between his fingers, since she was an artist.

His thoughts kept going back and forth between Novah and Laura. Novah was a year older than him, with the striking blue eyes and natural white-blond hair, unlike his almost-mousy blond hair and grey eyes. They took the same honors classes in high school, but they rarely spoke to each other.

Josh never found the courage to ask the bookish girl out. Besides, she treated everyone as if she were too good for them.

Don't even know why I'm thinking about her. We never got along. Still don't. But she is gorgeous.

Josh sighed and shrugged, remembering those days. Because he was an artsy type, he didn't fit in with the rest of the kids. The jocks played sports and hung out, along with the cheerleaders. The “hoods” seemed to live for breaking the rules, smoking in the bathrooms and sneaking off to light up a joint.

A few were into the arts, including the music kids, but they hung out in their cliques, too. He didn’t mind. He was too absorbed with his creations to bother with kids from school. As an adult, he still was, but at least he wasn’t rude to people and did have a few friends.

Josh had dated a few women during his late teens and early twenties, but nothing ever lasted more than a couple of dates. He was too focused on his work, and women didn’t want to hear about his newest project.

He sighed as he backed out of Novah’s driveway. Just as he started down the road, movement caught his eye. Novah stepped out onto her porch. “Got out of there just in the nick of time. Now to go home and wash this smoke off me,” he mumbled.

Before he’d left, the Chief let him know the fire was out, but they wouldn’t allow him inside yet, as they were still looking for hot spots and trying to figure out what started the fire. He shook his head when they’d asked him if he had left the kiln on. He knew he hadn’t, besides, as he explained to the Chief, it came with an auto shutdown. If the sensors didn’t sense movement in the room for thirty minutes, the kiln would shut itself down.

Chapter 2

Novah Quinney peeked out the window to see what all the noise was about. Someone parked a truck in her driveway. Just as she opened the door, it backed out and left. “That looks like Josh’s vehicle,” she thought to herself, noticing it was a black RAM. “Wonder what he was doing here.”

As she turned to go back inside the house, the acrid odor of something that burned filled her nostrils as the wind picked up. She stepped off the porch to check the sky for smoke, but it was clear. Novah walked toward the street and saw the few emergency vehicles still parked on the side of the road. *What burned?*

She headed down the street to see what was going on. The sirens never woke her because she had been up almost all night working on the next book in her series. The smell of smoke hadn't woken her, either. *That could be dangerous. What if it were my house on fire?*

When she had finally decided to crash, she'd put noise-canceling earmuffs on since even the slightest noise would wake her.

When she reached the police line, which the emergency personnel had moved to the edge of Gann Studio & Gallery, her eyes widened in surprise at the charred building. She didn't know Josh that well, other than from high school, and they didn't speak to each other. They hadn't spoken much in high school, either. She thought he was too full of himself. *I'm sure he thought I was just another book nerd.*

She shook her head and headed back home. While she didn't know him that well and really didn't like him, she still wished him no harm. She knew several in town who didn't think highly of him, thanks to his attitude.

Seems as though that hasn't changed since high school. I wonder how that fire started. I sure hope he didn't do something stupid, like leave the kiln on. I bet everyone is thinking that. Or, at least, those who don't think highly of him. They'll sure buy his pottery, though.

"Like I should be thinking like that. I have a few of his pieces in my house, too."

Novah shook her head again. No. I overheard him in the consignment shop talking about that kiln when he upgraded it a few years ago. That thing has some sort of shut-off switch.

She shrugged as she walked across her lawn and back into the cool house. "Feels damned good in here. It's hot as hell outside," she muttered to the television as she passed it to go into her office to work on her book. "Maybe I can do just as much tonight as I did last night."

Josh walked into Rowan's Hearth Bakery to pick up an apple fritter and a large coffee before he went through his studio to see what was salvageable. *If anything is.* He ordered and turned to leave, bumping into Novah, who was stepping up to the counter. "Sorry," he muttered without lifting his head as he continued past the long line of people who were behind him.

Novah huffed with impatience. "Watch where you're going, Josh..." Before she finished her sentence, the bakery door snicked shut behind him.

"Damn it. This is a brand-new shirt." She pulled her pale lavender shirt out to stare at the offending drops. There were only a couple, but she knew they would leave a stain. When she glanced up, a couple of people she didn't know that well were staring after Josh.

"Sorry," Jaxxon apologized for Josh. "He's not usually like that, but I guess he has other things on his mind. I guess you know his studio burned yesterday."

Novah huffed a laugh. "Yes, he is. I've known him since high school. We've never gotten along much. Well, truly, he kept to himself, and I kept to myself. I always thought he was full of himself, and I'm sure he thought I was nothing but a boring book nerd. And, yes, I drove past the studio this morning."

Jaxxon raised his eyebrows. "You think? I don't get that vibe from him."

The man sitting at the counter huffed a "Yeah, right."

Jaxxon ignored the man since Josh had always been polite to him.

Novah shrugged. "Maybe he doesn't give you that vibe, and that's all good. I'll take two each of the apple, blueberry and raspberry danish to go, please."

Jaxxon nodded and bagged up her Danish.

After paying, Novah walked toward her home office. When she passed Josh's studio, she didn't see him there and kept going. "Better off, so I don't have to make nice with him," she muttered.

She walked up her front steps and ran her fingers over the sign that said, "Willow Ridge Writer's Loft." She listed her books as being published by Willow Ridge Publishing. The name came from a cabin her parents owned when she was a kid.

The front of the house was on land, and the boathouse attached to it was over water. The original owners kept two huge boats they stored in there, so it was about the size of a three-car garage that was fifty feet deep.

Novah spent the money she inherited from her grandfather to have all the wood pilings replaced with concrete. She kept the structure the same, but replaced the old and battered wood siding on the boathouse and the house with composite siding that would withstand the elements much better than wood. She'd replaced the old shingle roof with a metal roof.

Because of the way the banks rose steeply out of the lake, she didn't have much of a beach, so she brought the lake inside. A steep flight of undercover steps allowed her to reach the surface, where Novah built a deck—big enough to entertain several couples. The deck and boathouse looked as though they floated on the water, but were built on pilings that held them just a few inches above the surface of the lake, unless it rose from flooding.

Framed Lexan windows ran from the deck to the ceiling in place of the garage doors on the lakeside. The flooring ended about ten feet before the windows, which left an open pool inside. The side walls featured wide windows to allow for views of the lake. A short set of steps led to a higher platform, where Novah built a small kitchen with RV-sized appliances to store coffee, snacks and light meals so she wouldn't have to go into the main house if she was writing. It also held a small writing table for her laptop, if she decided to write in the area when the weather was beautiful.

The back wall held a staircase to the second level, which was fully insulated and protected against the elements. It also featured expansive windows on the three sides that didn't connect to the main house. The upstairs contained a furnished office that took up the whole space, except for a bathroom and storage area on the rear wall.

While she placed a few short bookshelves in the office, she kept most of her books in the main house, in a room she'd converted to a library. It had floor-to-ceiling bookcases and a pair of comfortable reading chairs. A floor lamp sat between the reading chairs, and an end table graced the sides of the comfortable seats.

Novah put two of the Danish in the mini fridge and brewed a cup of espresso. It was cool enough this morning, so she decided to write in the lower level of the converted boathouse. She set the coffee and pastry on the table and went upstairs to grab her computer and notes. She started where she'd left off the day before, but she couldn't stop thinking about the burned studio down the street.

Chapter 3

The next morning, Josh met Chief Townsend and Sheriff Hank McAllister at the studio. The firefighters had boarded up the place to keep curious onlookers out. The Chief handed Josh a key for the padlock on the door. “It could have been worse, Josh. Someone set this fire intentionally.”

Josh turned to Sheriff McAllister. “I take it that’s why you’re here, Hank?”

The Sheriff nodded. “It is. Let’s go in, and we’ll explain it to you.” He handed Josh one of the hard hats and put the other one on. The Chief put his fireman's hat on.

They walked through the door into the charred retail area. "There's damage throughout the building, but this area took the brunt of it," the Chief explained. "Don't ever come in here without a hard hat," he added as he pointed up.

Josh adjusted the hard hat as he tipped his head to follow the Chief's finger. His heart sank when he saw that the whole front half of the second floor was gone.

The burned ceiling exposed the building's second-floor trusses. They made their way across broken bits of pottery and chunks of wood that had partially burned and fallen from the walls, ceilings and the second floor. Scorched shelving lay scattered everywhere.

Josh's eyes moved to the charred pieces of wood and clay under his feet, and he shook his head. Tears at the loss of hundreds of hours of work threatened, but the Chief's voice worked through the haze in his mind.

"It's a good thing you closed the door to the studio, and whoever did this didn't bother to open it." Chief Townsend walked through the entry that was now open and into the smoke-stained hall. The closed hall entrance had significantly limited the damage, as the fire hadn't spread to the rear of the building. The bathroom and kitchen were intact, but would need complete refurbishing due to smoke and water damage.

Josh's hopes were up when he realized what the Chief was saying. They walked into the studio where the odor of smoke burned Josh's nose. The heat and water that leaked in when the firefighters hosed the rear part of the building ruined much of his work, and his heart sank again.

"Damn it," he muttered, shaking his head. "I'm going to have to rebuild the entire building. That smoke and water damage..." His voice trailed off as it got thicker with emotion.

"'Fraid so," the Chief said. "You might get away with refurbishing this area, but I doubt you'd ever remove the smell of smoke. We checked it out, and this part of the building is structurally sound. If you go upstairs, stay in the back half. Don't walk too close to the front, as the bearing wall down here burned out. Anything past this point," the Chief pointed up at a point near the kitchen, "is not safe."

Josh nodded. "I've seen enough. Let's go outside, and you can tell me how you know this was arson."

The Chief and Sheriff nodded, and they made their way back through the mess and out the front door. Josh put the tailgate down on his truck and grabbed a bag of pastries and three coffees he picked up from Rowan's this morning. He motioned toward them, and the Chief and Sheriff grabbed theirs and a muffin. All three sat on the tailgate.

Chief Townsend said, “I’ll get right to it. First, we found unusual burn patterns. You’re lucky you installed sprinklers and the alarm that notified us. If we hadn’t gotten here as soon as we did, the whole building would have been gone. The fire spread fast and in multiple directions, which in itself tells us it was not accidental.” The Chief paused to sip his coffee.

“There were also burn marks in several places on the front wall and one of the side walls. Either the arsonist was interrupted, or he thought it might be enough. We believe that by the time he set the two fires on the left wall, the sprinklers must have come on and triggered the alarm.”

“Additionally, our chemical tests detected traces of an accelerant in all the places we found the V-shaped burn marks. And finally, they broke the front window. The glass was inside the store instead of outside. If the window shattered due to the heat of the fire, the glass would have been outside.”

Hank handed several papers to Josh. “I saved you the hassle of ordering our report online so you can contact your insurance company sooner. I suggest that you hire a lawyer before you even speak to them.”

Josh nodded. “Thanks. I know how they work. Even with all the premiums I’ve paid them over the years, they’re still going to look out for their bottom line, not me.”

Hank clapped his hand on Josh's shoulder. "We'll get out of your hair. Be careful while you're working in there." He handed Josh a card. "She's excellent at what she does. She'll take care of you."

Josh looked at the card. Hailey Lawson. "I thought she only did family law or something like that?" he asked.

"She does family, bankruptcy and personal injury. She has the cash to back you up, even though she's a sole proprietor. I've had to testify as an expert witness in more than a few of her cases."

Josh nodded. "Thanks. I'll give her a call as soon as I get back home."

After Chief Townsend and Sheriff McAllister left, Josh dragged his feet, walking toward the building with his shoulders slumped. He snapped photos in silence, moving through the wreckage, jotting down broken items one by one. Every step revealed more scorched and broken pottery and hundreds more dollars down the drain.

Standing in the middle of what was once familiar, the exhaustion pressed heavier with each discovery, settling on him until even the camera felt too heavy in his hand. The sight of the charred clay, twisted metal, and the blackened remains of pieces he'd put his soul into caused him to sink into the wall. The control he'd been barely hanging onto cracked, and his hands trembled at his sides.

Ava Sterling tapped the button on the earpiece to end the call. She saved the notes in the client's file and lifted her eyes as the front door snicked shut. "Josh Gann, right?"

Josh's shoulders stiffened. "Yes. Ava, right? I've seen you around."

"Yup. I can't seem to stay away from Rowan's."

Josh huffed a polite laugh. "Same here."

Ava glanced at the schedule on her screen. "You're a few minutes early, but I think Hailey is ready for you." She tapped the earbud and said something into the earpiece.

"She's ready for you," Ava said as she walked around the desk. "Follow me, please."

They walked down a short hallway to a door at the end. They passed three other doors, two of them marked with restroom signs. Josh assumed the other was a breakroom or small kitchen.

Hailey's door was open. Ava stepped inside, but before she could introduce Josh, Hailey stood. "Hello, Josh. It's good to see you again."

Josh nodded. "Hailey."

Ava tilted her head toward the door.

"Close it, please," Hailey said in response to Ava's silent question.

She motioned for Josh to take a seat in one of the comfortable chairs in front of her desk. "I heard about the fire. I take it, since you're here, Chief Townsend determined it was arson?"

"Yes. I'm going to need a complete rebuild. He warned me that the insurance company would probably fight me on it."

"Nothing personal. All insurance companies are like that. It keeps me in business."

The corner of Josh's mouth lifted in a small smile. "I bet." He handed the file with extra copies of the report, his inventory, and pictures that he took over to Hailey.

As she reached for it, her eyes widened. "You're actually one of the few people who organize evidence. Saves me a lot of work."

"And saves me a lot of money," Josh said, winking.

"That it does," Hailey said as she flipped through the file. "It looks as though you have everything I need that you can get your hands on. I'll draft a demand letter for the insurance company, and then have you come in and review it.

She paged through the documents again. Do you have a recent appraisal?"

"No, the newest is two years old, and it was before the renovations."

Hailey dug in her desk and came up with a card. "Okay, I've used this guy before. He's used to doing business appraisals in cases like this. I won't be able to complete the demand letter until I receive his appraisal. If you hadn't done all the renovations I know you did, we could have worked from the old one."

"No problem. I wasn't sure what you needed in that area, so I waited. I'll give him a call as soon as we finish up here."

When they ended their discussion, Hailey had a better idea of the value of Josh's loss. Josh stood and shook her hand after he signed the retainer contract.

Chapter 4

Josh walked down to the edge of the lake to take a break from going through the burned remains of his studio. He was able to salvage some of the pottery and statues from the upstairs gallery. Since these pieces had a thick glaze on them, they may not retain the smell of smoke. He was able to save his kiln and many of his tools, including his potter's wheel, but the fire had ruined the scraps of material he used to create different textures.

He turned his gaze up the shore to Willow Ridge Writer's Loft and found himself wondering if Novah was in her office writing. Since he parked in her driveway, he hadn't been able to get her out of his mind. *I don't know why I'm thinking about her. We didn't get along as teens. And she's still prickly. That bookish girl turned out to be gorgeous.* "But she still has that attitude," he muttered.

Sighing heavily, he trudged back up to his studio. The insurance adjuster was out the day after the fire. Now, a week later, he had another two or three truckloads to move into storage. "Might as well get to it. It's not going to move itself."

Novah caught movement out of the corner of her eye and moved to the window, watching as Josh stopped and stared across the lake. Her eyes moved from the dark shadow of a beard on his face and across his broad shoulders. His sweat-soaked shirt clung to the muscles she knew were hidden underneath.

Her eyes fixated on the worn jeans that pulled taut against a well-rounded ass. He turned toward her, and she ducked out of sight, smashing her elbow on the wall, even though she knew he couldn't see inside the tinted windows.

She rubbed her elbow. "Ow. That's what I get for staring. What the hell am I doing, anyway? We don't even like each other. And what would he want with someone like me?"

I don't know where that came from. I haven't even thought about people liking or disliking me for how I look for a couple of years after high school. That was when I finally figured out that you only need to make yourself happy since you're never going to be able to make everyone happy all the time.

"That doesn't mean you can't look," the romance writer in her argued.

She returned to her desk and put her fingers on the keys, but the words wouldn't come. Ever since he bumped into her at the bakery, she had a hard time writing. She stared at the word count in the top right of her screen. **50 words added today.**

Even more alarming was the next stat that said, **2,019 words deleted today.**

"Maybe a walk down to the bakery will settle me enough to get back into writing."

No. You'll run into Josh and make a fool of yourself. The anxiety of a run-in with him caused her chest to tighten. She didn't know why she felt as though she had to help him, especially since they barely knew each other as adults. She'd only make things worse, and he'd probably take her sympathy as pity. Her cheeks colored at the thought of coming off the wrong way to him.

"What the fuck," Novah muttered as she leaned back in her chair.

Well, you can't avoid going to town forever.

Novah closed her laptop and grabbed her keys and purse. She needed a few things at the store, plus she didn't have any more of that decadent triple chocolate cake from Jaxxon. She bought a whole cake and stored it in her freezer since she couldn't eat the entire thing before it would go bad.

Josh had just three more boxes of stuff to haul to storage. Grunting with effort, he wedged one against the passenger seat, then twisted the second sideways. Sweat dripped down his face as he tried to maneuver it around the gearshift. The last box teetered precariously as Josh attempted to jam it into the last sliver of space.

He stepped back and slammed the truck door, only to have the pile shift and the door bounce open. "Damn it," he muttered as he leaned against the side of the truck, his forehead pressed into his folded arms. He felt something drip down his hand and lifted his head to check. His knuckles were raw and bleeding from cardboard cuts. He shook his head in frustration and pulled the three boxes out of the truck before they fell and broke everything in them.

"Three boxes. That's all. You'd think I could find room in here for three fucking boxes." He angrily kicked a larger piece of gravel, sending it bouncing along the parking lot.

His eyes watered in frustration, but he refused to let the tears fall. He still hadn't processed his beloved studio burning, never mind trying to figure out who hated him so much that they burned it. He was being stubborn, and he knew it. He didn't know how long he stood there, but he knew that he could have been to the storage unit and back again, but his heart wasn't in it.

Novah slowed as she drove by. Josh never even looked up. She sighed and pulled into the parking lot on the other side of Josh's truck. She took in the boxes piled high in the bed and the full cab as she walked around to the other side.

"Josh." She narrowed her eyes when he gave no indication of hearing her. He had to have heard me slam the door, at least. It's not like I'm sneaking up on him.

"Josh."

When he still didn't respond, she reached out to touch his arm.

He jumped as a hand reached out to him and lifted his head. *Novah.* "You scared the shit out of me, lady."

Novah rolled her eyes at him. "I wasn't exactly quiet when I pulled in and shut the car door. Or, when I called your name more than once." She lifted one eyebrow at him.

"It's not a good time, Novah. I need to get this shit to the storage lot." He turned and tried to rearrange the boxes for the umpteenth time, knowing it wasn't going to happen.

Novah put her hand on his shoulder. "Turn around, Josh."

"No. Just leave me alone so I can get this done."

"Josh," she said softly. "I know we don't get along that well, but at least let me help you as a neighbor. I can put those boxes in my truck and follow you to the storage if it's close. I have groceries in the car, but they'll be fine in the cooler bags if the storage unit is close."

He turned around to face her. "Why would you even want to help me? We can barely say a civil word to each other." *And it's going to be even worse today, since I'm already in a pissy mood.*

"You're a neighbor, Josh. You know that people in this town help each other out, even when someone doesn't ask. I don't want anything in return. It's late. I have the time. I-I- can't concentrate on what I'm writing anyway."

Novah looked into his eyes when he finally lifted his head again, and was surprised to see the light gone in them and the hunch in the shoulders of someone who always stood tall. She'd never known the reserved but stubborn man to show defeat over anything.

"Okay," Josh said softly. "They're kind of heavy. You want to back over here?"

"Sure." Novah pulled her keys out of her pocket and headed to her truck. She followed Josh's hand signals as she backed up toward the boxes.

Josh waited for her to open the tonneau top since it had a lock on it. She twisted it and lifted the cover. "I don't keep it locked. No reason to. We'll have to tie the cover down since the boxes are higher than the sides of my truck."

They both reached for the tailgate handle at the same time. "Sorry," Josh muttered.

"No problem," she answered as she opened it.

He lifted one of the boxes and slid it in. When he turned to grab another one, Novah slid the second box onto the tailgate. Josh grabbed the last one. "You're pretty strong. These things weigh fifty-sixty pounds a piece."

"That's about all I can lift without struggling. I work out, but can never seem to lift more than that."

Josh nodded and pulled the tonneau cover down so Novah could tie it off. "The storage unit is close by. It's the one at the other end of Main."

"Okay. I'll follow you."
"Thanks, Novah."

Josh slid into his truck and started it, and then waited for Novah to climb into hers before he pulled out.

Once they arrived at the storage unit, Josh pulled to the side so Novah could back up to the door. He unloaded the boxes and thanked her as she climbed into her truck. Instead of taking off, she pulled out of the way so he could back in.

"You don't have to help. You've got groceries to put up, and these boxes are heavy. You're going to tear up your back."

"It won't take but a few minutes."
"Suit yourself," Josh said.

Her vowels stretched just a little, the mountains softening the edges of her words, a gentler echo of his own drawl that tugged at the corners of his mouth. When their hands brushed on the tailgate latch, a jolt snapped through his palm, and he pulled back a heartbeat too late.

Did she feel that, too, or was his brain just inventing fireworks where there'd only been skin and metal?

Once they pulled all they could reach out and stacked them in the storage unit, Novah climbed into the back of his truck to push boxes toward the tailgate while Josh hauled them into the room.

“Thanks for the help, Novah. Uh, do you want to grab a bite to eat at Hensley’s?”

“Maybe another time? I need to get these groceries put up, and I have to cook up the chicken I thawed yesterday.”

Josh nodded. “Okay, that works. Thanks again for your help.”

Novah smiled and nodded. “See you around.”

The next morning, Josh met with the appraiser. Luckily, he’d taken many pictures of the construction process when he remodeled the building into the retail, studio and gallery that it had become. He had also saved receipts and invoices for expenses, including the cost of the construction crew.

“Do you have digital files of these pictures?” the appraiser asked. “I don’t want to take them out of their sleeves since they’ve been in there for a while.”

Josh nodded, so the appraiser wrote down his email on the back of his card.

"If you can send them sometime today, I can have this done by tomorrow morning."

Nodding, Josh said, "I can send them now. They're in the cloud. I'll just move them into a file that I can give you access to." His head bent over his phone as he worked. Once he got the files copied into another file, he sent the share link to the email the appraiser had given him.

Pulling a portable wireless printer out of his oversized briefcase, Josh set it on the table and turned it on. He printed the summary of all expenses, which included the total he'd put into the renovations.

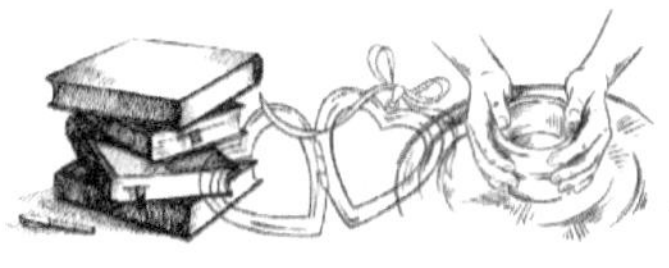

Chapter 5

Josh's eyes followed the water as it drained from the sink. Ever since the day Novah helped him move into the storage unit, all he could think about was the electricity between them and wondered if she felt it, too.

He braced his hands on the counter, the cool laminate tacky under his damp palms, and pictured her in the bakery the week before. She'd had her hair twisted up in a lazy knot, pen tucked behind one ear as she'd traded smart assed comments with Jaxxon while rattling off an order big enough to feed half the town.

She'd stood there in her faded jeans and book quote T-shirt, teasing the baker about his "carb peddling" with a grin that crinkled the corners of her eyes, then turned around and tipped big anyway, like it was a habit and not a performance.

He'd seen her truck parked at weird hours, lights burning in the boathouse when most people had gone to bed, and more than once he'd watched her haul in grocery bags with one hand and a banker's box of manuscripts with the other, shoulders set in that stubborn line that meant she'd been at the keyboard too long.

That wasn't someone too good for anyone. That was someone grinding just as hard as he did, someone who emptied her own trash, carried her own boxes, and still somehow had enough left over to show up for a neighbor with a trunk full of his broken life.

"I made a fool of myself for asking her out. That was a polite way of saying, 'No way.'" He shook his head as if that would erase the thoughts that played through his mind over and over.

He leaned into Novah, and before he knew it, his lips touched hers for a brief second. When she didn't pull away, his lips touched hers again. All or nothing. Josh slid his tongue between her lips and rubbed against her teeth.

Novah moaned as she pressed into Josh, and his tongue dueled with hers as her hands found their way to the back of his head. Her fingers ran through his hair as she pulled him closer. His hands moved from her hips, past the dip in her waist, and up to her breasts. He forced his thumbs between them to rub her nipples as he walked her backward to the wall.

He felt the moan at the back of her throat as he ground against her and bit her bottom lip. He sucked her tongue into his mouth before kissing her again. His hands moved back down to her hips to pull her against his rock-hard cock as he ground into her.

"Damn," he moaned. Josh's cock pressed painfully against his fly. He moaned again as he reached for it, rubbing himself. He stroked himself exactly three times and came in his jeans. He reached for the sink with his other hand to steady himself as he continued spurting and moaning. When he finally finished, he sank to his knees as he tried to catch his breath.

"Oh, God. If I came that hard just thinking about her, I wonder what it's like with my cock buried deep inside of her."

With that thought, he felt himself getting hard again. "Well, hell." He stood and headed down the hall to the bedroom to change, but his mind—and his cock—had other ideas. He fumbled in the nightstand for the

Masterbator toy he rarely used. There was no way his hand was going to cut it this time.

He shoved his jeans and underwear down to his knees and lay back on the bed, sliding his cock into the toy. Josh pumped the masterbator twice, and his hips jerked into it as his hand forced it down onto his cock. He let out a long, low moan as his hips bucked into the toy again, and ribbons of hot cum filled it.

He lay there with his arm over his eyes, skin still damp and sticking to the warm sheets. The sharp odor of sweat and sex was so strong it felt like Novah was in the room with him. His pulse hammered in his throat, and he didn't know what to do with the low, unnerving pull in his chest.

I have never, ever had it that bad. What the hell is this woman doing to me? She doesn't even want me like that.

When he finally caught his breath, he turned his head toward the clock, squinting until the red numbers stopped swimming. For a second, the thoughts of her mouth made something tight twist in his gut—want and panic knotted together—before the time actually registered.

"Fuck. I need to get going. I'm already late."

He peeled the jeans off his legs, the fabric rough against his oversensitive skin, and tossed them into the washer. The sharp scent of soap cut through the humid air as he splashed cold water over his face, the shock biting down his nerves, like it could rinse out thoughts of her if he just scrubbed hard enough. He dragged on clean underwear and fresh jeans, the cool, dry fabric grounding him even as that unwanted ache for her sat heavy in his chest.

Novah shifted in her chair as a wave of heat rolled through her, starting low in her belly and sparking out to her fingertips. Her thighs pressed together on instinct, the worn cushion suddenly too soft, too warm beneath her. “Now, where the hell did that come from?”

She could understand it if she were writing a particularly steamy scene, but she was elbows deep in dry medical texts on her screen. The lines of symptoms and terminology blurred into a gray hum. The blue-white glow of the monitor felt harsh against her eyes, and the clinical words did not match the pulse drumming between her legs.

She knew she was wet, a slick, insistent awareness every time she shifted, but had no idea why. When her muscles clamped down, a tight involuntary squeeze stole her breath, and she shifted again, letting out a low moan. “What the hell?”

She'd been thinking about Josh earlier. The way his jeans hugged his perfectly rounded ass. The way his shirt stretched across his back. But he wasn't even on her mind right now. Still, the ghost of that image clung to her, like her body had filed it away and pulled it up without asking.

Novah shook her head and forced her gaze back to the text on the screen, her fingers tense on the mouse as she scrolled.

After several minutes, she realized that she didn't remember a word she had read. Sighing, she saved the links and opened the file for her book. "If I can't concentrate on research, maybe I can write the next steamy part."

Josh 00walked out of Watauga Books & Brews with a large coffee in his hand. He'd run out of coffee at home, and they made the best. As he was walking out, someone brushed past him with a scowl. Josh narrowed his eyes as he continued to his truck. When the man didn't say anything, Josh continued across the parking lot. *What the hell did I do? I don't even know that guy. Seen him around, but don't know him.*

He shrugged and backed out of the parking spot.

As he pulled into the accountant's parking area, Josh craned his head to the nearly empty lot across the street. "They work fast," he said to himself. He parked and then walked across the street to watch the construction company raze the rest of the building he'd spent so much time, energy and money on.

He knew Hailey was working with his insurance company to get the funds to rebuild. Since it was arson and he had all of the proof, it would most likely settle. Hailey wanted to sue the arsonist when they caught him—or her, but Josh figured a criminal didn't have much money, so he wasn't holding his breath.

Josh watched for another couple of hours while the construction crew loaded what was left of his life into the back of several dump trucks to haul off to their burn lot. Each slam of metal and crunch of debris thudded into his chest. Dust and the faint, acrid scent of burned wood hung in the air, clinging to his clothes and coating the back of his throat.

Once they left, the silence rushed in around him, broken only by the distant buzz of insects and the soft lap of water against the shore. He made his way down to the lake, taking care not to slip on the loose gravel in the walkway.

Just down from where his property was, several large rocks jutted out to form a dyke into the lake. Years of waves and weather had worn their surfaces smooth. It was a favorite place for him to sit and think as he allowed the cooler air and the clean, earthy smell of water and wet stone to wash away his troubles.

He took off his shoes and his toes curled against the damp, packed earth. Josh rolled his pant legs up, the denim scratching lightly against his calves, and then stepped into the cool water. He made his way to the dyke and climbed the rocks, feeling the smooth stone under his bare feet and taking care to stay upright when he hit slick spots caused by algae.

After making his way to the end, he sat on the edge of the last rock, the hard surface pressing into the backs of his thighs, and wrapped his arms around his knees. He rested his chin on them as a faint breeze brushed his skin and rippled the water below.

Novah saved the document and pushed back from her desk, the chair's worn cushion hissing softly as the air shifted under her weight. The words on the screen swam together. Symptoms, dosages, side effects, and none of it stuck in her brain.

She scrubbed her hands over her face and blew out a breath. "Useless," she muttered to the empty office. "You can write a three-chapter chase scene in one sitting, but you can't keep your mind on blood thinners for ten minutes."

She stood and crossed to the window out of habit. The lake lay flat and pewter gray, a sheen of light clinging to its surface. Down the street, she could make out the flattened shape where Josh's studio had been, now nothing but scraped earth and piles of debris waiting for a dump truck.

A week ago, she would've looked at that building and thought about his smug expression in high school, the way he'd always seemed a little removed, like the rest of them were background noise. Too good for the book nerd with the spiral notebook and ink-stained fingers.

But the image that rose now wasn't teenage Josh leaning against a locker. It was the man from two nights ago, shoulders slumped in the parking lot, forehead pressed to his arms on the side of his truck like someone had turned gravity up just for him.

She could still feel the weight of the box they'd lifted together, the rough cardboard biting into her palms as he'd tried to apologize for snapping at her. He'd looked…small. No, that wasn't the right word. Stripped, maybe. Exhaustion and soot dulled the sharp edges she'd built entire internal arguments around.

Her mind flicked to Rowan's. She'd been in there enough to see him on his good days, laughing with

Jaxxon over the counter about whose pastries sold out first, trading barbs about "sugar art" versus "real art" while he paid for coffee and tipped like it was muscle memory. Jaxxon didn't laugh like that with people he didn't like.

She remembered another morning, from months back, when she'd ducked into the bakery in an oversized hoodie, hoping nobody would want to talk. Josh had been at the front of a small knot of tourists, explaining the difference between wheel-thrown and hand-built pieces with his hands moving in the air.

He'd stayed patient as the couple asked the same question three different ways. When their toddler knocked over a display of napkin holders, he'd dropped to his haunches and helped the kid stack them again, making a game out of it while the parents apologized. She'd watched from her table, notebook open but untouched, and told herself the warm pinch in her chest was just professional curiosity. Good raw material for a character.

Now, standing in her office with the taste of too-strong coffee still bitter on her tongue, that excuse felt thin.

"Full of himself," she said under her breath, testing the old label. It didn't sit right anymore. Not with the memory of his hands shaking around the box in her truck bed. Not with the way he'd insisted on unloading most of the weight himself, even when his shoulders were already trembling.

She crossed back to her desk and stared at the open document. Medical terminology glared up at her. None of it drowned out the memory of his voice in the storage unit, low and rough around the edges when he'd thanked her like she'd done something monumental instead of the easiest kind of neighborly favor.

Maybe he wasn't the aloof jerk she'd spent a decade being annoyed at from a safe distance. Maybe he was just…like her. Tunnel visioned. Married to his work. Awkward as hell at anything that required vulnerability instead of clay or words.

Her fingers hovered over the keyboard, then dropped. The scene on her screen didn't stand a chance.

She shut the laptop with a decisive click. The quiet that followed wasn't the usual comforting hush of her office. It felt restless, like the room was holding its breath with her.

On impulse, she grabbed her hoodie from the back of the chair and shrugged into it. The soft cotton skimmed over her bare arms, carrying the faint smell of detergent and the smoky tang that had hung in the air since the fire.

"Just a walk," she told herself as she headed for the stairs. "Clear your head. Check the sky. Maybe see if he's…okay."

Her sneakers squeaked faintly on the wooden steps as she descended to the lower level and stepped out onto the deck. The air was cooler here, coming off the water with a damp edge that raised goosebumps along her forearms. Across the small cove, movement caught her eye.

Josh was barefoot, picking his way out along the dyke rocks. Her gaze followed his jeans as they rubbed his calves where he'd rolled them up. He carefully made his way across the natural dock, his shoulders rounded against a wind that hadn't picked up yet.

The old anxiety fluttered in her chest. *What if he snaps? What if I say the wrong thing?* It threaded through something steadier this time. She'd seen him carry boxes without complaining, stand in a bakery full of people and make a kid feel like the most important person in the room, and build his life piece by piece ever since he was a teenager.

If anyone had earned someone just sitting next to him for a while, it was him.

Chapter 6

Novah glanced up at the storm clouds building across the lake and stepped inside the first floor of the converted boat house to close the watertight lid across the pool. Intense storms tended to cause large enough waves that the water splashed on the upper part of the deck. As she made her way back up, she noticed someone sitting on the rocks between her place and Josh's.

Instead of going back to her writing, she stepped out on the deck and then on the trail that followed the top of the bluff and wound its way down to the shore. She stood at the end of the dyke, watching Josh. When his shoulders slumped even more, she couldn't help herself. She made her way across the slick rocks and lowered herself to sit next to him.

The front of Josh's jeans tightened, despite his sour mood and what his mind told him about Novah. He shifted to a more comfortable position, but kept his knees up. *That's all I need is for her to notice me getting hard.*

"Novah. What are you doing here?" Josh asked.

"I don't really know. I saw you sitting out here, and my feet seemed to bring me here."

"I'm not really good company right now," he muttered.

"Lucky for you, I'm not that good at taking hints," Novah said with a smile.

"Suit yourself." Josh could feel the heat from Novah's body as she cast her gaze over the lake.

"Storm's coming," she said lowly.
"Yup."
"Do you still want to get that dinner?"
"Not tonight, Novah. Maybe tomorrow."

She nodded, her throat too tight to push any words out. She doubted he saw her. Heat rolled slowly through her chest and down to her stomach. Without realizing it, she wrapped her arm around his shoulder and pulled him into a side hug, her palm brushing against the firm line of muscle along his upper arm. "You'll be back up and running before you know it," she whispered, her breath stirring the hair near his ear.

Josh nodded and leaned against her, letting more of his weight settle into her side. It felt so good with her breasts pressed against his arm, the soft give of her body a sharp contrast to the hard rock beneath them. He closed his eyes and turned his head just enough to catch a whiff of something floral, yet musky. *Musk mallow and jasmine. Smells so good on her.* The familiar scent wrapped around him, grounding him.

His mood mellowed a bit, the tight band in his chest easing as the rhythm of her breathing brushed against his shoulder.

Novah couldn't suppress the moan at the back of her throat when Josh turned his head, and the faint scrape of stubble near her temple sent a shiver down her spine. Embarrassed, she lifted her arm from around his shoulders. The loss of contact made her skin ache. "I should get going," she said, wincing inwardly at the low, husky edge to her own voice. "It's getting darker, and I walked along the trail."

Before she could stand, Josh's arm snaked around her waist, his fingers splaying across the small of her back as he pulled her against him. "Novah," he groaned as he turned his head. His lips were inches from hers, his breath warm against her mouth, and he lowered his gaze to her flushed and slightly parted lips that he knew had to be soft.

When he lifted his eyes, his breath hitched at the raw desire shining in hers. His lips inched toward hers, and when she leaned into him, closing that last sliver of space, he claimed her mouth. Her lips were warm and pliant, and when her tongue pushed past his, he felt, more than heard, a low, desperate moan vibrate between them. He didn't know if it came from him or her. Pressure built tight in his jeans, forcing him to straighten his legs as the front grew painfully snug. Josh leaned back onto the rock, the stone digging into his shoulders as he pulled Novah with him.

Her hand found its way to the top button on his jeans, fingers trembling slightly as they brushed the worn metal. As she unfastened it, Josh broke the kiss, his breathing rough and uneven. "Jesus, Novah," he groaned, his voice ragged. "Are you sure?"

Novah couldn't answer. Her throat felt thick, and her pulse was a steady roar in her ears. Heat coiled low in her belly, building and tightening with every brush of his body against hers. She claimed his mouth again and unfastened the second button, her fingers slipping beneath the edge of the denim as Josh slid his hand under her shirt.

His palm was hot against her bare skin as he cupped her breast, his thumb and forefinger closing gently around her nipple. The sharp, electric pull of sensation made her break the kiss, and she tipped her head back as she cried out when the waves of pleasure rolled through her in aching, insistent pulses.

"Fuck," Josh mumbled rough and low, dragging the word from somewhere deep in his chest as he pushed her hands away and unfastened the rest of the buttons on his jeans. His breathing was uneven as he slid them down his thighs and then sat up and pulled her into his lap, pushing her skirt out of the way.

"I need to hear you say it, Novah. Are you sure you want this?" His lips hovered near her ear, his breath hot against her skin, sending a shiver down her spine.

"Y-yes," she huffed. "I've never felt a pull like this toward anyone. Hell, fucking yes, I want it." Her voice shook, a mix of raw nerves and want.

His fingers slid her wet panties out of the way and found their way into her opening. "God, Novah, you're so wet. So ready for me."

Novah threw her head back and arched into his hand as her muscles clenched his fingers. She let out a strangled cry as her hips ground against his hand, seeking more contact, more pressure, more of *him*.

Josh's control frayed with each ragged breath, every tremor that ran through her body where it met his. He grabbed his throbbing cock with his other hand, squeezing the base, trying to keep from blowing his load all over the front of her shirt. He pulled his hand out before she came down and lifted her over his turgid cock.

Her muscles gripped him as she slowly stretched around him. As soon as he was seated inside her, Novah ground her hips against him. He turned his head slightly and captured her nipple in his mouth. He sucked on it while his other hand slid between them to find her sensitive nub.

Josh made greedy grunting noises as he sucked and teased her nipple with his teeth. He felt Novah tighten against him. "Now, baby, now. Let me feel it. Jesus, Novah, I need—"

She loudly moaned his name as she let loose and ground her hips into him, and then stiffened as waves of red-hot heat rammed through her.

Throwing his head back, he let out a yell, and Novah felt his hot cum filling her as he stiffened under her. The sensation sent a jolt through her, making her breath hitch. Her muscles tightened more, and her body trembled as a fresh wave of pleasure crashed over her—deeper and more intense than before. Her cries grew louder as she fisted his shirt in her hands, the climax refusing to release her for what seemed like hours.

Josh groaned as her spasms caused him to harden again. He was so sensitive that when he ground his hips into her, he cried out each time he pounded against her, as pleasure spiked so sharply that it bordered on pain and forced raw sounds from his throat. His muscles trembled with the effort to keep moving, each deep, rhythmic thrust sending heat spiraling through him until it felt like his whole body was nothing but pounding heartbeat and ragged breath.

Novah reached between them and found her overly responsive nub. "I'm going to cum again, Josh," she moaned raggedly.

He was so lost in the feeling of her that he never heard her. Tears streamed from the corners of his eyes as he ground into her once more and held her against him. "Oh, God, baby," he moaned over and over as the flashes of light behind his eyelids burned into his brain.

Novah collapsed on top of him, his chest rising and falling hard against her as they both tried to catch their breath in the darkness of the night. The air around them felt thick and still, filled with the faint scent of lake water and sweat from their tangled bodies.

She finally rolled off of him and snuggled against his side on the hard rock, the surface digging into her hip and shoulder while his body was a solid, living warmth. She pressed a soft kiss to the side of his face, and her fingers slid slowly through his damp hair. She tasted the salt from his tears. “Josh...”

“Don’t let go, baby. Don’t let go.” His voice was raw, and the words vibrated through his rib cage where her palm rested.

“I won’t,” she whispered.

I wonder if he felt that crazy connection. Is that why he’s crying? Or is it that he’s overwhelmed with life in general? I know it was good for me, but was it good for him? I’ve seen his girlfriends around town. I’m nothing like them. He dates women who must wear a size zero. I’m far from that. The thoughts tumbled over each other, her stomach tightening as insecurity prickled under her skin.

After a few minutes, Josh finally got his emotions under control, his breathing evening out as the trembling in his chest eased. He could feel the way she shifted beside him, the tension in her body like a hum against his side, and he knew her mind was running a hundred and fifty miles an hour. “Novah.”

“Yeah, Josh.” Her voice came out soft and unsteady.

“Too incredible for words.” His fingers flexed lightly on her arm, giving her a gentle squeeze.

“Yeah, it was.” Warmth spread through her at his sentiment, loosening something tight in her chest as she let herself sink a little closer into his side. The night wrapped around them like a heavy, comforting blanket.

Chapter 7

"Who the hell is calling me this early?" Josh reached for the phone on the nightstand, only to be met with air. Memories of last night flooded through him. *Novah.* She flung an arm and a leg over him.

"I have to get that, Baby. That was Hank's ringtone." He extracted himself from her and sat on the edge of the bed, reaching down to grab his jeans. He pulled the phone out of his pocket and leaned back against the pillows as he dialed Hank's number. He listened to the Sheriff for a few minutes, and then said, "Let me think. I had an apprentice who developed a weird attitude after a couple of years, but I haven't heard from him for three or four years. I don't know if he's still in the area. Other than that, I don't think I have any enemies."

He felt Novah's hand circle his semi-hard cock and took a deep breath, trying to concentrate on what Hank was saying. "Uh, I'll think about it some more and let you know if I can come up with any other names. Otherwise, I can be there in about thirty minutes. Uh, make that an hour and thirty. I have something to do first thing."

"I'm sure you do. I saw your truck at Novah's a couple of hours ago. I guess you're getting along now?" Hank asked.

"I guess so," Josh mumbled. "I gotta go. I'll see you in a bit." Josh ended the call and threw the phone on the floor.

"Jesus, Novah," he mumbled as he leaned over and kissed her.

"Now, Josh. I need to feel you inside me *now*."

His blood raced as he pushed her onto her back and entered her in one swift movement. He held still as Novah arched her back and ground against him, her muscles already milking him. "Jesus, Baby, I'm not going to last."

His hips moved against her as he fought through her spasms. They slammed into her once more as he yelled her name, dragging it out as he filled her with his essence.

Josh collapsed on top of her, his weight pressing her into the mattress as his chest heaved against hers. Both of them dragged in ragged breaths. “Can’t move,” he barely whispered, his words warm and shaky against her ear.

After a few seconds, he rolled off of her, the cool air rushing in where his body had been, and Novah couldn’t stop the soft whimper that slipped out at the loss of his weight as he pulled out.

“I have to get going. I need to shower and grab a bite to eat before I meet Hank. He has a suspect.” His voice was steadier now, but still rough around the edges.

She leaned over and kissed him again, catching his lower lip between hers before her tongue pushed past his lips. He tasted like salt and the faint tang of coffee. He moaned as he pulled her closer. His fingers pressed into her side as if he could memorize the feel of her.

He broke the kiss after several long seconds, their breaths mingling as he hovered over her, staring into the depths of her eyes as if he were trying to hold on to something he didn’t want to let go of.

“I have to go. I don’t want to, but I have to.” He kissed her quickly and then dressed. He patted his pockets, feeling for the familiar shapes of his phone and keys. "I'll call you in a bit. Maybe we can get a bite to eat for lunch?"

Novah nodded, her throat too tight for a second before the words came. "That sounds good." The promise of it settled warm and slow in her chest as her eyes followed his every movement. Even after he walked out the door, the scent of his cologne and their shared heat hung in the air.

Josh walked out of the sheriff's office into the bright morning glare, blinking as the sun hit his eyes after the dim, stale-coffee air inside. The faint scent of burned wood clung to his nose, even though he'd changed his clothes and the building wasn't nearby as a reminder of the footage they had just watched.

A street camera had caught grainy images of a figure strolling past his studio minutes before the alarm screamed to life.

He checked his watch, the metal cool against his wrist, and exhaled when he saw the time. His stomach wasn't even grumbling yet. The parking lot lay quiet, heat already starting to rise off the asphalt, so he angled toward his truck with the dull, practical thought of groceries and a couple more errands filling the space where panic had been.

The sheriff had promised to dig into the former intern's name, but the idea sat wrong in Josh's gut. That kid had been unreliable and annoying, sure, but when Josh searched his memory for anything truly mean, he found only missed shifts and half-finished tasks, not the kind of cold malice it took to torch someone's life's work. His mind kept circling the empty space for a motive, but he came up blank.

If the cops hit a wall, he could always call Cory Phillips. Just thinking his name brought up a mental snapshot of the man. Crisp posture, quiet voice, the kind of watchful stillness that came from years in uniform. Cory had contacts tucked away like tools in a well-packed kit, and Josh knew if he brought him in, things would start moving in the shadows where official channels couldn't reach.

The real problem was how clean the crime was. Nothing left behind to hold onto. No convenient cigarette butt. No tossed glove. No tool with a smear of sweat. Everything that might have carried a print had gone up in the blaze.

The items that survived weren't any better. Shelves, frames and counters had a coating of history from kids' sticky fingers to hands carefully cradling pottery to tourists leaning in to point something out.

Every surface was a blur of overlapping ghosts from the millions of fingerprints layered from years of being open to anyone who wandered in.

On his way out, he walked past two people standing just outside the doors. Their conversation stopped as soon as he opened the door. He'd heard his name, but didn't know either person that well. They'd been in his shop once or twice over the years, so he nodded at them. The man facing him averted his eyes.

Well, hell. What's going on? I know he saw me. He's been in the shop a couple of times. He always seemed friendly. Come to think of it, there have been many conversations that just stopped when I walked into places or got close to people talking.

His brow creased as he slid into his truck, thinking about all the times he'd noticed people turning away from him or ending conversations only to pick them up after they thought he couldn't hear. He was always too far away to listen to the words, but he could hear their voices.

Josh shook his head and started the truck to head home. He drove into his driveway and checked his watch. Just then, a deep, rumbling noise came from his gut. The breakfast sandwich he'd had was long gone. He carried the groceries in and set the bags on the counter while he called Novah. "Hey, Baby, are you ready for lunch?"

"Yeah, but I'm hungry, and I have lunch made. Do you want to come over here?" Novah asked.

"Sure. I'll be there as soon as I finish putting these groceries up," Josh responded. He ended the call after a few pleasantries and freshened up a bit before he climbed in his truck to head over to Novah's.

On his way to Novah's, Josh received a notification. When he pulled into her driveway, he checked his messages.

NOVAH: *Come around to the office.*
JOSH: *Just pulled in. Will do.*

He walked around the outside of the house and entered through the door to the second floor of the converted boathouse.

"Down here!" Novah called.

He walked through her office to the steps leading downstairs. She had spread a blanket on the lower deck and had a picnic lunch spread out. Josh kicked his shoes off and rolled his pant legs up before he walked over and sat next to her. "Hey, Babe." He leaned in to kiss her.

Novah broke the kiss. "I'm hungry."

Josh adjusted the front of his jeans. "I am, too, but not necessarily for food." He turned as Novah grabbed a plate and loaded it up with cold fried chicken, mustard potato salad and cole slaw.

"Beer, pop, wine or water?" she asked.

"Beer, since it's past noon."

She handed him the plate and walked up the steps to grab two beers.

Josh twisted the cap off his and took a long sip. "Ahh, that's good."

As they ate, the only noise was the lapping of the lake on the pilings and the metal clank of their forks against their plates. After they finished, Josh pointed to the water. "How deep is it here?"

Novah shrugged. "About twenty feet. At least it was when I had the new support columns put in."

"The water is really clear here. You can see the bottom, but it's deceiving. It doesn't look all that deep." Josh grabbed the hem of his shirt and lifted it over his head.

Novah's eyes moved from his face to the muscles in his arms—those created by lifting heavy blocks of clay and working them all day, and then down to his rock-hard abs. She suppressed a moan as she felt the tingling in her core.

When Josh's hands moved to his waist, her eyes followed them as he slowly unfastened first one button and then the next, showing a flash of deep purple—almost black—low-cut briefs. The bulge under his underwear twitched as Novah moaned, "Jesus, Josh."

He unfastened the last button, lay back and slid the jeans over his hips and off his legs, leaving the briefs in place. He rolled to his side, watching her. When her eyes remained on the large bulge his now fully erect cock made in his briefs, Josh flattened his hand over it and rubbed up and down.

While he wanted to see what her reaction would be, he wasn't so sure he wouldn't lose it while she watched him rub himself. "You have too many clothes—" He broke off with a moan when he felt the drop of pre-cum through his briefs.

Novah licked her lips and lifted her T-shirt over her head without moving her eyes away from Josh's hand as he continued to rub himself. When his cock jumped, she moaned and hurriedly stripped her jeans off.

"Take it all off. I want to taste you, Novah. I need to taste you."

She unfastened her bra and let it slide off her shoulders, and then slid her matching silk panties over her hips. When Josh pushed her back, she shook her head and reached for him. "Take them off first."

Josh freed his cock, lay back on the blanket and then lifted his hips to slide his briefs off.

Novah licked her lips again and then straddled his face. She leaned forward and licked the tip of his cock before sliding it as far into her mouth as she could.

Reaching up to spread her open, Josh pulled her hips down to his face and licked her from her clit to her entrance. He almost lost it when he felt the vibration of her moan on the tip of his cock. Reaching between them, he rubbed circles on her nub while he flicked his tongue in and out of her entrance. He tasted a new wetness and moaned as he lapped it up.

He couldn't stop to warn Novah, and his hips bucked as hot cum filled her mouth.

Novah arched her back and adjusted her hips over Josh as her spasms continued. She couldn't get enough and ground her hips into his face, wanting even more. "Jesus fucking Christ, Josh!" she yelled, his name turning into a long, low moan.

Before her muscles stopped spasming, Josh pushed her hips up. "Turn around," he gasped, trying to catch his breath. He was already hard again. He grabbed the base of his cock and rubbed up and down while Novah turned and straddled him.

She lowered herself onto him and ground out, "I need you now. I need it rough. Fuck me as hard as you can, Baby." Novah's hips pushed against Josh as he met her stroke for stroke. He grabbed them so he could pull her down onto him with more force. Every time he met her, his cock rubbed against her nub, sending her into oblivion. Her screams turned into a long, low moan as she spurted on him while her muscles pumped his cock dry.

Josh yelled as streams of hot cum filled her. His breath caught, and it seemed as if his brain forgot to tell him to breathe.

Novah collapsed on him, trying to catch her breath, her muscles still pumping him.

Chapter 8

Josh groaned at the stiffness in his neck and shoulders. The crisp, damp earthiness of the lake settled gently in his nose, and a peaceful confusion washed over him. When he turned his head slightly, he caught a whiff of musky jasmine and opened his eyes, taking in the strange ceiling.

"Shit." He reached for his jeans to grab the phone out of his pocket.

"What time is it?" Novah asked sleepily.

"Nearly ten. The next day," Josh said, shaking his head.

Novah opened her eyes and winced as she pushed herself up from the floor. "Oh, hell. I can't believe we fell asleep right here. That crick in my neck will mess with me all day." The muscles along her spine twanged as she rolled her shoulders to ease the dull throb at the base of her skull.

Josh rubbed the back of his neck, his fingers pressing into a tight knot just below his hairline. "Me, too. It's what woke me up. I can't believe we fell asleep here, either."

He stood and helped Novah up, and pulled her into him as he kissed her. "Novah," he said hoarsely as he broke the kiss, his breath rushing hot against her cheek.

She raised an eyebrow at him, but he didn't say anything else. Instead, he wrapped his arms around her and pulled her into a tight hug, pressing her against his chest until she could hear the steady thump of his heartbeat.

Oh, hell. What am I doing? I almost said those three little words. But do I love her? Josh's stomach gave a slow, uneasy twist as he analyzed his feelings. I know I care deeply for her. I'd do just about anything for her. But where did this come from? A few weeks ago, we couldn't stand each other. Now, I can't get enough of her. The way she laughs. The way her fingers always smell faintly of citrus from the soap that she likes. The way her presence settles the static buzzing in my head.

"Josh." Novah shifted, moving her upper body away from him, but keeping her arms looped around his waist. When his eyes met hers, she said, "You were in outer space there for a few minutes. Are you okay?" Her voice was soft, still husky from sleep, and her brows pinched together.

"Yeah. I was just thinking about what I need to do today," he said, the lie feeling thick on his tongue. He could tell by the tight set of her mouth that she didn't believe him. The wooden floor felt cool under his bare feet as he pulled on his jeans and reached for his shirt, the fabric dragging over his skin while she turned away to dress.

"Come up to the house and get cleaned up before you go home," she whispered, her fingers threading through his as she took his hand and led him up the stairs. Warm light from the window spilled down the stairwell, carrying the faint scent of coffee left in the pot.

"I have to go. I need to work on a piece I'd promised someone." He leaned over and gave her a quick, almost absentminded kiss. His lips barely brushed hers before he straightened and walked across the upper part of the lower level to the door. "I'll see you later," he said as he let the door snick shut behind him with a muted click that sounded more final than it should have.

Novah stood there, rooted to the spot, the cool draft from the closing door brushing over her bare arms. *What did I say? One minute, he was fine, and then the next, bam.*

The echo of his expression, his eyes wide and unfocused as the color drained from his face, played in her mind repeatedly, and it didn't look like disgust so much as pure, unfiltered panic. She'd seen that look before when people got bad news and on fans at signings who suddenly realized they were about to cry in public, not on a man who'd just made her feel cherished with every touch.

Maybe he realized that I'm not the prettiest woman or that I have a few extra pounds. Damn. The old, familiar sting of that insecurity burned hot and fast, but even as it flared, a quieter, steadier voice pointed out that his hands hadn't hesitated on her hips, that he'd looked at her like she was something he'd found instead of settled for.

He hadn't flinched when she'd been naked in full light. He'd come apart in her arms on a cold rock, tears hot against her skin. That wasn't a man suddenly noticing a soft belly. *That was a broken man.*

Her throat tightened as she swallowed hard. She couldn't pretend she hadn't heard the strain in his voice lately, or seen the way his shoulders hunched whenever someone mentioned the fire, or how he'd gone quiet when the subject of his parents came up, his gaze turning inward and far away.

Whatever had just flashed across his face had roots deeper than her thighs or her curves. It felt more like he'd hit some invisible tripwire in his own head and bolted before it snapped shut on him.

Her throat tightened as she swallowed hard. She shook her head, pushed her hair away from her face with a sharp, irritated swipe, and went into the main house to wash up and change.

After her shower and grabbing a bowl of cereal, she went back out to her office to clean up the dishes they'd left out there. She brought them into the house, rinsed them and stuck them in the dishwasher. Back in her office, she picked up the blanket where they had made the most tender, yet rugged love. As she folded it, she caught a whiff of his scent—the scent that was uniquely Josh—intermingled with hers.

It sent a shot of electricity through her core as she remembered the feeling of being loved and protected when he'd wrapped his arms around her or as he'd raised himself over her to take her flying. She brought the blanket to her second-floor office and laid it across her chair.

It was too muggy to work in the first-floor office, so she'd enjoy the view with the air conditioning. Having the blanket on the back of the chair wasn't enough. She pulled it around her shoulders as she opened her manuscript. As her arms moved while she set up her desk to start writing, Josh's essence filled her nose, causing her to moan.

"I love his smell. I love his stormy gray eyes. I love..." Novah's breath hitched, and she shook her head. "No. I don't love him. I can't. He doesn't love me. It's too soon to know that. And besides, I can't mean much to him. Not the way we treated each other all these years."

Josh turned on the shower, making sure the water was cold. He'd been hard for Novah since he woke up, but when thoughts of love infiltrated his mind, he'd gotten out of there as fast as he could. "No wonder you can't keep a woman. As soon as you think one of them is getting too close, you bolt."

He stepped into the cold shower, but it wasn't helping. Turning the water to warm, he took himself in his hand and braced himself against the wall with the other hand above his head. He couldn't help but let thoughts of Novah run through his head, even though he knew that wasn't going to help, either. She had the perfect amount of softness about her, yet he could still feel the muscles when she held him. And that...that...from last night. Josh shuddered, arched his back and yelled.

He turned and leaned against the wall, breathing heavily, while the water rinsed his seed down the drain. When he caught his breath, he finished his shower and put on a fresh pair of Levis and a T-shirt.

Josh stepped into the sheriff's office, the scent of burnt coffee and old paper hitting him as the door clicked shut behind him.

"Hank."

The sheriff nodded at him and stood to shake his hand. "Come back to my office. We had an anonymous tip that led us to the person who might have burned your studio."

Josh followed Hank down the narrow hall, passing bulletin boards cluttered with wanted posters, memos and sun-faded flyers. Their footsteps echoed off the cinderblock walls, and somewhere a phone rang. They entered the sheriff's office, and Josh closed the door behind him. "What do you have?" he asked.

Hank reached for the stained coffee pot on the filing cabinet, the glass clinking lightly against the burner as he tipped it. The bitter, over-strong smell drifted across the room as he poured himself a cup and held the pot toward Josh.

"Sure. Black, please," Josh said, easing down into one of the surprisingly comfortable chairs in front of the sheriff's desk.

Hank handed Josh his coffee and plopped down into his chair on the other side of the desk, the old seat whining in protest. He logged into his computer and hit a few keys. Turning the screen toward Josh, he asked, "Know this guy?"

Josh leaned forward, setting his coffee on the edge of the desk, and squinted at the screen. The man had red hair, cut short in a military cut, but not quite a buzz cut, heavy-set shoulders straining the collar of his shirt, and a face crowded with freckles. The wire-rimmed glasses made him look a little crazy—at least, Josh thought so.

He leaned back in his chair, causing the leather to sigh. "Can't say I've ever seen him. I definitely don't know him."

Hank leaned forward, resting his elbows on his desk and propping his chin on his fists. "We got an anonymous tip in the form of a typewritten note that was shoved under the door and addressed to 'Sheriff Watauga Lake.' We went to talk to him just to get a feel for where this guy's head is at, and he was acting mighty suspicious.

"A couple of days later, we went back out to his place with a warrant. He lives not too far from you and Novah—up off Windward Lane in a camper. We found all kinds of suspicious stuff, but it's all circumstantial." Hank's voice roughened slightly with frustration on the last word.

Josh leaned back and rubbed his chin, feeling the rasp of stubble under his fingers as he thought. A faint image of his charred studio flashed in his mind. The acrid stench of smoke. The skeletal beams. The warped metal.

"If he's far enough back up in there, he could see my studio and Novah's place with a good pair of binoculars. That road goes up on that ridge." He glanced back at the monitor, the man's freckled face staring back at him, and a cool weight settled in his gut.

Hank nodded. "He's far enough back. We also found a trail through the woods right across from his place. Looks like he only used it for walking, and he never cleared it. It went around bushes and trees. I know these woods like the back of my hand, and that trail has never been there.

"We followed it, and it goes a bit higher on that bluff, and yes, there's a perfect view of both of your places. We found cigarette butts and other trash where he must have been sitting for hours, watching."

Josh leaned forward, as if he was going to leave, but sat back in his chair again. "Wait a second. What's Novah got to do with any of this, other than you can see her place? From that spot, you can see Cassidy's Accounting, too. Why would you mention Novah and not Skylar Cassidy?"

Hank pulled his cell phone off his belt and opened the gallery. He handed it to Josh. This doesn't leave this room. You can't even tell Novah. Not yet. We'll be keeping an eye on her place. There's no telling how long he's had this, so we don't think it's going to come to anything within the next day or so."

Josh swiped through the pictures. "What the fuck, Hank?"

Chapter 9

The lump of clay took shape as Josh's hand caressed the side, while the fingertips of his other hand helped to shape the bowl from the inside for the sixteen-place dinnerware set he was making for a new client. Josh's mind kept going back to the photos on Hank's phone. He'd taken them at that Eric guy's house. Camper. He had lined the walls with hundreds of pictures of Novah. He shuddered as he remembered the way every scrap of wallpaper disappeared beneath her duplicated smile.

Josh still couldn't connect the whacked-out guy's obsession with Novah to the burning of his place—nothing about it fit in his mind. *I could see it if Novah and I were seeing each other before the fire, but we weren't.*

He shook his head, the faint earthy scent of wet clay grounding him as his fingers moved over the spinning bowl. The cool, pliant mass yielded under his touch, slick against his hands as he shaped and trimmed the rim before carefully setting the piece aside, its surface still damp and fragile, ready for the kiln.

He grabbed another hunk of clay, the weight of it solid in his palm, and slapped it onto the wheel, the soft thud echoing in the quiet make-shift studio. As the wheel hummed beneath his hands, a dull ache in his shoulders and the fog in his thoughts made him pause. After a moment, he peeled the clay off the wheel and tucked it into the plastic bag, sealing in the moisture. A break suddenly felt more necessary than another perfect bowl.

After pouring a cup of coffee, he stepped out onto the rear deck. The steam curled into the morning air, and the rich scent mixed with the scent of lake water and wet sand. The breeze brushed against Josh's face and ruffled his hair.

A few people were walking in the beach area and their voices carried as soft, indistinct murmurs over the lapping waves, but he saw them without really seeing them. He dragged in a breath and tasted lake water, and sun-warmed stone, the air clean and sharp on his tongue, and it threw him back to other nights, other women.

Laura's perfume had always sat heavy in the air, florals and vanilla that clung to his clothes long after she'd gone, her laughter too loud in restaurants as she checked her phone between kisses. The women before that had blurred together. Bars, dim light, the slick feel of sweat and cheap body spray, hands sliding over him while their eyes kept darting to the clock or the door.

With Novah, the air had smelled like coffee and books, like the faint citrus of her shampoo when she'd tucked her head under his chin on the dyke, her weight settled against him as if she'd known exactly where to fit. Her silence hadn't been a wall. It had been a soft, steady hum that let his shoulders loosen and his jaw unclench. It allowed the noise in his head to drop from a roar to something closer to rain on a roof.

He couldn't remember the last time he'd sat with a woman and noticed the rhythm of her breathing more than the shape of her body and the warmth of her palm resting on his thigh.

His mind stopped on the images of Novah and the way her smile lit up her face, and slid straight to the way his tongue had almost formed those three little words.

The memory made his chest tighten, and a strange weightless drop in his stomach formed. He'd never even come close to saying them to anyone else before, and that realization sat heavy and sharp under his ribs, startling and unnerving him.

I know she's an artist, too. Yeah, writers are artists. But would she really understand the hours I spend in the studio working on a sculpture? Sure, I can whip up a sixteen-place setting in several eight-hour days, but one of those sculptures?

There were times he'd spent over twenty-four hours working on one, only taking short breaks to grab a coffee or go to the bathroom. Most of the time, he didn't even stop to eat.

I have to call her. I can't just run out on her, not after a night like that. She's ruined me for anyone else; that's for sure.

Novah glanced at her phone when it rang. Alexis's name lit up the screen, and she thumbed it on. "Hey, girl," she said, her voice softer than usual.

"Uh, oh. You don't sound like your normal, chipper self. What's going on?"

Novah shrugged, even though Alexis couldn't see it through the phone. "Nothing, just involved in writing." The words felt thin to her, and she knew Alexis would pick up on it.

“This doesn’t sound like the ‘I’m-distracted-because-I’m-writing-a-super-steamy-scene’ Novah that I know. Do I need to come over there?”

Novah paused for a minute, pressing her nose into the blanket, inhaling deeply. It still smelled like Josh, and the scent tugged at something low on her chest. “No, I’m really okay,” she mumbled.

“Now, I know you’re not okay. I’ll be there in ten with a gallon of ice cream.”

“Uh, is there something going on with you that you need a gallon of ice cream?” Novah asked, trying to lighten the conversation.

“Not necessarily.”

Novah sighed. “Come on then. I’ll meet you at the main house.”

They ended the call. No way she can come into the office. Her gaze dropped to the blanket as her fingers absently smoothed the fabric. Yeah, all the evidence is gone...except that blanket. She’d pick up on that right away. Better to stay up at the main house.

Novah saved her manuscript and headed up the stairs. She decided she needed a little more nourishment than ice cream and pulled the fixings for sandwiches out of the fridge. She’d just laid everything out on the counter when the doorbell rang. “It’s open!” she called.

Alexis strolled in wearing a pair of her favorite short-shorts and a cropped T-shirt. She saw Novah making sandwiches, so she put the ice cream in the freezer.

"Ham or turkey?" Novah asked.

"Both?" Alexis asked, her shoulders hunching as she grinned.

"Sounds good to me." Novah slathered four slices of bread with mayo and piled lettuce on them. She then added tomato slices with salt and pepper—but just a touch of salt because the ham was salty enough—on two of the slices. She added a layer of turkey, piled on some cheddar cheese, and then a layer of ham, and then covered it with the top half of the bread and lettuce.

They took their sandwiches to the dining room table, where Novah had already placed two bottles of water.

"So," Novah said as she tilted her head at Alexis. "What's going on?"

Alexis laughed. "No, you tell *me* what's going on."

"I'm not the one who called me looking for someone to binge on ice cream with. I know you too well, Alexis."

"Can't a girl just have a good time with some killer ice cream and her bestest bestie?"

"Oh, sure. Because nothing screams 'totally casual hangout' like desperation ice cream before it's even lunch."

Alexis laughed as she grabbed two spoons and the ice cream from the freezer. "Let's go. I wanna sit and dangle my feet in your 'inside' lake."

Oh, hell. I should have known. If I say no, she's gonna know for sure something is up. Maybe she won't notice the blanket.

Novah sighed to herself as she grabbed her phone and another couple of bottles of water.

Alexis raised her eyebrows.

"I haven't refilled the fridge out there yet," Novah said.

They walked down the steep stairs to the second-floor deck, the wooden steps creaking under their weight. "The bottom is locked, since I hadn't planned on coming back out here today," Novah said as she keyed the code in for the second-floor entry. As she walked through the upstairs office, she glanced at her cell to make sure she hadn't missed any texts or calls, her thumb brushing over the screen out of habit.

She didn't notice Alexis cutting her eyes at her, watching the way Novah's gaze kept darting back to the phone.

They walked down to the lower level and kicked their shoes off. Alexis set the sweating carton of ice cream on the deck between them and handed Novah a spoon. "Dig in, girlfriend."

Novah scooped up a bite of the cherry ice cream, making sure to snag a dark chocolate chunk with it. The bright sweetness and creamy chill hit her tongue, followed by the slight bitterness of the chocolate as it melted. She swallowed it and asked, "Okay, what's up with you?"

"What? Nothing. I told you."

Novah rolled her eyes, the familiar motion loosening some of the tension in her shoulders. "I know you better than that."

"Well, this absolutely gorgeous guy called in to the real estate office, looking for real estate around here."

"And you know he's gorgeous, how?"

"I kinda looked him up online."

"So, when's he supposed to come here? What's his name?"

Alexis shrugged, tapping the spoon against the carton. "Denver. I don't know. I sent him a bunch of listings around the area. Not just here, but in nearby cities."

Novah cut her eyes to her best friend, a smirk tugging at one corner of her mouth. "And that's a crisis, why?"

"Because he's gorgeous?"

Shaking her head, Novah said, "There's something else. That's nothing."

"I told you nothing was up. But...there's something up with you."

"No, there's not."

"Novah. You're checking your phone a zillion times, and you always ignore it. You have a blanket on your chair upstairs. You're never cold."

Alexis sniffed the air. "And it smells like a man in here."

Laughing, Novah said, "I checked my phone once since you've been here. I was using the blanket for my back because I was sitting too long in a marathon writing session. And I have no idea where you got the idea that it smells like a man in here. I smell lake water."

Alexis tilted her head and lifted her eyebrow at Novah. "Word through the grapevine is that you're seeing Josh. Mr. 'I-don't-like-anyone-I'm-a-high-and-mighty-artist' Josh."

The corner of Novah's lip lifted as she tried to hide a smile. "I don't know about that. I helped him move some stuff to his storage unit. He took me to dinner for a thank you."

Alexis let out a belly laugh. “Oh, my God, Novah. You two can’t stand each other. I can’t even picture you helping him in the first place.”

“Then you know we’re not seeing each other.” Novah’s fingers tightened a little around her phone as she said it.

Just then, the phone buzzed against her palm and the vibration jumped up her wrist. She swiped it active and pulled up the texts, the bright screen glaring in the softer light of the room.

JOSH: I’m sorry I ran out on you. Can we talk?
NOVAH: Yeah. Give me a few minutes. Alexis is here.

Before she could hit the send button, Alexis’s hand shot out, and her nails lightly scraped Novah’s skin as she snatched the phone away. “Oh, so you *are* seeing him?”

“Damn it, Alexis. Yes. No. I don’t know. Give me that.” Heat climbed into Novah’s cheeks as she lunged forward, her fingers closing around the smooth case. Novah jabbed the “Send” button and jammed the phone into her pocket.

Her phone notification tone chimed again, a bright ping that seemed louder than usual in the quiet between them.

JOSH: *Meet me on the beach behind the studio?*

NOVAH: *Okay. I'll walk up the beach. Should be around 15 to 20 minutes.*

She turned to Alexis. "I need to meet him in fifteen minutes. I have to get going. We did put a dent in that ice cream."

"Nice way to change the subject, Novah."

Sighing, Novah gave in. She knew her friend well enough to know that unless she got at least part of the story, she'd delay her.

"Okay, so we might have kissed. More than once. But he ran out on me the other night. Now he's apologizing for it."

"And you're falling for him, Novah. I can see it on your face. He never hangs around for more than a few dates. That guy is allergic to commitment. Be careful, or you're going to get hurt."

Novah shrugged. "I don't really want a commitment, either, Alexis. Besides, what man wants someone who is thirty pounds overweight?"

"You are not fat, so don't start that. Not everyone can be a size zero. You have curves, and a lot of men like curves. I wish I had those curves instead of this straight up and down man-looking bullshit," Alexis said as she motioned up and down her narrow body. "Hell, unless I get a boob job, I'll never be more than a 34-B.

At least you have some good-looking boobs that'll fit a guy's hand. Especially nice hands like Josh has."

"Well, I've seen the women he's normally with. They're all like size zero or size two. Not my size 14."

"Maybe that's why they never last. Have you ever thought of that?" Alexis asked.

"No. Then why bother going out with someone you're not attracted to? That doesn't make sense. Let's get going. I'm going to be late, and I want to get some writing done today, too. Call me later?"

Alexis handed the ice cream to Novah. "You can bet on it. Stick this in your freezer."

They made their way upstairs and into the main house. Novah stashed the ice cream in the freezer. "Call me later."

Alexis grinned. "Uh, maybe *you* should call me later, if you're not busy."

Novah rolled her eyes and locked the door behind Alexis. She glanced at what she was wearing. "This'll have to do. I don't have time to change."

She grabbed her cell and sent a quick text to let Josh know she was on the way.

Chapter 10

Josh was sitting on the beach with his arms around his legs when he saw Novah in the distance. She was wearing short jean cutoffs and a tight T-shirt, and was carrying her shoes in her hand. The longer he watched her, the more uncomfortable the front of his jeans became. He finally stood up to relieve the pressure and walked toward her.

Josh shoved his hands into his pockets and fell into step beside her, close enough to share the chill without brushing Novah's sleeve. His shoulders folded in against the wind as it worried at their clothes, the beach stretching ahead in gray silence. Between them, the crunch of sand and shells under their shoes said everything they didn't.

The space of a few inches between them felt a lot wider. They walked for several minutes before he stopped and turned to her. "I really am sorry for running out on you the other day. I, uh, have issues with, well, you know. Feelings. I was being an ass." His voice came out rough, the words scraping his throat on the way up.

"What were you feeling?"

"Uh," Josh stuttered, his gaze flicking away toward the water.

"Kiss me, Josh."

"I-I-. I can't. I get too lost in you." Josh lowered his head and stared at the sand.

"And there's something wrong with that?" Novah asked with sarcasm, heat creeping into her tone. He was starting to piss her off. "Or is it that I'm not a size zero?"

He lifted his head quickly, widening his eyes. "No, never think that. It's not you. You're perfect the way you are. I never would have been able to, uh, do what we did if I didn't think you were beautiful just the way you are." His hands curled tighter in his pockets as he spoke.

"You have to admit, I'm not like the girls you are usually with."
"This is true, but you notice I'm not with any of them?"
"You acted like you weren't with me, either."
Josh shook his head. "Yeah. I know. I'm sorry."

They stood in silence for several minutes before Josh said quietly—so quietly that Novah barely heard him over the light wind—"I know I have issues that I have to work through, but I can't be without you."

Novah's heart softened, the tight ache in her chest easing just a little. "I think we all have issues," she whispered.

"I can't promise you I won't do something stupid again. One of those issues is being too self-absorbed in my work. It's not something I can help, at least so far." His shoulders sagged at his admission.

She put her arm around him, but his muscles went taut under her fingers. Novah removed her arm so they were no longer touching, the loss of contact leaving her feeling suddenly cool. *Is it his issue, or does he really think I'm too heavy for him? Damn. I don't know if this is going to work. What if I get more invested than I already am, and he decides I'm not for him?*

"I have to go, Josh. I have a deadline to meet." She didn't, but she couldn't stand there with him, knowing he may not be able to stand her touch.

Novah walked down the trail to her office, the gravel crunching under her feet. The air grew stiller as the trees closed in around her. She didn't let the tears fall until she was inside, the door clicking shut behind her, and she wrapped herself in the blanket that still carried Josh's scent.

Josh rolled over and groaned when his phone rang. He glanced at the time as he reached for it. Seven in the morning. He hadn't been able to fall asleep last night and had just drifted off at five. Instead, he thought about Novah all night. The way he treated her. The way she walked off. The way she felt in his arms. He also thought about what was wrong with him and why their relationship—such as it was at this point—scared him.

"Damn it," he said as the phone stopped ringing and then started again.

"Hello," he mumbled, his voice rough with sleep.

"Josh, Hank. Sorry to wake you. Have you spoken to Novah?"

"Not about the case. You said not to mention it to her." And then, under his breath, "Evidently, not about much else, either." He sat up, rubbing his forehead with the heel of his hand as a dull throb settled behind his eyes.

Hank narrowed his eyes. "What?"

"Oh, nothing. Just mumbling to myself."

"Josh, if you're not seeing her anymore, we need to tell her. You won't be there to protect her if this guy decides to get even nuttier. His cheese already fell off his cracker..."

"And what makes you think I'd be there all the time, even if we were seeing each other, Hank?" Josh swung his legs over the side of the bed.

Hank opened his mouth to say something, but changed his mind. It didn't make any sense to get into it with Josh. "Point taken, buddy, point taken."

"What's that guy's name anyway? You never did tell me."

"I'll tell you later if you don't know. Wait until we get enough on him to arrest him. We're working on it."

"Well, fuck, Hank. Those pictures ought to be enough, don't you think?"

"No. It's not a crime to have pictures hanging up. It's only circumstantial evidence. And, we don't have enough to tie him to the fire. Just sit back and let us do our investigation, okay?"

"I don't like it, but I guess I don't have a choice."

"Not if you want what we get to stick so we can put this guy away for good."

They finished the call, and Josh lay back down, the mattress creaking softly. After thirty minutes of tossing and turning, the sheets twisted around his legs. He swore and sat up. "Might as well take a shower and see if I can get more done on that dinnerware service. I'm sure as fuck not getting any more sleep."

He rubbed his face with his hands and then stepped into the bathroom. After his shower, he refused to look at himself in the mirror and didn't even shave. He didn't want to see if he looked as bad as he felt. "Damn, I need to get some sleep. Famous last words."

After staring at a lump of clay for several minutes, Josh shook his head. He knew it was bad when he didn't even have the ambition to work the clay. That was his go-to whenever he was out of sorts. He packed the clay back up and made sure the kiln was off, even though he knew he hadn't turned it on this morning.

I guess I could take a hike up the trails. I really don't feel like doing that. Can't take the boat out. My buddy won't let me go alone, and I don't want company right now. He's right, since I don't have a lot of experience, but I can't be around people. Josh shook his head.

He walked into the kitchen and grabbed a beer. He knew it was only nine in the morning. "Fuck it. Five o'clock somewhere." He took it outside and plopped into one of the chairs, resting his feet on the railing.

Novah leaned forward in her chair and read the last few paragraphs, so she'd make sure she hadn't forgotten where she left off the day before. After she read the paragraphs, she poised her fingers over the keyboard.

After a few long seconds, nothing came to her. "Well, fuck. I don't have time for writer's block. I've taken enough off the last few days to hang out with Josh."

Josh.

He smells so good. Clean soap and something warm and masculine that clings long after he leaves. Just enough muscles to show them off, but not enough to look disgusting. The faintly outlined abs and the sexy swirl of hair that disappeared under the waistband of his jeans.

Novah shifted in her chair, pressing her thighs together, trying to ease the slow, intense heat that was gathering low in her belly.

The way he kissed me. His soft lips on my skin. She shivered as she remembered his mouth moving along her neck, lingering at the curve of her shoulder, then lower, across the top of her chest, each brush of his lips sending a line of goose bumps racing over her before he grabbed a nipple between his teeth and pinched the other one between his fingers.

His tongue as it flicked my clit and pushed into my entrance...

She dragged in a breath, but her mind slipped back to the way his touch had turned her whole body into a live wire.

She shoved herself away from the desk, the chair casters squeaking in protest. “Jesus fucking Christ. I can’t even write because I can’t think about anything but him.” She stalked into the main house and yanked open the fridge, the cool air spilling over her flushed face. “I’m not even hungry,” she muttered as she slammed the door shut. “Eating isn’t going to help the situation.”

Josh stepped into the bakery. It was later in the afternoon, and he knew it would be nearly empty, since it was after the lunch rush. He’d waited purposely because he wanted as little contact with others as possible. He knew he had an attitude since most people gave him a wide berth when he was like this.

It’d been two weeks since he last spoke with Novah. He knew she was pissed, and she had a right to be, but he didn’t know how to fix it. He’d tried to talk to her and knew he’d handled it poorly.

He jerked his head up when he realized someone had called his name a few times.

Jaxxon had a grin on his face. “Damn, son, you look like shit. Lose your razor?”

“Whatever, dude. Can I get some of those danishes to go? And the largest coffee you have. Black.”

Jaxxon shrugged. “Sure. But you might want to get your head out of your ass. People have been mumbling about your attitude, about how you won’t even respond to them.”

“I don’t give a fuck what they think,” Josh snarled.

Jaxxon handed him a box with six of the danishes he knew Josh liked best.”

Josh shook his head. “Sorry, man. Bad couple of weeks. I shouldn’t be yelling at you.”

“No, you shouldn’t. A word to the wise. Get your head out of your ass. Pay attention to your building, too. I caught them using shit wood and made them take it back.”

“What? Are you kidding? That business comes with a stellar reputation.”

“That doesn’t mean they won’t try some shit behind your back. It’s not like they’re locals, so...” Jaxxon lifted his hand in a wave. “See ya, and get some sleep. Keep an eye on them over there, and I will, too.”

“Thanks, Jaxxon. I’ll see you around.”

Josh slid into his truck, set the danishes down on the passenger seat and his coffee in the holder in the console. He banged the steering wheel. “Fuck. Just something else to worry about.”

He took a sip of coffee and grabbed a pastry. “Apple. Good man, Jaxxon.”

After he finished eating, he wiped his hands and headed to the job site. He knew he was looking for a fight and probably shouldn’t be there, but they needed to see that they had to do a good job, even if he wasn’t there twenty-four-seven.

Pulling into the parking lot, he reached in the back to grab the hard hat that the super always required on-site. Josh jammed it on his head and slid out of his truck, slamming the door behind him.

Before the foreman knew what was happening, Josh closed the distance between them in three long strides, heat rolling off him as he got in the man’s face. “I don’t want ever to catch you or hear of you using inferior materials on this job again. You’re getting paid top dollar, and I expect top-quality materials and work, not fucking grade B lumber!” His voice cracked across the site, sharp enough to make a couple of workers glance over.

The foreman held up his dusty hands. “Calm down, it won’t happen again. They sent the wrong stuff—”

"I don't want to hear it! I know that's bullshit. This ain't my first rodeo with builders, bubba. Now get to work and do it right. You get inferior shit, you return it—and don't say they sent it when I know you ordered it to cut corners!" Spit flew with the last words, and Josh jabbed a finger toward the stack of lumber.

He stalked off without giving the man time to respond, his boots thudding against the packed dirt. He walked over to the pile of materials and yanked boards free, the rough grain scraping his palms as he checked stamps and labels, mumbling under his breath the whole time.

Nails clicked and plastic wrap crinkled as he moved from stack to stack. An hour later, sweat darkened the back of his shirt, and he'd gone through everything. He'd call the insurance company when he got home and give them an earful, too, just in case they'd been the ones pushing cheap substitutions. "Lord knows they cut costs wherever they can. Greedy bastards."

He slid into his truck and slammed the door, the hollow bang rattling in the cab. He was still muttering about inferior materials and slop-shod work as he jammed the key in the ignition. He pulled out and headed toward home. His jaw clenched so tightly that it ached. Just as he pulled into his driveway, his phone rang. Without looking at it, he swiped the call active. "What??!!"

Chapter 11

Novah had finally been able to write. She was on a roll and had just finished two more chapters, and was starting the next one when her phone rang. "Damn it." She ignored it and wrote the next paragraph. The phone rang again. With a sigh, she hit the keys to save her work and glanced at the display.

She narrowed her eyes. She answered. "Hank. How can I help you?"

Hank sighed and rolled his eyes. Josh had just ripped his head off, too. "Not you, too."

"Sorry?"

"Everyone sounds grouchy today. But anyway, I hope your day isn't as bad as you think it is."

Novah sat up straighter in her chair, the seat cushion creaking under her as a prickle of unease slid over her skin. "What's wrong, Hank? Who's hurt? Is Josh okay?"

"Nothing like that. No one's hurt. I, uh, didn't say anything before because I thought you'd be spending more time with Josh, but, ah..."

Novah waited, listening to the faint rustle on the other end as he gathered his thoughts. It didn't take long.

"We think someone may be stalking you. We got a tip several days ago about someone who may have either had a hand in or burned Josh's studio. When we went to check it out, the guy had his walls covered with pictures of you. It looks as though he's been watching you for some time."

Novah rolled her eyes, even though he couldn't see it, her fingers tightening around the phone. "I'm sure more than just he has pictures of me all over their walls. I am a popular romance writer."

"No, Novah. This wasn't like that. I mean, the walls were covered. Like the pictures were wallpaper."

A slight chill slid down her spine, but she forced her tone to stay light. “And you didn’t warn me before. Why?”

“We don’t have any concrete evidence. It’s all circumstantial. We have no evidence that he was stalking you other than the pictures, and as you alluded to, there’s no crime in that. I’m asking you to keep this under your hat for now. We’re actively investigating it, along with a possible link to the studio fire.”

Novah took a deep breath, holding it for a few long heartbeats. “And you haven’t arrested him, yet, right?”

The sheriff made an agreeable noise in his throat. “And why not, Hank?”

“We don’t have enough to arrest him on. We’re pretty sure he’s the one who started the fire at Josh’s studio, but without fingerprints and only pictures on the wall, we really don’t have anything.”

Novah remained silent for several long seconds, staring at the cursor blinking on her screen. “Okay, I’ll be careful. Is that all? I was in the middle of writing.”

“No. Call us if you see or hear anything suspicious, even if you think it’s nothing. We don’t know what we’re dealing with yet, but there is an active investigation that the state is involved with. If it goes further, we may have to bring in the feds, depending on what we find. We do have someone tailing him, so you should be safe."

"Yeah, until he loses his tail," she muttered.

"Well, we sure hope that won't happen."

"Oh, hope? Really? Great. I'll sleep like a baby knowing the fate of my safety rests on wishful thinking."

Hank sighed, the exhale crackling faintly through the line. "No need to get sarcastic. Between you and Josh. You need to—"

"Don't even go there, Hank."

Hank knew when to shut his mouth. "Just be careful, Novah. Talk to you later."

"Sure, Hank. I will. Talk to you later."

She leaned back in her chair. She'd managed to get Josh out of her mind, and now he was in it again, tangled up with the image of some stranger's walls lined with her face. "Damn it," she muttered.

Novah sighed as she went back to her book. She wrote another paragraph, fingers tapping out the words in a quick burst, and then deleted it with a few sharp keystrokes. She tried a few more times before she swore under her breath, the blinking cursor starting to feel like it was mocking her.

She'd been on a roll, and that phone call had knocked her clean off it, leaving her thoughts scattered. The cool weight of her phone pressed into her palm as she scrolled to Josh's number, fingertip hovering, screen light washing her skin. "Nope. Not going to do it." She threw it onto the desk, where it landed with a thud and slid across the wood.

Josh glanced at the makeshift shelves in the room he'd converted to a temporary studio. "I might be able to fit this piece on there." Nothing was ready for the kiln yet. They were all bisque-fired, but he had to paint them. He pointed at each piece as he counted them. "Not even half done with that set. I really need to get my space back. This is slowing me down."

He fisted his hands several times and tried to go back to the piece he was working on. His restless fingers put too much pressure on the piece. He pulled his hand away from the warped bowl. "Fuck. Now I have to reshape it." Shaking his head, Josh turned the potter's wheel off and covered the piece so it wouldn't dry out.

After cleaning up, he decided to check on the progress of his building. Grabbing his keys, he stepped out onto the porch, planning on walking. As he reached the road, he thought better of it. "I'd have to walk right by Novah's house." His face colored just remembering how they'd ended their last conversation.

"She must be pissed since she hasn't called me since." *Phone works both ways,* he argued with himself. The stab in his gut told him how wrong he was. He knew he should call her and apologize. "Not today. I can't handle much else right now."

Instead of cutting across the lawn to take the walk he wanted, he ambled toward the driveway. "Too hot to walk anyway," he muttered under his breath. *Excuses, excuses.*

When Josh arrived at his building a few minutes later, the parking lot was full, so he pulled into the accountant's office across the street. Luckily, Skylar didn't mind.

He found the foreman and asked if he could get a tour. The first floor exterior and interior frames were up, plus the first floor dried in. The exterior frames were up on the second floor.

"We'll have the whole second floor dried in today. Tomorrow, a crew will be here to do the exterior, and my crew will work on the interior," the foreman said.

Josh nodded. "It's going faster than I thought. I'm glad of it. It's hard work in that tiny space at my house."

The foreman walked Josh through the first floor, their footsteps echoing dully on the unfinished subfloor.

Sawdust hung in the air, mixing with the sharp scent of fresh-cut lumber as the foreman pointed out the bare studs, open wiring runs and skeletal framing that would eventually hold walls. It was clear from the exposed pipes and tangled cords that the building still needed a lot of work.

By the time they stepped back out into the daylight, Josh's head hummed with measurements and timelines, the promise of "a few more weeks" still ringing in his ears.

Josh slid into his truck, shutting out the clatter of hammers and shouts from the crew. He turned the key, and the engine rumbled to life. He pulled away from the site, the tension in his shoulders easing a bit as the construction noise fell behind. The thought of hot coffee and something sweet tugged at him as he steered toward the bakery.

Chapter 12

Just as Josh pulled into the parking lot at the studio, his phone rang. He took a sip of his coffee, the heat biting his tongue, as he checked the display. Hank.

"Yeah, Hank."

"Josh. Got a question for you."

"Yeah?" Josh shifted the cup to his other hand.

"What chemicals do you use in the studio?"

"Usually turpentine, why?" The word tasted bitter as he said it, the memories of its sharp, piney reek ghosting through his mind.

"Hold on a second."

Josh heard the sheriff talking to someone in the background. The muffled voices and the faint scrape of something hard against a desk sifted through the line. Since he couldn't hear the other person, he assumed Hank was on another phone.

"He uses turpentine."

Josh heard Hank say, "Hold on, I'll ask."

Hank came back on the line. "Do you ever use paint thinner?"

Josh shook his head as if Hank could see him, his eyes fixed on the soot-stained outline where his old doorway used to be. "No, just turpentine to clean the brushes if I have to use oil-based paints."

"Okay, let me call you back. We might have something."

They ended the call, and Josh finished his Danish, licking a smear of glaze from his thumb before taking another sip of his coffee. He slid out of his truck, grabbed the coffee and hooked the phone to his belt before walking toward the building.

"Fuck." He turned back to the truck as the realization hit. He'd forgotten his hard hat. He unlocked the door, grabbed the scuffed orange hat from the passenger seat and shoved it on his head. As he turned back toward the building, his phone vibrated against his hip.

When he saw Novah's name on the screen, he sent it to voicemail. "I'll have to call her later," he muttered guiltily. "No time right now." He knew he was making excuses.

The construction crew was working in the front room, which would be his new retail space. Josh walked through the front area to the rear. Instead of putting the gallery upstairs, he decided to combine the retail and gallery spaces into one large room. The actual footprint of the building was larger than the old building by a few feet on either side and by several feet toward the rear.

The change in size gave him room enough to have just the one retail space. He would put sets of pottery in the middle of the room, and then line the walls with various types of shelving and hangers for display and one-off pieces, such as his sculptures.

Because he had several hundred feet of property in the back before it hit the lake, he was able to add the public restrooms, a small commercial kitchen and a patio. He would keep pastries from Rowan's Hearth Bakery and sandwiches from Hensley's Cafe and Bakery in the kitchen. Both businesses would deliver daily, so he'd have fresh product. It would have a microwave and a toaster oven, plus a large coffee machine and espresso maker.

Hensley's used fresh bread for their sub rolls, and they were better than any other kind of sub rolls Josh had ever put in his mouth. Mia, the owner, said her friend, who lives in Connecticut, called them grinder rolls.

They were chewy on the outside and softer, but still chewy on the inside. They were a long roll, much like Italian bread. She'd finally gotten her hands on a recipe and perfected it so that the rolls tasted just like a grinder roll from Remy's Grinder Shop in Willimantic—a place that used to be known as Thread City because of the American Thread mill. No one in the south—hell, no one outside of Connecticut could make grinder rolls as they did there.

He would get coffee beans from Rowan's so people could grab a coffee and a light lunch or snack while they were browsing the gallery. Josh would have a few bistro tables inside and several outside on the patio.

The workers hadn't finished the rear section yet since they were working from front to back. He went up the steps that were behind a wall that separated the kitchen and bistro area from the rear entry. The upstairs would hold his studio and his office. The front retail area would also have a set of steps that would lead to his office in the front of the building. The studio would take up about three-quarters of the rear of the second floor—that part would not be open to the public.

Josh glanced around at the stud walls upstairs. He could see where a large wall would separate his office and a private bathroom from the studio. The office area also held a small kitchenette with a fridge, coffee maker, a large air fryer and a microwave. The bathroom would have a walk-in shower for when he stayed all night working on projects.

As he headed down the stairs, Josh's phone rang. He glanced at the screen and swiped the call active. "Hey, Hank. Hold on a sec until I get outside."

Josh ran down the half-finished staircase at the front of the building, staying close to the wall, since the railing wasn't up on the open side. Once he went through the front door and reached his truck, he put the phone to his ear. "Sorry. Too many ears in the building. What's up?"

He listened as Hank explained that the lab tests showed the arsonist had used paint thinner to start the fire, the words coming through the line in a flat, measured tone that made them feel even colder. A phantom sting of the chemical's sharp, acrid smell seemed to burn in Josh's nose, taking over the cleaner scents of coffee and sawdust around him.

Heat climbed up from his stomach, tight and twisting, until it sat like a hot stone under his ribs as the sheriff went on about what the lab had found. His grip on the phone tightened until the plastic dug into his palm, jaw clenching so hard his teeth ached while anger roiled in his gut, thick and heavy, begging for somewhere to go.

Josh stopped at the grocery store to pick up something for dinner. He had the staples at home, but he wanted a good steak and didn't have any left in the freezer. He needed to make a trip to the city to hit Sam's Club. As he wandered down an aisle, he overheard someone talking about the fire and how fast it spread. He caught other pieces of the conversation and stopped so quickly that the person behind him almost ran him over.

Josh shook his head and moved out of the man's way. He pretended to look at something on the shelf as the man went by him. He didn't recognize the person, but noticed he had a smirk on his face. *What the fuck?*

He hurried to the meat counter and picked up a couple of steaks, then over to the fresh vegetables to grab some mushrooms and onions. He was thinking about inviting Novah over for dinner, but he needed to get the hell out of the store. As he turned up the next aisle, he saw a couple of people he'd seen around but didn't really know.

One of the women shushed the other one, who was still rambling on about the fire. They had a guilty look on their faces as he passed by them. Josh was ready to say something sarcastic, but instead kept his eyes ahead and his face passive, as if he hadn't heard their gossip—their incorrect gossip.

Once home, he put the groceries away and thought about the hushed tones and the silence when the women noticed him. He realized that it wasn't the first time people had stopped speaking with a guilty look on their faces when he walked into a business. "Why the hell would they think I started the fire in my own place?"

He'd just gotten to the point where he could control his feelings about the fire, and then not only had Hank brought them back up with his call, but the women and his realization that people were talking behind his back fueled the anger again.

Chapter 13

Since his attitude wasn't the best, Josh put the steaks in the fridge for another night. He wasn't in the mood for company, and he knew he'd just snap at Novah. He decided to walk the trail to the shore. Instead of heading away from town, he headed toward it, which meant he had to go right by Novah's house.

As he approached it, he shook his head. *What the fuck am I doing? If she sees me... Well, hopefully, she's in her office and doesn't see me.* The trail went up to the road to miss the cliffs that surrounded Novah's house, and then wound down between the next two properties.

Josh made it past Novah's house without her seeing him. At least, he thought so, since she didn't come running out. He'd made it back down to the beach and walked until he was behind his gallery. The construction workers had gone for the day, so he meandered up to the building.

Sitting on the steps that led up to the incomplete studio, he rested his elbows on his knees and hung his head as thoughts about Novah, the construction process, and people talking behind his back ran through his mind.

Novah was sitting on the rear deck, taking in the fresh lake air while she waited for the potatoes to boil for the salad she wanted to make. She tilted her head when she thought she heard someone step on a large stick on the trail just past her house. She was tempted to see who was on the trail, but remembered that Hank hadn't arrested the alleged stalker yet. Besides, she had potatoes on the stove.

Once the potatoes finished cooking, she drained them and left them in the strainer to cool. She mixed the sauce for the salad—she liked to use mayonnaise, spicy brown mustard, salt, pepper, garlic and onion powders, and parsley. She added chopped ham, frozen peas, small cubes of cheddar cheese and dried onion to the mix and set it in the fridge.

The boiled eggs were cool enough to peel. After peeling them, she put them in the fridge until she was ready to fold them into the salad. That done, Novah went back out on the porch with her phone. She still hadn't heard from Josh, and wondered for the billionth time if she should call him.

Shaking her head, she tapped over to her author page on Facebook. She responded to a couple of messages from readers and had several more to read and respond to, but couldn't make herself sit still. Finally, she pocketed her phone and headed toward the trail. It was open enough so she could see someone a couple of hundred feet ahead of her, since the rocky part of the cliffs didn't allow large trees to grow.

As the trail made its way down to the water's edge, the woods became denser, but she still didn't see anyone. She decided to walk down the beach since it was such a nice day. Kicking off her shoes, she stepped onto the warm sand.

Just before she reached Josh's section of the beach behind the gallery, she heard a noise. Novah stopped and listened, but didn't hear it again. After she walked several more feet, she heard it again. Stopping and glancing around, she finally saw Josh sitting on the steps that led from the gallery to the beach.

Novah stopped where she was. He never lifted his head, so he didn't see her. Should I walk up there or turn around before he sees me? If he wanted to see me, he would have called me, plus I don't feel like dealing with his attitude. But is he all that bad? He was very nice to me once we got to know each other.

She stood there, arguing with herself for a few more minutes, and then her feet—seemingly of their own accord—walked toward the steps where Josh was sitting. He still hadn't lifted his head when she reached the bottom of the stairs. She went up the few steps to where he was sitting. He still hadn't noticed her. *Damn. He is really stuck in his mind.*

She turned and sat next to him, close enough so that their arms and legs touched. "Josh," Novah said quietly.

He mumbled under his breath so softly that she barely heard him. "I'm not very good company, Novah." His voice cracked on her name, sounding rough and thin.

"You always say that. How about you let me decide if you are or not?"

Josh shrugged, his shoulders lifting and falling in a small, tired motion, but he didn't say anything. The night air pressed cool and damp around them, carrying the soft rush of waves and the distant call of a bird.

Novah sat silently for a few minutes, listening to the steady rhythm of his breathing and the faint creak of the wooden steps under them. She moved up a step, so she was behind Josh. Sitting on the edge of the tread with him between her legs, she wrapped her arms around his shoulders, the warmth and solid weight of him filling her embrace, and gently pulled him against her, her cheek brushing the back of his head.

Josh's muscles tightened as Novah pulled him into her. After a long beat, some of the tension eased out of his shoulders, and he finally caved, leaning back against her. He let the warmth of her body steady him.

He kept his gaze fixed straight ahead. Looking at Novah felt impossible when she was part of the reason he was sitting there, feeling sorry for himself, instead of working on new orders.

His breathing hitched as he tried to get himself under control, each inhale catching in his chest, but the thoughts kept circling like vultures.

The charred ruins of his gallery.

His tangled, too-intense relationship with Novah, something he'd never planned on, but somehow walked into anyway.

The low buzz of voices behind his back, especially from people he'd once called friends.

The memory of how he'd bolted after the most passionate night of lovemaking he'd ever had.

He couldn't hold back the sound that escaped him, a half-whimper, half-groan that scraped his throat as he became acutely aware of the pressure building at the front of his jeans, his body reacting despite the chaos inside his head. Heat crawled up his neck, and just as he started to push himself to his feet to move away from Novah, his stomach let out a long, loud growl that cut through the tension.

Novah laughed, the sound puffing warm against his back. "When's the last time you ate, Josh?"

"I don't know," he said, shrugging as his stomach rumbled again.

"Josh."

"I'm not hungry, Novah. I really need to be alone." His word came out flat and rough around the edges.

"No." She stood and caught his hand, her fingers wrapping firmly around his, and tugged him down the steps and across the cool sand with her. "I'm going to feed you, and then you can talk about what's bothering you."

I have no idea why I'm being so nice to him. Her grip tightened, her knuckles whitening against his tanned hands. He keeps pushing me away. But I can't help it. I love him.

Josh tried to pull away, his arm giving a short, resistant jerk, but she held on. If he broke free now, that would be it. He was stubborn as a mule, but she could dig in just as hard. The memory of his panicked face that morning on the boathouse floor and the way he bolted like the dock was on fire flashed across her mind. *Does he love me, too? Is he afraid of falling for me? For anyone?*

That thought lit a spark in her chest. She stopped and gave his hand a sharper tug. “Come on. We don’t have to talk. Just eat. You’re going to waste away to nothing.” Novah kept her tone light and teasing, even as something tight and fragile pressed against her ribs at the idea of him walking away for good.

Novah turned to him, stepping into his space. She put both of her hands on the knotted muscles of his shoulders, and he still wouldn’t look up. “Baby, let’s get you something to eat. You can leave after, or you can sit and watch TV with me. We don’t have to talk if you don’t feel like it, but you do have to try to eat something.”

She lifted one hand and brushed her knuckles across his cheek. His warm skin, rough with stubble, met her touch, and she felt the wet track of a single tear slip free. *Oh, baby.* Every instinct screamed to pull him into her arms, but she knew he needed the illusion of holding it together, so she let the tear slide without saying anything.

"You'll make me feel better if you eat something, Josh. No pressure for anything." Her voice came out low and husky, thick with everything she wasn't saying, and she hoped he heard only concern, not the love humming under it.

Taking a step backward, Novah gently kept hold of his hand and tugged until he took a step. *Like taming a wild animal. A little bit at a time.*

As they entered the woody trail, Josh's hand tightened on hers, and another groan escaped. "I can't do this. I'm losing my fucking mind," he thought. He slowed his steps without letting go of Novah's hand.

She turned, and before he could school his face, she took in the clenched jaw, haunted eyes and the tight lines around Josh's mouth. The sight twisted something inside her. Instead of pulling him into the hug she ached to give, she kept her distance and said lowly, "We're almost there, Josh. Come on, baby."

When they stepped into her house, the cooler, shaded air greeted them along with the faint scent of coffee and something savory from earlier. Novah pointed toward the sofa. "TV clicker is there on the coffee table. Make yourself at home. I'll be right back with something to drink."

She went into the kitchen, the tile cool under her feet, and pulled the bowl of potatoes from the counter, folding the now-cooled chunks into the creamy sauce.

The soft thud of her knife on the cutting board echoed as she chopped the eggs, then gently turned them into the salad and slid the bowl back into the fridge.

She grabbed two beers from the fridge, along with the bottle of fourteen-year-old Batch 1 Jack Daniel's she'd been saving.

If not now, when?

She cracked the seal, poured two shots of the amber liquid, and put the bottle back in the cabinet. She didn't want to get drunk, and Josh only needed something to take the edge off.

When she walked back into the living room, Josh was still standing exactly where she had left him, shoulders slumped and his hands loose at his sides, like he wasn't sure what to do with himself.

She set the drinks on the coffee table with a soft clink of glass on wood and stepped up to him. Her fingers curled around his hand again. "Come on, sit."

He let her guide him down onto the sofa, the cushions dipping under his weight. Once he sat, she pressed one shot glass into his hand and picked up the other. "To better days," she said, tilting the rim of her glass toward his, the faint chime of glass on glass a slight, hopeful sound in the quiet room.

Chapter 14

"What the fuck am I doing?" Josh asked himself as Novah pulled him over to the sofa, her hand warm and insistent around his. He let himself sink into the cushions, the soft give swallowing some of the tension in his shoulders as he crossed his arms against his body.

She handed him a shot glass with dark amber liquid in it—whiskey, he guessed—that he hadn't seen her bring in. The glass was cool against his fingers as he lifted it, one eyebrow ticking up while he brought it to his nose. Whiskey. Expensive whiskey, if the rich, smoky scent and faint vanilla bite were anything to go by.

She lifted her own glass in a small toast, so he gave a short nod and tilted his toward hers, the rims clinking together. They both swallowed the shot. The burn slid down his throat and bloomed warm in his chest, taking more of the edge off.

"Need another one?" Novah asked.

Josh shook his head, still not trusting his voice. He noticed the cold bottle of beer waiting on the table, but he let it sit, not wanting to drown out the heat still curling in his stomach.

Novah leaned over to grab the TV remote from the coffee table, her shoulder brushing his as she stretched. She flicked through the channels until she found an old movie that almost everyone had seen a million times. "Anything you want to watch, or is this okay?" she asked.

"This is fine," Josh mumbled, the words rumbling low as he let his head tip back against the sofa.

"I'll go plate us up some dinner," Novah said softly, her voice gentler than the movie's background chatter as she pushed herself up and padded toward the kitchen.

When she returned to the living room, Josh was leaning against the back of the sofa, tilted slightly toward the middle, fast asleep. Novah sat on the other end to eat a couple of bites before she took both plates back into the kitchen, wrapped them and put them in the fridge for later.

Josh never even woke up when she sank into the sofa beside him. She slid closer to him and put her arm around his shoulders. He grunted as he adjusted his position in his sleep and put his head on her.

When the movie ended, Novah didn't want to wake Josh, so she turned the television off and leaned back. After a few minutes, she swore under her breath. "Shit. I have to pee, and I'm hungry. And thirsty. Maybe he won't wake up."

She gently moved her arm from behind Josh, being careful to support his head. He groaned as she leaned him back against the couch. Novah stood quietly and made her way down the hall to the bathroom. When she came back, he was still sleeping in the same position, so she went into the kitchen to heat up her dinner and make a cup of coffee.

She sat at the bar so she could see if he woke up. When he hadn't by the time she was done eating, she washed the dishes and turned the coffee maker off.

Josh had tipped sideways, so he was lying on the sofa with his feet on the floor. She went down the hall to grab a pillow and an extra blanket. He stirred when she slid it under his head, but didn't wake up. She quietly removed his shoes and lifted his legs onto the couch.

Damn. Now I know he's tired. She covered him with the blanket and went down the hall to her room.

It took her a while to fall asleep while thoughts of the man in the other room ran through her mind.

Novah suddenly woke up. It was still dark outside. She glanced at the clock and groaned. She'd only been sleeping for an hour. She rolled over to go back to sleep when she heard the noise that must have woken her up in the first place. It took her a minute to place it.

She grabbed a robe and stole into the living room. Josh's head was turning back and forth, and he was muttering in his sleep. She couldn't understand a word he said. When the nightmare didn't stop after a couple of minutes, she sat on the edge of the sofa and put her hand on his chest.

"Josh," she said quietly.

He didn't wake up, so she rubbed his chest. "Josh," she said a little louder.

Suddenly, Josh sat straight up and yelled, "No! You leave her alone!"

Novah grabbed Josh's shoulders and pulled him into her as he fought to get away from the imaginary demons. "Josh! It's me! It's Novah. Wake up!"

His eyes opened, but stared through her. She knew he didn't see her. "Josh, wake up. I'm here."

He wailed, "No," drawing out the word.
Novah shook him. "Josh!"

His eyes finally became clear as tears ran down his cheeks. "N-Novah. Fuck. Where am I? What's going on?" He scanned the room and finally realized he was in her living room. His shoulders sagged in relief as Novah pulled him into a hug.

"I'm here, baby. I'm right here."

His body shook with silent sobs as she held him. When he finally quieted, she lifted his chin with her finger. "Come to bed. Just to sleep." She took his hand and stood.

Josh resisted. "I can't. I should really go home. I didn't mean to fall asleep here."

"No, Josh. It's late. You haven't been able to sleep until tonight. Come on." Novah tugged at his hand.

Josh sighed and finally stood to follow her down the hall. Once in her room, he removed his jeans and his shirt, leaving his boxers on, and climbed into the bed next to her, turning his back to her.

Novah wrapped her arm around his waist. "Slide over here. I'll hold you. Maybe you won't have the nightmare again."

Josh slid against her warm body. He lay awake for a few minutes, and the next thing he knew, the sun was shining. He rolled over and felt Novah's side of the bed. He could smell her scent, but the sheets were cool, so she'd been up a while. He sat up on the edge of the bed and rubbed his eyes. *Damn, I'm hard. I guess I need a cold shower because this is more than a piss hard-on.*

He found his clothes and headed into the master bathroom. He turned the water on and adjusted the temperature. When it warmed up, he got into the shower, washed, and then turned the hot water off. "That did it," he muttered.

He grabbed a towel Novah had left for him on the vanity and dried off. Once he dressed, he followed the smell of coffee, sausage, and eggs to the kitchen. Josh leaned against the wall in the large entry, hoping Novah didn't notice him quite yet. He'd thought about sneaking out because he was embarrassed about last night.

"Have a seat, Josh. You didn't eat last night, so I made a big breakfast. Sausage and gravy. Biscuits. Eggs. Pancakes. Coffee."

When she didn't hear him move, she turned away from the stove. Her breath hitched when she saw his red eyes, but she didn't say anything. Instead, she smiled and pointed to the table in the breakfast nook, which already held a cup of coffee for him.

Josh sighed and stepped over to the table. As he sat down, he blew on the steaming coffee and then moaned as he took a sip. "Thanks. This is good coffee."

"Thanks," Novah said as she plated breakfast for both of them. She set the plates on the table and then reached into the fridge for maple syrup and butter. They ate in silence, except for the couple of times Josh grunted as he shoveled food in his mouth. "So damned good," he said as he finished. "Is there more?"

Novah grinned. "Yeah, there's more biscuits and gravy. Want more eggs?"

"No, the biscuits and gravy'll do. Thanks," Josh said as he carried his plate over to the stove.

When they finished, Josh helped Novah clean up. After she put the last plate into the cabinet, Novah dried her hands on a soft dish towel and then rested her palm lightly on Josh's forearm, feeling the tense line of muscle under his skin. "We need to talk. Here, boathouse or a walk along the beach?"

"I don't really want to talk about it—anything." Josh stared at his feet, studying his boot.

"You corrected yourself. There *is* something bothering you, isn't there?"

When he didn't respond, Novah exhaled and said, "Come on. Let's take a drive." She led him out to her truck, and he slid into the passenger seat. She headed north out of town.

"Where are we going?" Josh asked, watching the familiar buildings thin into trees and open stretches of road.

"You'll see. You'll like it." Her lips curved into a small, secretive smile.

About ten miles out of town, Novah turned down an old dirt track that used to be a logging road. "This land belongs to a friend of mine. When I need to decompress, I come out here. It's quiet, and no one can bug us, since it's private."

A couple of hundred yards in, the trail split. Novah took the right trail and drove for a half-mile before pulling up in front of a gate. "Wait here."

She slid out of the truck and fiddled with a lock and chain. The barrier creaked as it swung wide enough to ease the vehicle through. She stopped just inside and hopped out to close it behind her.

Novah slid back into the cab and pointed. "That road goes to her neighbor's land. After a few hundred yards, there's a boundary line, and they have a gate."

Josh nodded. Novah put the truck in four-wheel drive and continued up the narrow trail. After about a mile of twisting corners and steep hills, the road opened into a small clearing. It had a swing under a large tree at the edge of the open space and a picnic table with a rock-ringed fire pit closer to the center. She turned around and pointed the nose of her truck out where the trail ended.

"They won't bother us. They have cameras pointing down the road. We have a code. When I park like this, they know I don't want to be disturbed. If they can't see my truck in that camera, then I'm open to company. There are no cameras in the clearing itself—just the one pointing down the road.

She grabbed a small cooler that Josh hadn't noticed. "Let's go."

They slid out of the truck, and Novah led him toward the wooden swing. Josh sat at the edge of it, shoulders hunched and his fingers knotting and unknotting in his lap as the chains gave a faint metallic creak.

"Sit back and relax, Josh. That's the point of this."

After several seconds, he eased himself back against the slats, the swing dipping slightly with his weight. Novah set her foot against the ground and gave a gentle push, causing the swing to move with a slow, rhythmic glide.

"I thought you wanted to talk?" Josh asked, his eyes fixed straight ahead of him.

"In due time. You said you didn't want to talk about it. This gives you some time to relax and think about your troubles. Maybe you can leave them here when we go." She nudged the swing again with her foot, sending it back and forth in a smooth arc.

Chapter 15

After several long minutes, Novah said, “Josh, I see you. You are kind and caring, no matter what you make people believe with your actions. I don’t know what’s bothering you, but you know you can talk to me. Granted, we didn’t get off on the right foot all those years ago, but both of us have changed.”

She sat back and continued rocking the swing with her foot. The air smelled of the forest, wrapping around them like a thin blanket. She didn’t expect an answer from Josh and didn’t get one. Not even a grunt of acknowledgment to say he heard her. Out of the corner of her eye, she caught the quick flick of his eyes sliding to her before dropping back to his hands, where they clenched in his lap.

Josh's gaze drifted away from Novah, as if the line of trees could soak up the emotion burning at the corners of his eyes. He blinked hard, letting his lashes shield the sudden shine before it could spill over where she might see it.

She slid closer to him, so their legs were touching, and the warmth of his thigh seeped through her jeans. Gently, she slipped her arms under his, wrapping them around his chest and pulling him back against her as the swing rocked in a slow, steady rhythm. She lay her head on his shoulder, breathing in the mix of soap, sweat, and the loamy forest air that clung to his shirt, and held him tightly, as if her embrace could keep him from coming apart.

Her heart beat a little faster where it pressed against his back. Every small shudder of his breath traveled straight through her. Feelings for him were rooting deeper with every quiet second, but she held them close and silent. He'd bolted once already, and she wasn't sure if he'd ever be ready for anything heavier than this borrowed moment. Still, as she tightened her hold just a fraction, she let herself hope that, given time, he might turn toward her instead of away.

Josh leaned forward, rested his elbows on his knees and buried his face in his hands, breaking Novah's hold on him. His back twitched when she began rubbing it, trying to comfort him.

I don't deserve her. The thought slammed into him so hard his chest actually ached. *Jesus, what must she think of me?* His fingers dug into his knees, his nails biting through the denim as his mind spun. *She must think I can't handle life. I'm having a fucking nervous breakdown over here, and I can't stop it.*

It was all stacked in a choking pile. The fire. The blackened ruins of his gallery. The way people's voices dropped when he walked into a room. The shadow of some faceless stalker-arsonist out there. Her. Again.

Heat crawled up his neck. But it's not her fault. Yes, it is. You know she's falling for you, but you just run away like a little sissy when emotions run high. Fuck, fuck, fuck.

Josh shook his head at himself, a short, sharp movement. His jaw clenched until it hurt.

Novah leaned in and kissed his cheek and then whispered, "Josh, no one can hear you out here. There's no one to see us. You need to let this out. Keeping it bottled up so much only makes it worse—more emotional. I know I'm probably part of that, but I really do care about you. I have thick skin. Cry. Yell. Bitch and moan. I don't care. Do what you need to do. I'm here for you."

Yeah, but will she be there when she feels all of my emotions? They're too strong for the average person. I know I'm going to screw up our relationship—if I haven't already. I can't even look at her, or I'll lose it. "Fuck my life."

Shit. Didn't mean to say that out loud.

Josh stood and stomped to the edge of the clearing, staring into the woods, thoughts of how fucked up his life was since the fire. Since Novah came into his life. *It's not her fault I'm fucked up.*

Novah kept her eye on Josh as he stalked off, waiting for him to blow up. When his shoulders slumped and his head dropped, she quickly moved toward him. Moving in front of him, she wrapped her arms around him and pulled his head into her shoulder and rocked him from side to side. She kissed the top of his head and whispered, "No judgment, Josh," and then laid her cheek on his head.

I can't do this. Not to her. I just can't. But damn, it feels so good to have her holding me like she really cares. She does care, Josh. How can she? No one cares this much about anyone else. And hell. I'm getting hard with her this close. Despite all this bullshit going through my mind, all I can think about is making love to her. No. You can't love her. She won't be able to handle you.

Josh lifted his head and stepped away from Novah. "I'm fine, Novah." He turned toward the truck. "Can we go?"

"No." Novah grabbed his hand and led him back to the swing. "You're not ready. You're fighting it. I don't know what part of everything that's either fucked up or what you're denying is going through your mind, but you're fighting it too much. Let's sit for a little while longer until you feel better.

As she turned to sit, he adjusted the front of his jeans, hoping she didn't see, but there was no way he could sit without doing it. He glanced at her from the corner of his eye. *Shit. She had to have seen that.*

Novah reached out with one finger to pull his chin toward her. "Kiss me," she barely whispered, the words catching in her throat.

"I-I. I can't. I'll l-lose control."

"I want you to lose control, Josh."

"Fuck, Novah. You don't know what you're saying. What you're asking for."

She leaned into him, and when their lips were barely an inch apart, she whispered, "Yes, I do. I want you, Josh."

The words were barely out of her mouth when Josh grabbed a fistful of her hair and pulled her into him. His mouth ravaged hers as he pulled her tightly against him.

She palmed the lump in his jeans and moaned as his tongue forced its way past her lips and tangled with hers. His hands pulled her head hard against him as his lips roughly plundered her mouth.

After several long seconds, Novah couldn't stand it anymore. She broke the kiss, causing Josh to cry out as he felt the loss of her against him. She pulled her shirt over her head. Her bra followed, and then she reached for the buttons on Josh's jeans. When she fumbled with them, he pushed her hands away, undid them himself and slid them down over his hips.

She freed him from his underwear and fisted him as she leaned in to kiss him.

Josh cried out again when her thumb rubbed the tip of his cock. He aggressively pinched her nipple, making her moan.

When his hips pumped into her fist, Novah let him go to stand and remove her jeans. "I need you right now, Josh. Right here." She sank into the soft grass, and he followed her. When he pushed her legs apart, she grabbed his shoulders, pulling him up against her. "I need your cock inside me now," she growled.

Josh didn't hesitate. He notched her dripping entrance, and as she arched her back to take him, his hips slammed into her. He stilled as Novah cried out. Her muscles gripped him so tightly, a strangled groan left his throat, but he couldn't stop. His hips pounded through the pleasure and the pain.

When Novah came down, she wrapped her legs around him as her hips bucked against him in a wild, desperate rhythm, and her gaze locked onto his, soaking up every flicker of hurt and turmoil in his expression, as if she could draw it out of him and into herself.

Something broke loose inside of Josh, a tight, jagged knot he'd been holding for far too long, and hot tears blurred his vision as they spilled down his face. The words tore out of him, raw and hoarse, ripped straight from the center of his chest. "Take me with you, baby!"

Novah's hips slammed into Josh again and again, her movements growing more frantic as the pleasure crested, both of them riding that edge and oblivious to the storm tearing through him. She screamed his name as her muscles clamped his cock, her whole body bowing toward him.

Josh didn't know what hit him. It was like something snapped free and surged forward. He ground into her like he couldn't get close enough, like there might be some way to crawl inside her skin and escape everything else, his back arching as white-hot release ripped through him. His head snapped backward as he screamed, the sound unrestrained, as ribbons of cum shot into her.

Afterward, his strength vanished all at once. He collapsed over her, arms shaking as he braced on his elbows to keep from crushing her, and buried his face in the curve of her neck. His breath came in ragged bursts against her skin, and for a few precious seconds, all the chaos in his head narrowed to the thump of her heartbeat thudding against his chest and the way her hands held on like she had no intention of letting go.

Chapter 16

Josh flipped the steaks while Novah brought the plates and salads out. It was the first time they'd seen each other since that day in the woods a few days ago. He still couldn't talk about everything that caused his breakdown, and still couldn't tell Novah his feelings for her.

Hell, I won't even admit it to myself. Yeah, denial. Even though I know it, I still can't do it. What if she leaves? What if she doesn't feel the same?

On top of that, he'd seen her talking to one of the women, someone he'd overheard saying he started the fire on purpose. They were at the coffee shop, and he caught sight of them as he passed the window, so he went down the street for his coffee instead.

Novah put some potato salad and green salad on each of their plates. He's going to have to come clean soon. He's not as tense as he was, but I can tell he's still holding back.

He'd cried on her shoulder for a long time after they made love in the clearing. She hadn't said anything, knowing he was one step closer to opening up, but not there yet. Since he refused to go to counseling, Novah had called her friend, Mary, a psychiatrist who helped her out when she needed to flesh out a mental health scene in her books.

Somehow, even though she was bipolar, Mary managed to get her degree in psychology and had a family. Her mental health condition wouldn't let her work full-time, so she often consulted with authors, both famous and indie authors, and movie producers to ensure their mental health scenes were realistic.

She had told Novah that she couldn't push Josh. He had to face his demons at his own will, though she could bring up certain subjects without pushing, as long as she backed off at the right time. Mary said she'd know when to push and just how much, since she had gotten advice for book situations just like this one.

Never thought I'd see the day when I'd be dealing with this in real life.

Josh put the steaks on a platter and carried them over to the table, breaking her out of her thoughts. "Blue rare, just like you like it," he said as he put one of the steaks on her plate.

She smiled at him. "Thanks, babe."

Since they were both hungry, they ate in silence. Novah cut into her steak and groaned when she put a bite into her mouth. After she swallowed, she said, "Ain't nothing better than a man who can cook the perfect steak."

Josh grinned at her and nodded as he chewed. "At your service, Ma'am."

For just a fraction of a second, his eyes gleamed with happiness and pride. His gaze went to his plate, and when he looked up again, the dim hurt was back. Even though he tried to hide it, Novah saw through him.

When they finished, Novah gathered the plates and brought them in to wash while Josh cleaned the grill. She grabbed two beers out of the fridge and went back out on the deck. She set them on the table and walked over to him, putting her arms around him from behind. "You about done with that?" she asked lowly.

"Yeah." Josh hung the brush on the side of the grill and turned the flame off.

Novah moved her hands up under his shirt, rubbing his belly and chest, causing him to moan lowly.

He pulled away from her. “Let’s grab these beers and sit over here,” Josh said, pointing to the double porch swing. He turned and kissed Novah on the cheek before he grabbed the sweating bottles and stepped over to the swing.

Novah sat next to him and curled her feet under her while she snuggled under Josh’s arm. “How was your week?” she asked.

Josh shrugged, embarrassed. He knew where she was going with this. “Better, but not quite there yet.”

Novah started to say something, but Josh held a finger up. She glanced at him, waiting for him to continue.

Finally, he took a deep breath. “Baby, I’m sorry I lost it. I don’t know what came over me.”

“I do. You bottle up too much shit inside. You have to break at some point.”

“It’s embarrassing.”

“No, baby. There’s nothing embarrassing about it. You can’t handle this on your own, not this much shit. It’s too much for anyone.”

Josh nodded and sipped his beer, deep in thought.

After a few long minutes, he asked, "Can I ask you about something?"

"Sure."

"That woman you were with the other day in the coffee shop. Did she say anything to you about the fire?"

Novah narrowed her eyes, trying to pinpoint what he meant. "Oh, you mean Taylor? That was the only time I was sitting with someone in the coffee shop. Why didn't you—" She stopped suddenly, knowing why he hadn't come in.

"No, baby, she didn't say anything. Why?"

"She's one I overheard talking to another woman about me starting the fire for attention. There have been a few similar conversations around town."

"Well, that doesn't make sense, Josh. Everyone knows the sheriff has a line on someone. Anyway, why would anyone think you'd do something like that in the first place? That's just stupid."

"I don't know, but they do. There have been many times when people just stopped talking when they saw me coming. The silence was really uncomfortable, and then they acted as if they didn't see me."

"What the fuck, Josh? That doesn't even make any sense. No wonder you're so stressed. Just ignore that shit. Those people are idiots."

"Even your friend?"

"She's an acquaintance I met a while back. We don't do much together, but we will have coffee if we happen to show up at the bakery at the same time. And besides, I wouldn't call someone who did that a friend. If she's talking behind one person's back, she can just as easily talk behind my back. I don't have time for that shit in my life."

Josh grunted his acknowledgment and continued pushing the swing back and forth with his foot.

When Josh didn't say anything else, Novah continued, "I know I have my issues about stuff like my weight and the way I look, but those are my issues. People are going to talk, and probably do, but I don't care. I only care what I think of myself."

Josh lifted his eyebrows at her. "There ain't a thing wrong with the way you look. I like you just the way you are."

She wasn't going to argue with him. He was as stubborn as she was. Instead, she changed the subject. "Have you seen Alexis around town?"

"That girl who was at your house a couple of weeks ago?"

"Yeah. She hasn't responded to my texts. I haven't really been out and about, so I haven't seen her. You're out more than I am."

Josh shrugged. “No, but I don’t always pay attention to people. Isn’t she supposed to be your best friend?”

“Yep. That’s what’s so weird. She always responds to my texts.”

Chapter 17

Josh groaned as he slapped the alarm. He'd been getting up an hour earlier for a while, so he could get that time in on the treadmill before he worked on orders. Around ten in the morning, he would go to the gallery to check on progress and, since the contractors were working on the interior, to ensure that everything was to his specifications.

He left at twelve-thirty to get lunch, which is when the builders also left for their break. Then, he would go back home to work on orders. Having a smaller workspace, plus the three hours he spent in town every day, was cutting into how much he could produce, so he'd been working later in the evening.

He knew Novah was working on her book, as she had a looming deadline. Though they texted every day, they hadn't seen each other for several. *Hmm. I wonder if she ever caught up with Alexis?*

Josh made a pot of coffee and then started a warm-up walk on the treadmill. He grabbed his phone from the holder.

> ***JOSH:*** *I meant to ask, did you ever catch up with Alexis?*
>
> ***NOVAH:*** *Yes. She never received my texts and was wondering where I had disappeared to. The cell company has no idea what happened, but they got whatever issues fixed.*
>
> ***JOSH:*** *Weird. If I ever disappear like that, you'd better come looking for me.*
>
> ***NOVAH:*** *Really?*

"Oh, shit, I probably shouldn't have told her that. Now she'll be stalking me," Josh thought as he typed a reply.

> ***JOSH:*** *Yeah. Since we're both alone, no matter what happens between us, we should keep an eye on each other. After all, we are neighbors.*
>
> ***NOVAH:*** *Agreed. Now get back to work.*

Josh inserted a laugh emoji and the sunglasses-face emoji.

JOSH: *You, too.*

Once he finished his workout, he took a shower and then poured another cup of coffee. After glancing at the time, he decided he didn't have time to cook breakfast this morning, so he scarfed down a bowl of cereal before he went into his makeshift studio.

"Damn," he mumbled when the phone rang. He glanced at the display. "I have to take this," he mumbled to the piece he was working on. He wiped one finger off on his jeans and swiped the call active, and then hit the speaker button. "Yeah, Hank."

Hank had pulled the phone away from his ear to hang up when he heard Josh's voice through the speaker. "I was just about to hang up and shoot you a message."

"Sorry. I have clay all over my hands. What's up?"

"Well, we got another tip. Do you know a guy who goes by Ray Singer?"

"Name sounds familiar. Hold on a second. Let me clean my hands."

Hank heard water running in the background. Even though he could tell Josh had him on speaker, he waited, as he didn't think Josh could hear him that far from the phone.

"Okay, I'm back. I think he might have been a student at one time, but I'm not positive."

Hank heard Josh pounding on the keyboard.

"Well, I'll be damned."

"What?" Hank asked.

"He was a student, but it was four, no, nearly five years ago. I've never heard from him since. He got an A in my class."

"Well, that doesn't make a lick of sense," the sheriff said

Josh shrugged, even though he knew Hank couldn't see it.

"Okay, we're going to look into this, but it doesn't feel right."

"Anyway, it could be a setup?" He didn't wait for Hank to respond. "My issue with that is I don't know that Eric guy from Adam, and it's a long shot that he knew Ray was a student, especially from so long ago."

"That would be one of the questions of the year in this case," Hank said sarcastically. "I'll let you know what we come up with."

"Thanks, Hank."

Josh swiped the display. "Well, hell. I might as well head over to the gallery. It's a bit early, but there's no sense in uncovering that piece for ten minutes of work," he mumbled to himself.

Novah clicked on the email, hoping it was the information she needed to finish the scene. The librarian in Johnson City came through. She pumped her fist in the air. "Yes!" She hated doing an incorrect scene, even if it was fiction.

She clicked the link and decided it would be a good time for coffee and lunch. She could read the information she needed while she ate. Novah flipped on the coffee pot and grabbed the lunch she'd brought down this morning. She stuck her leftover homemade chicken fettuccine alfredo in the microwave while the coffee brewed. It didn't take long to heat up and was ready by the time the coffee was. She set the lunch on her desk and filled her mug.

Sitting in front of the computer, she took a sip of the hot drink and muttered, "Damn, that's good." She picked up her fork in her left hand and scrolled the page with her right hand as she read. Setting her fork down, she took a few notes and then resumed eating and scrolling.

She was just about to close the site, now that she had the information she needed, when a headline caught her eye, and she moved the mouse over to click the link.

1997 Vehicle Accident Ruled as Homicide 28 Years Later

BUTLER, TN—Aug 5, 2017. In a stunning turn of events, authorities have officially reclassified a 1997 vehicle accident that claimed the lives of a local couple as a homicide, closing a decades-old mystery that left their infant son, Joshua, orphaned.

Tragedy Revisited

On the evening of April 9, 1997, emergency services responded to the scene of a single-vehicle wreck on Hwy 67W. The victims, Steven and Heidi Gann, were pronounced dead at the scene. Their infant son, Joshua, was not in the vehicle at the time and was placed in foster care, beginning a life irrevocably altered by tragedy.

At the time, investigators attributed the crash to driver error and poor road conditions. They closed the case within weeks.

New Evidence Emerges

An anonymous person submitted a request to reopen the case after nearly three decades. Cold case detectives uncovered inconsistencies in the initial investigation. Subsequent advances in forensic science allowed investigators to re-examine physical evidence from the crash site, including tire marks and vehicle debris, which law enforcement had kept due to minor inconsistencies found at the time.

Investigators refused to comment on new inconsistencies and why the "minor" inconsistencies found at the time were not further investigated, other than to say that it became clear that it was not a simple accident.

They have also not released information regarding motive and suspects, citing an ongoing investigation. However, authorities confirm that developments include witness interviews previously overlooked and new forensic leads.

We have not been able to contact Joshua Gann to verify this information since it has come to our attention. Joshua Gann would be in his early twenties at this time.

Novah printed the article and searched for additional articles regarding the alleged murder of his parents. I wonder if he knows? I can't believe Hank would let this slide. Though it happened in another town and another county, so he wouldn't have any reason…He may not have even seen this article.

Josh was only two or three. He wouldn't remember that. He's never talked about being adopted or going through the foster system. His attitude makes a lot more sense, though. The fear of getting too close to someone, almost as though he thinks they'll leave him, too.

Her eyes moved to her phone, which was sitting next to the computer. *Three in the afternoon. I have a few minutes.*

She searched by name for other articles and came up empty. She tried several other search terms that might bring up articles about the accident, but struck out. *I wonder if they even found him after all those years. Or solved the case, for that matter.*

Novah sighed when her phone binged. She finished the sentence she was typing and glanced at the screen.

Swiping it with one hand, she hit the keys to save her work with the other. "Hi, Josh."

After they hung up, she checked the time. I have enough time to finish this chapter. Maybe start the next one. I'm on a roll.

Josh was bringing the ingredients for a spaghetti dinner, and he'd be there in about an hour. She really should have declined so she could work on her book, but she hadn't seen Josh for several days. Her core tingled when she thought about what she wanted to do to him right about now. *But it'll have to wait.*

Chapter 18

Novah had just gotten out of the shower and was making cheesy garlic bread to go with the spaghetti. It was a good way to use up the rest of the loaf of Italian bread she'd purchased the day before yesterday. Just as she finished spreading the cheesy garlic mixture on the two halves of the loaf, she heard Josh pull in.

Setting the loaves on a sheet tray, she slid them into her air fryer. It wouldn't take but a few minutes to melt the cheese, so all she had to do was plug it in and turn it on before the spaghetti finished cooking.

She went to the front door and opened it, just as Josh stepped up on the porch. She grabbed one of the bags out of his hands and leaned in for a kiss. Placing her other hand at the back of his neck, she pulled him into her, pressing her tongue past his lips.

Josh moaned as his tongue dueled with hers. He'd gotten hard as soon as he'd seen her standing on the porch. He placed his free hand at the small of her back and pulled her against him. Holding her tight, he ground his hips against her. Breaking the kiss, he said lowly, "Fuck, Novah. I need you. Now."

Still holding her, he guided her backward into the house. He took the bag out of her hand and dropped both of them on the floor. Turning her around, he said, "Brace yourself against the door." He slid her shorts and underwear down, and then unbuttoned his jeans. He slid them down just far enough to free his throbbing cock.

Grabbing Novah's waist, he pulled her hips toward him. He reached one arm around her to find her nub. "Damn, baby, you're ready for me."

When he touched her sensitive clit, Novah's hips jerked into Josh. "Now, Josh. I need to feel you in me right now."

Using his other hand while he continued worrying her clit, Josh guided himself into her. He moaned deeply as he felt her muscles clench him as soon as he was all the way inside of her. He grabbed her waist, but waited a long heartbeat before he slid almost all the way out and slammed into her.

Every time he slid into her, her hips ground into him. He knew he wasn't going to last. Josh moved his hands next to hers against the door as he pressed himself against her back. "I can't get close enough to you," he ground out as his hips pumped into her.

He felt her muscles quiver around his cock as she moaned his name. "Take me with you, baby." As he pushed himself into her again, the quivering turned into a strong grip that squeezed his cock so tightly, it was almost painful. He ground into her one more time and shouted as every muscle in his body tightened up and rivers of hot cum flooded her.

Josh leaned into her, holding her against him as her muscles continued to grip him for several more long heartbeats.

Between breaths, Novah said, "My legs aren't going to hold me up much longer."

He turned them together, remaining inside of her and took two steps back and then turned again, pulling her into his lap as he collapsed on the chair next to the door.

Novah leaned into him, resting her head on the back of the chair, her cheek against his cheek. "Damn, Josh," she huffed as she tried to catch her breath.

Opening the fridge, Novah grabbed two Heinekens and handed one to Josh. “You’ll have to teach me how you make your homemade spaghetti sauce.”

Josh shrugged. “Sure. It was my mom’s recipe.”

He turned to walk out to the deck. He hoped she wouldn’t ask about his parents.

Novah followed him out and sat on the swing next to him and leaned her head against his shoulder. “It’s really nice out.”

“Sure is,” Josh grunted.

She took a deep breath, leaned in, and let the question fall between them in a hushed murmur. “You know how you told me about hearing whispers and people stopping talking when you walked near them or into a business?”

He went still, breath pausing mid-inhale, the air between them tightening with him. “Yeah. What about it?”

“I heard it, too, except they didn’t see me around the corner. I was in the library.” She hesitated for just a second. “How can they think you started that fire? Do they not understand that an artist’s work is more than just his or her next dollar? Do they not understand how much each piece means to us?"

Novah shook her head. "I didn't know who these people were. I peeked around the corner, but I didn't recognize them. I know I keep mostly to myself, but I thought I knew just about everyone in town."

"I don't know, baby. Some people just don't get it. If they did, it would never cross their minds that I could destroy my dream and for what?"

Novah turned her head to kiss Josh's cheek. "How's your new building coming along? How much more until it's finished?"

Josh shrugged his free shoulder, the worn boards of the deck pressing faintly through his jeans as he shifted his weight. "I don't know. They say they're still on time, so I'm guessing a couple more months."

"I know you can't wait to get back into a spacious studio to work."

Josh grunted his agreement. The lake moved in slow breaths against the shore, lapping at the rocks. He was content to sit in silence, taking it in, warmed by the solid line of Novah's warm thigh against his.

Novah tried again. "Heard anything else from Hank?"

"No. He said something about another lead, but he hasn't said anything else."

Josh tipped his beer bottle, watching the pale liquid slide against the green glass, and finished the last quarter of it in one big sip. The lukewarm fizz scraped down his throat, bland and heavy, but the familiar burn loosened something knotted behind his ribs. The glass clinked softly as he set the empty bottle between his boots.

"Want another one?"

Josh shook his head. "But if you have any more of that whiskey, I wouldn't mind a shot or two of that."

"You're not one to drink the hard stuff. Are you okay, baby?"

Josh turned to see the concern on Novah's face, her features softened by the dim light behind them. Her brows pinched slightly, and her thumb brushed once over the back of his hand where it rested on the dock.

"Yeah, baby. I'm good. I guess I'm just in one of those moods."

"Okay." Novah let the word hang there, trusting that he was okay, and reached for his empty beer bottle.

When she came out, the bottle of whiskey and two shot glasses clinked as she moved. Even though she had half of her beer left, she poured a shot for each of them, the amber liquid catching a faint glint of moonlight as it rose in the glass. Sitting next to Josh again, she let her shoulder lean into his and lifted her tumbler. "Cheers."

Josh nodded and drained the glass, the whiskey searing a path down his throat before blooming into a slow, heavy warmth in his chest. He leaned forward and poured another one and downed it, not savoring the smoky warmth this time. He sat back in the swing and put an arm around Novah's shoulders, tilting his head against her. He wrapped his other arm around her waist and tried to pull her even closer.

Novah slid her hand onto Josh's cheek and rubbed his lips with her thumb in slow, unhurried passes. "Josh," she said lowly, her voice a hushed vibration he could feel more than hear.

"Don't, Novah." He leaned forward enough to grab the whiskey, her hand falling away with a reluctant drag, and took a slug right from the bottle. He offered it to Novah, but she shook her head. Putting it between his legs, he leaned back, pushing the swing with his foot so it rocked them in a slow, soothing arc.

Novah kissed the side of his head, her lips lingering in his hair for a heartbeat, then she trailed kisses past his ear, the whisper of her breath sending a shiver skimming over his skin, and down onto his shoulders, where his T-shirt had slipped just enough for her to press her lips to the bare patch.

Josh moaned roughly as his muscles loosened under her touch, and took another slug of whiskey, letting the heat of it mingle with the warmth she was drawing up under his skin.

She kissed his neck and then sucked it for several seconds, giving him a hickey. When she saw the mark she left, she moaned, "Touch me, Josh."

He tipped the bottle up and took several gulps of whiskey, his throat working hard as the burn rushed down, hot enough to make his eyes water. It knocked dully against his teeth on the last swallow, and he set it on the floor at the end of the swing.

When he turned to her, his gaze swayed just a fraction off-center, and he gave her a sloppy, wet kiss that landed more on the corner of her mouth, but broke it right away. "I don't think this is a good idea right now. I'm dr-dr—"

"Yeah, you are. Think you can walk?"

"You want m-me to l-lea—"

"No," Novah interrupted again, squeezing his knee to steady him as he listed a little. "I want to get you inside. It's going to get cool out here. Better that you're inside while you can get there than to freeze out here if you pass out."

Josh leaned down and picked the bottle up, his fingers fumbling once at the neck before they closed around it. “Drinkin’ all your good sh-shit.”

“No worries.” Novah stood and took his hand, her grip firm and warm around his unsteady fingers. “Come on, baby. Let’s get you inside.”

Josh stood and wobbled on his feet as he took another large sip of the whiskey. He stumbled after her when he felt her tug on his hand.

It was still too early for bed—at least for Novah, so she settled Josh in the oversized recliner with a heavy blanket thrown over the chair and a lighter one to cover him if he passed out. She figured it would soak up any mess he might make, and the floors in the room were tile, so overall, it would be easy to clean up.

It was her favorite chair, and she’d had it specially made one-and-a-half times as wide as a regular recliner, so she could curl up in it with a good book. Novah turned the TV on, but kept the volume low. As she walked past Josh, he reached out and took her arm.

“Sh-sh-sh-sit with me,” he slurred.

Novah grinned. “You’re shitfaced. Go to sleep, Josh. You know you’re going to be sorry in the morning.”

“I know. Please,” he slurred again, and then took another long slug out of the bottle before he handed it to her. “Take dis away. Drunk.”

Novah took the bottle and put it in the kitchen, in a different cabinet where he hopefully wouldn't find it. When she went back into the living room, he was channel surfing. She sighed. She wasn't ready for bed yet, so she went back into the kitchen and made a pot of coffee. *Might as well start sobering him up now.*

She carried the coffee into the living room and put the foot on the recliner down.

"Whatcha doin'?"

"Gonna sober you up a little bit."

"Don't wanna."

"Sure you do. You love coffee."

"Coffee? Mmmm. Good."

Novah sat next to him in the recliner and handed him a cup. "It's hot, Josh. Two hands."

Surprisingly, he blew on it and sipped. "Yeah. Good stuff."

Chapter 19

Novah woke up to the wet, miserable sound of retching echoing down the hallway, each heave followed by a hollow pause and the faint splash of water running in the bathroom sink. She rolled over and squinted at the glowing red digits on the bedside clock. *Five.* The gray light of early morning leaked around the edges of the curtain, flattening the room into soft shadows. *Might as well get up.*

She took a quick shower, letting the hot water beat the sleep from her muscles and rinse the faint cling of last night's whiskey from her skin. She padded to the kitchen along the cool tile. By the time she got there,

Josh was sitting at the island bar with his head resting on his arms, shoulders slumped, and his hair sticking up in uneven clumps. She kissed the top of his head as she walked past to make a pot of coffee.

Josh moaned, his voice muffled against his sleeve. "Remind me never to do that again."

Novah laughed, trying to keep her voice low. "I warned you last night you were going to pay."

"Shh. Don't yell. I remember. I should have listened." His words came out thick, as if his tongue didn't quite know where to sit in his mouth.

"I'm not yelling. You're hungover. Maybe still drunk." Novah grinned and continued, "You remember? How? You could hardly walk and were slurring your words."

"Sometimes, no matter how hard I try to drown out shit, I can always seem to remember. It's a curse. I don't do it often, because I don't like the two-day hangover, but even more because I still remember." He shifted, and she heard the soft crack of his neck as he tried to loosen it. A faint wince pulled at his features.

Novah poured two cups of coffee and placed them on the bar, the steam curling up in thin, fragrant ribbons that smelled dark and slightly burnt. She pulled a barstool closer to Josh and slid the coffee over to him.

"Drink some. It'll help. Did you take anything for the headache?"

"Yeah. I found some aspirin in the bathroom." His hand groped for the mug with clumsy fingers and took a sip before groaning and putting his head back down.

Novah waited until he drank a second cup of coffee, watching a little color creep back into his face even as his eyes stayed half shut. "Do you want breakfast?"

"Uhh. Probably not a good idea right now." His stomach gave a low, protesting churn that he didn't bother to hide.

"Dry toast?"

Josh slightly shook his head. "Maybe in a bit."

"Do you want to talk about why you decided to get trashed last night?"

"Not really. It's old shit. I thought I had it handled." His fingers tightened briefly around the warm mug, causing his knuckles to whiten, before he eased his grip.

After a few minutes, Josh said, "I guess you figured that my parents never really bonded with me. Sometimes, that kind of stuff rears its ugly head. They made me go to therapy for a while in my teens, but it never really helped. It also didn't help that they worked opposite shifts. Now that I look back on it, they had enough money to hire a sitter or even a full-time nanny. I think they did that on purpose."

“I don’t know, Josh. How can you be sure? Have you ever talked to them about this?”

“I tried a few times, but they always shut me down.

“I know you don’t have siblings. What about aunts, uncles, cousins?”

Josh shook his head. “Not that I know of.”

Novah debated with herself as to whether she should show Josh the article or ask about the accident. Finally, she said, “Wait a sec. I want to show you something.”

She went into her bedroom and took the folded copy of the article out of her purse.

“I have a feeling you don’t remember this, and your parents never told you about this. My parents remember this happening. It might piss you off, Josh, so promise me you’ll stay calm. I’m here for you and will always be here for you.”

“This must be something bad,” he mumbled.

“Well, it was bad. But it’s not bad now, at least only because you don’t remember. Are your parents still alive?”

Josh’s voice came out flat. “My mother is, but I haven’t spoken to her in over ten years. I didn’t even go to my father’s funeral because they didn’t act like my parents.”

Novah put her arm around Josh's shoulders, her fingers spreading lightly over the tense muscle as if she could smooth it down. "That's because they weren't your real parents," she said softly, her words careful and reluctant.

Josh sat up straight so fast that her arm slipped from his shoulders as his whole body went rigid. "What the fuck are you talking about, Novah?" His jaw bunched as he spoke, his eyes narrowing on her as if she'd just thrown a punch.

"Have you ever wondered why you have a different last name?"

"My mother told me it was because it was before they were married, so she gave me her maiden name." His voice shook at the edges, a mix of disbelief and something darker, and his hands curled into loose fists on his thighs.

Novah closed her eyes briefly. "Damn." She took a deep breath, her chest rising and falling as if she were bracing for impact. "No kid should ever be treated like you were." She reached for his hand, her touch gentle, and brushed his knuckles with her thumb. She handed him the article with the other. "Remember. I'm here. We'll figure this out together."

As Josh started reading the article, she stood and moved behind him. Wrapping her arms around his waist and leaning into him, she whispered, each word slow and sure, "I love you, Joshua Gann."

His shoulders climbed toward his ears, knowing he still couldn't say them back to her. As he read more of the article, the words seemed to blur, and he started rubbing his forehead with his hand. "What the fuck is this?" he asked under his breath.

He shook his head as if to clear it and read the article again, his eyes moving faster and blinking, as if he'd misread it the first time.

"Josh," Novah whispered, her hands sliding up to rest against his chest, feeling his heart thudding too fast beneath her palms.

"Where did you get this?" he asked, his voice low and his words clipped as he tilted the paper like he wanted to tear it in half.

"At the library. It was in the Butler paper. I was doing some research for my book. I was going through the local newspapers. This headline caught my eye." Novah kept her tone even, but her fingers tightened slightly in his shirt, unwilling to let go.

"How long have you known?" Josh was still growling.

"Since yesterday. I wanted to talk about it last night, but it—ah, wasn't the right time. I thought maybe you knew, and that is why you were drinking. I only realized that you may not have known this morning after you started talking about them." Her gaze searched his profile, looking for signs that this hurt less than it clearly did.

"No. And that's another reason to drink, but I won't." His voice broke on the last word, and his throat worked as he swallowed it down.

Josh crumpled the article in his hand and stared stoically at the wall, his eyes glassy but unblinking.

"Do you want me to see if Hank can get us more information? Maybe they found who killed them? I couldn't find any other articles." Her voice softened around the words, and she stayed close, one hand rubbing slow circles between his shoulder blades.

"No. Yes. No. Fuck. I don't know. Just leave it for now," Josh said as he abruptly stood and walked with clipped strides to the window. The chair scraped against the floor, and Novah grabbed it before it could fall. He stared out of the window, his shoulders hunched and his fist crushing the paper.

Novah stayed where she was, watching him with a helpless aching tenderness.

Two Days Later

Hank lifted the phone. He didn't want to make either call he had to make this afternoon. He pressed the call button for the first call. "Damn. Typical. No answer," he grumbled.

He moved the file and grabbed the next one. Just as his finger hovered over the call button, his cell rang. "Do you ever answer your phone?" he asked in greeting.

Novah laughed. "No. But I didn't do it on purpose this time. I was across the room and had my hands full. Did you find something on Josh's birth parents?"

Hank leaned back in his chair and rubbed his forehead. "Does Josh know you asked me about this?"

"I told him we should, but he couldn't make up his mind. He never mentioned it again, and I didn't want to because of the pain it caused him. Why?"

The sheriff shook his head. "I found the file. It took some time, since the case is ancient and they had to dig it out of another warehouse."

"Wait," she said.
Hank could hear her typing something.

"Well. The Butler police generally don't keep files past the statute of limitations. That means there's something up with that case if they still have the file."

"Yeah," Hank said quietly. He flipped through the file again, not saying a word.

Novah opened her mouth to speak, but Hank finally said, "Sorry. I took a quick look through the file again." He shook his head.

"And?" Novah asked.

"It's never been solved. It's a cold case. Worse yet, it's a cold case that was sitting and collecting dust—at least until they reopened it in 2017. It hadn't seen the light of day prior to that, nor since. Normally, at least for the first few years, there are notes in the file showing when someone worked on it. This one doesn't have one note or anything else showing that it was worked on since the *day of the accident.*"

Novah sat back in her chair and sucked in a deep breath. "Shit, Hank. You think there's a cover-up or something?"

"I don't know. Something's not right. There are a few notes from 2017, but you can tell someone only gave it some half-assed attention due to the tip, and then put it back on the shelf. And now we have Josh, the victim of a fire."

A cold chill crept over Novah, causing her to shiver. "That's supposed to be public record. Can I get a copy?"

Hank shrugged, even though Novah couldn't see him. "Let me do some checking on it first. At first glance, there doesn't seem to be anything that needs to be kept under wraps. I'll see if they kept any kind of evidence or something."

Novah held her finger in the air. "Hank. Don't let this sit. I have a bad feeling about this."

"Yeah, Novah. Me, too. Josh is a good friend. I won't let it sit. I'll be in touch."

Hank never made the second call. Instead, he signed out of the building and drove over to Butler.

Chapter 20

I wonder if he's okay. I know we text a couple of times per day, but he's not even tried to visit and hasn't invited me over since I told him I loved him. I wonder if he even heard me. He had to have. I whispered it in his ear. Maybe he was too pissed about the article to remember. Damn. That's twice he's ignored it.

Novah leaned back in her chair. She was trying to write a steamy scene, and all she could think about was Josh. That wasn't working because her character didn't make sure his partner was satisfied. Josh always made sure she was satisfied. "Ugh," she groaned.

She leaned forward and read what she'd just written. "No. Nope. This just isn't right. Since I met Josh, I can't write these sex scenes as they should be. Fuck my life." Novah highlighted the last thousand words she wrote and hit the delete button. "So much for that."

She stepped down to the lower level and sat on the edge of the opening, sticking her legs in the water and leaning back on her hands. *It's no wonder Josh doesn't talk about his parents. They never treated him like a son. At least, from what he's told me. And now he knows why. I hope the sheriff finds something today. On the accident and the fire.*

Her phone chirped. "Damn." She'd left it on the desk and didn't feel like moving. The phone chirped again. "Fuck me." It was Alexis's notification tone for a text. *I can't ignore her.* Novah pulled her feet out of the lake and padded up the steps to her desk. She flopped into her chair and swiped the screen active.

> ***ALEXIS:*** *Hey, girl. The town is organizing an event to raise money for the volunteer fire department. We need your expertise in organizing.*

Novah sighed. She helped organize various events throughout the year, especially for the fire department.

> ***NOVAH:*** *When is it? I'm behind on writing.*

> ***ALEXIS:*** *The event? Not for another few months. Organizing it? First meeting tonight.*
>
> ***NOVAH:*** *Okay, count me in. I'll see if Josh wants to help, too.*
>
> ***ALEXIS:*** *Great. I think Jaxxon is going to talk to him about it, but you can ask him anyway.*

Novah sent a thumbs-up emoji and shoved the phone into her pocket.

Josh walked into the town hall. Against his better judgment, he'd agreed to help Jaxxon at the fundraiser. They were organizing the crafters and the food tables. He lifted his hand in a wave when he saw Novah and Alexis at the front of the room.

Novah checked the time and turned to Alexis. "We'll give it another five minutes to see if anyone else shows up. We still need someone to organize people from the banks and insurance companies. We have the lawyers and real estate covered. Hailey's doing that. Skyler's doing the accountants and bookstores, and Jordyn's doing the rest of the businesses. You know her, right? The pet store owner?"

Alexis nodded. "I do. Not well, but I see her around town."

Novah felt a warm tingle trace the back of her neck, a soft prickle that spread across her skin like the brush of invisible fingers. The low murmur of conversation and distant clink of glassware faded at the edges as she glanced around the room, following the pull she didn't quite want to acknowledge.

Josh stood with Jaxxon near the far wall, his head tipped slightly as he spoke, shoulders relaxed in that easy way that always seemed to settle a space around him. With his back to her, it should have been simple to look away, but her gaze lingered, drawn by his familiar lines and the comfortable way he fit into the room.

Her eyes slipped to his finely rounded ass before she could stop them, catching on the shape of him, and something in her chest tightened, small and warm. Her breath hitched a quiet stutter she felt more than heard, as if her body had noticed him a heartbeat before her thoughts would let her admit it.

"Uhh, Novah."

She blinked and turned to her friend, the buzz of voices and the faint sweetness of cider rushing back in. "Hunh?"

Alexis laughed, bumping her shoulder against Novah's. "You haven't heard a word I said, have you?"

"Sorry, no. I was thinking about something."

"Thinking about that sexy ass over there," Alexis said, tilting her chin in Josh's direction.

Novah's face colored at the wicked grin on Alexis's face and her teasing words. "Stop, Alexis."

"Pay attention, Novah. You can mess with him later. Preferably when I'm not mid-sentence."

Novah gave her friend a friendly shove. "I haven't seen him in a few days. I can look all I want," she said, bending over the table to go through the list of who they still had to contact.

An hour later, they had divided the list, and Novah grabbed her notes. "I'm heading out. I'm getting hungry, and I need to get a few hours in on the book today."

Alexis grinned. "I don't know about that."

Novah jumped as she felt hands grab her around the waist. Alexis's grin turned into a laugh. As Novah turned to see who was behind her, she caught Josh's unique smell and let out a little moan. She turned toward him. "You smell so good," she whispered.

Josh leaned down to kiss her chastely, and Novah's hand snaked around the back of his neck, pulling him into her. Her tongue pushed past his lips.

Alexis mumbled, "Get a room."

Josh raised his eyebrows, and Novah broke the kiss, laughing.

She turned to her friend and said, "We just might."

He turned her and pulled her against him. *That was a mistake. I was already getting hard, and this is making it worse.* Leaning to whisper in her ear, he said, "Let's get out of here."

Novah waved at Alexis. "See ya," she said as she grabbed Josh's hand and pulled him across the room and out the door.

Josh woke up to an empty bed and a strip of cold air against her back where her warmth had been. The sheets were still warm and faintly scented with her shampoo, so he knew Novah hadn't gone far. A sharp crash from the kitchen shattered the quiet, followed by the clatter of something metal skidding across the tile, and he jolted upright, his heart thumping hard against his ribs.

"What the hell is she doing?" he muttered, scrubbing a hand over his face as he squinted at the red digits of the clock. Two in the morning. Josh shoved his legs into his jeans and padded down the cool hallway toward Novah's living room.

Novah heard the soft thuds of Josh's feet on the floorboards and the faint rustle of fabric, so she lifted one hand up to stop him. The other gripped a .45. She held up one finger, her breath tight in her chest, and then reached around the corner and turned the lights on.

"Oh, shit! Go shut all the doors, Josh! Hurry! A fucking raccoon got in here!" The animal hissed from the countertop, its claws scrabbling on the marble as its tail twitched in the sudden light.

Josh ran down the hall, slamming the doors shut while Novah tried to herd the raccoon out the back door. When he got back to the kitchen, she'd traded the pistol for a broom, its bristles rasping over the floor as she shoed at the beast. Josh grabbed the mop from the corner, and together they got it back outside.

"How'd he get in here?" Josh asked, his heart still beating a little too fast.

"We must not have latched the door," Novah said. "Sometimes it sticks and doesn't latch right, so even though you think you locked it, it's not locked."

"Damn, that's dangerous. At least with this whacko around," Josh said, referring to Eric. They still hadn't heard from the sheriff about the fire, the stalking or Josh's parents.

Novah closed the door, double-checking that it latched and locked. She turned to look at Josh. "I know we should go back to bed, but I'm not really that tired right now. And I have an early day, too."

"I do, too. Let's go. Even if we just lie there talking, we'll get some rest, and maybe we'll fall asleep."

Novah nodded. "Okay." She put the broom and mop away and grabbed her .45 off the counter.

"Would you have shot someone if they broke in?" Josh asked.

"Damn straight," Novah said adamantly.

Josh raised his eyebrows.

"I was taught as a kid never to pull a gun unless I was going to use it. My father drummed it into my head. I'd have no problem pulling that trigger if someone was coming after me."

"Now I know why you said you could take care of yourself," Josh mumbled.

"Damn straight," Novah repeated.

The alarm's shrill buzz cut through the dark at five-thirty, and Novah grumbled as she blindly reached over to her nightstand to shut it off.

Josh rolled toward her, his arm snaking around her waist and drawing her back into his arms. His sleep-rough breath brushed the nape of her neck. "Morning," he mumbled.

"Morning. I guess we did fall asleep after all," she replied hoarsely. The dim gray light leaking around the curtains told her dawn was not far off. She felt his lazy nod.

"Yeah, but I don't want to get up." His words slurred together, and his grip tightened as if he could keep her in the bed and stop the day from starting.

"I could stay here all day, but we both have meetings this morning," Novah said as she eased from under his arm and rolled out of bed. "I'll make us some coffee."

When Josh didn't respond, she glanced back at him. He was sprawled on his stomach, one hand hanging off the edge of the bed, breathing deep and even. A small smile tugged at her mouth as she set her alarm for another hour. His meeting wasn't as early as hers.

Steam fogged the bathroom mirror as the hot water beat against her shoulders, washing away the last of the sleepiness. After her shower, the house filled with the rich, bitter smell of brewing coffee as the machine gurgled and dripped its goodness into a pot.

Novah pulled some leftover biscuits out of the fridge, along with eggs and sausage. She cooked enough to make three sandwiches. She ate one with her coffee and wrapped the others. Glancing at the time, she swallowed the last bite of her biscuit with the now lukewarm coffee. She grabbed a pen and left Josh a note.

When the alarm went off again, Josh grumbled. "Novah."

When she didn't answer, he sat up and reached over her side of the bed to shut it off. His hand knocked a piece of paper to the floor. Josh sat on the edge of the bed, rubbing his eyes.

"Oh, fuck. What time is it?" He turned to glance at the clock and shook his head. Then, he remembered the paper he had knocked on the floor. Rolling across the bed, he reached down to pick it up. The corner of his mouth lifted as he read it. He'd take the biscuits with him. He had to shower at his house, since they hadn't planned on getting together the day before, and he didn't have a change of clothes.

> Josh,
> I left two sausage biscuits in the fridge for you. Pop them in the microwave for about 40 seconds each.
>
> Please turn off the coffee pot when you're done and lock up. I'll call or text between meetings.
>
> Love, Novah

He found a large travel mug in the kitchen and filled it with the rest of the coffee. He grabbed the two biscuits and then remembered the note. He wanted to keep it. Josh folded the note and tucked it into his wallet. He made his way out with the biscuits and coffee, ensuring the door was shut and locked.

Chapter 21

Novah glanced at her phone when Josh's notification tone rang. They'd both had a busy couple of weeks and hadn't seen each other, except in passing and at meetings for the firehouse fundraiser. She glanced longingly at her computer screen and decided she was in a good place to stop for a few minutes.

JOSH: Can you come over for dinner? Got some news.
NOVAH: Yes. About six?
JOSH: That works. I'll get the grill going. Burgers good?

NOVAH: *Yes, that will be great. I'll bring some potato salad that I have left over.*
JOSH: *Perfect. I have beer.*

Novah ended the conversation with a quick thumbs-up emoji, the glow of her screen washing her fingers as the chat bubble popped out of view. The time in the corner made her mouth twist. Not much evening left.

She knocked out two more chapters, the keys clicking in a steady rhythm until the words on the monitor began to blur and the muscles at the back of her neck protested. With a slow exhale, she saved her work, pushed back from the desk, and headed up to the house.

In her bedroom, she dragged her small overnight bag from the closet and tossed it open on the bed. A clean blouse, spare jeans, travel-size toiletries, and an extra pair of panties went in first, followed by her makeup bag and charger. She chose each item with a quick, practiced efficiency that kept her from having to think too hard about why she was packing "just in case."

She paused at her dresser, fingers resting on the handle of the top drawer, then grabbed an extra T-shirt and stuffed it into the bag. The thought of driving home half-asleep in the gray light just to shower and double back made her shoulders sag. Leaving straight from Josh's tomorrow would be easier on the eyes and the nerves.

She could smell the burgers before she even killed the engine, the smoke and char drifting down the drive to meet her. The low sizzle of grease and the muted thump of music from inside followed her as she walked around the side of the house and up onto the deck.

Josh stood at the grill, a faint sheen of sweat on his forearms. She gave Josh a chaste kiss and said, "Let me put this in the fridge."

"Okay. Bring us a beer when you come out?" He flipped a burger, and a curl of the fragrant smoke rose between them.

"Sure, babe." The cool air from the open fridge rolled over her as she set the dish on a shelf and grabbed two bottles. The metal caps bit into her palm as she twisted them off.

She stepped outside and handed one of the beers to Josh, and then sank into the swing. The cushions gave with a soft sigh as the seat rocked and a light evening breeze threaded through her hair. "It's nice out tonight."

"It is. Did you get anything done on your book?" He took a pull from his beer, his eyes flickering to her over the rising smoke.

"Yeah. I finally got several chapters done." She tipped her head back, feeling the tension ease from her shoulders. "I even got two more done after you texted.

Did you finish that order you were working on the other day?"

"Yep. Got another one. And I'm working on a statue, too. These are about ready if you want to bring that salad out. There's a Cole slaw in the fridge, too."

When Novah came back out with the tray of salads and condiments, Josh had the cheeseburgers on buns on the plates he'd set by the grill. He brought them over to the table and put one in front of Novah.

"Oh, you made those meatloaf burgers. Those are so good."

The side of Josh's mouth lifted in a half smile. "Yeah, they are." He took the spoon Novah handed him and scooped some of the potato salad onto his plate. They both added coleslaw and to their burgers, lettuce, tomato, onion, ketchup, relish and mustard.

Both were hungry, so they ate in silence. Novah leaned forward, resting her elbows on the table and sighed. "That was good, babe. I'm good and full now."

"Me, too. Let me get this cleaned up, and I'll tell you what I heard today."

Novah nodded. "I'll help you." They grabbed the plates and the leftover salads and brought them inside. She put the salads in the fridge, and then dried the dishes that Josh washed.

Josh stepped back, the screen door giving a soft squeak before it snapped shut. His phone buzzed, and he took it from his pocket. An anonymous number glowed on the screen. He swiped the call active, putting it on speaker. "Josh Gann."

"Fucking pyro," the caller growled. The voice came out of the speaker, rough and distorted, wrapped in a thin hiss of static that scratched at the edges of each word. Faint background noise murmured under the growl—just enough to sound wrong.

Josh's shoulders locked. "Excuse me?" he said, narrowing his eyes, his teeth clicking together on the last syllable.

"The whole town knows you burned down your own shop." The sentence slid out slowly, each word separated by a tiny beat of dead air.

Josh shot a look at Novah. The steady chirp of crickets and the far-off hum of the TV in the caller's background suddenly seemed too loud compared to the tinny voice they couldn't place. Novah swallowed hard, the small sound feeling huge in the tight silence between them.

She reached across the table and grabbed the phone, the speaker crackling under her grip. "Listen, you cocksucker," she snapped, her words hitting the mic in sharp bursts, "you have no idea what you're talking about. Stop harassing him. We'll find out who you are and sue you." Her breath came fast and audible now.

"Listen, you fat bitch." The insult landed in a low, almost conversational tone, made uglier by the calm. A faint snort of laughter ghosted over the line. "He's only with you because no one else likes him. He can't keep a girl, and he won't keep you either." The last words thudded out in a steady rhythm, separated by soft clicks, as if the caller's fingers were tapping the phone while he spoke.

Josh reached across the table and took the phone back. "Fuck off and grow up," he growled and then hung up. He stood and walked around the table to sit next to Novah. "You know that's not true, right?"

Novah leaned away from him and raised her eyebrow. "Well, I might be fat, and I *can* be a bitch, but you seem to like it enough."

Josh reached behind her head and pulled her until their foreheads touched. "First, you're not fat. You're just right. Second, yeah, you can be a bitch, but so can I. I think everyone can when they're having a shit day."

"And we all know you didn't start that fire. But more importantly, the fire chief knows, and so does the sheriff. He is the one who woke you up with that phone call."

Josh grinned. "And how did you hear about that?"

"Aha. You don't remember everything from the night you got drunk. You were going on and on about that."

Josh's face reddened. "And how else did I make an ass of myself?"

Novah opened her mouth to say something, and Josh held up his hand. "No. Never mind. I don't want to know. I'm already embarrassed. Oh, and by the way, don't let me forget. I got you a new bottle of whiskey."

"You didn't have to do that. I rarely drink it anyway."

"Yes, I did. I don't think you planned on me drinking most of it."

Novah laughed. "You ready to try that again?"

"Hell, no. It's not bad getting there, but the next morning is hell on wheels. I'm not ready to do that again for a while. Probably never again."

Josh opened two more beers and handed one to Novah, and then pulled her over to the swing. "Okay, Hank called. They still don't have anything on Eric the stalker. They cleared Rob. He had a solid alibi. They don't know who left that anonymous tip, and they don't really have a way to find out."

"Sometimes I wonder if Eric didn't have anything to do with the fire. You'd think they'd be able to pin that one down," Novah said.

"They have a mess of circumstantial evidence, but nothing that a good lawyer won't shoot down in court."

Novah glanced at her phone when it rang. She narrowed her eyes as she answered. "Josh, are you okay?" He never called—he always texted, as he knew she'd answer when she wasn't writing.

Josh glanced at his watch as he waited for Novah to pick up the phone. Just as he'd suspected, she thought something was wrong. "No, baby, nothing's wrong. That storm is pretty nasty, and they didn't cancel the fundraiser meeting. Want me to pick you up?"

Novah glanced at her watch. "Yes. That would be great. I'm ready any time you get here."

"I'll be there in a few. I'm heading out now."

When Josh pulled into Novah's driveway, she was standing on the porch. He reached across the cab and opened the door as she pulled her hoodie over her head and made a dash for the truck.

"We're gonna freeze in there. They always have the air conditioning cranked, and we're going to be soaked," Josh said.

"Nope," Novah said and held up a plastic bag. "I have another hoodie for both of us. Mine should fit you since I buy them a size too big for me."

Josh grinned. "Now, why the hell didn't I think of that?"

"I'm taking the fifth on that one."

Josh gave her a light shove in the shoulder. "You ain't right."

"Never said I was," she countered.

Josh leaned against the door of the meeting room, waiting for Novah to finish with her meeting. Hank waved and walked over to him. "Let's step into the hall for a minute."

The two friends stepped out and made their way toward one end of the nearly empty hall, where they could speak in private. "Still nothing on the fire. Nothing on your parents' wreck, either. I'm putting out a county-wide notice to see if anyone remembers anything about that wreck. Maybe the Butler police missed something back then."

Josh nodded. "Sounds good."

"I also went over the evidence again. Just on the off-chance that their car still exists, I called the junkyard where they towed it. Because they were driving a 1969 Chevelle, the junkyard didn't junk it. People are always looking for parts. They took a few parts off it, but it's still there. They said it's probably pretty rusted now, but we're more than welcome to check it out. I'm heading out there tomorrow with some forensic guys."

Josh's eyes widened. "Really. Wow. Maybe we'll get lucky."

"Don't get your hopes up, Josh. I have no idea what parts they took of the car to sell or how bad the rust is. If the weather got inside, we probably won't find much," Hank said.

"At least we have something, though."

Hank nodded just as Novah walked out of the meeting room.

"Did the investigators find the car back in 2017?" Josh asked as Novah walked up to them.

Hank turned to Novah. "Hi, Novah." He turned back to Josh. "No. They never thought to check to see if the vehicle had been crushed. I only checked because of the year, make and model."

"Were you able to determine what the additional evidence was that they found in 2017?" Novah asked.

Hank shook his head. "No. It almost looks as though they opened the file to make someone happy, and then closed it a couple of months later. There are no additional notes in the file, no indication that anyone signed out the little evidence the police had."

Josh narrowed his eyes. "That's weird."

"Yes, and it makes me want to look even harder," Hank said. "Let me get out of here and finish up that pile of paperwork on my desk, or I won't be going anywhere tomorrow."

"Thanks, Hank. I'd ask to go with you tomorrow, but I know better," Josh said.

"Yeah, the state could use that against us if we have to bring this to a trial," Hank said.

Hank stepped into the office at the junkyard. The man glanced up from his paperwork and smiled. "Hi, Hank!"

"Hey, Jerry. I didn't know you worked here. How've you been?"

Jerry nodded. "Hanking in there."

Hank laughed at the play on his name. "Still as smart-asserey as ever, are ya?"

"Sure am. Might be worse, according to my wife." Jerry grabbed a notepad. "I got a note here that a sheriff is supposed to look at that old '69 in the back. That happen to be you?"

"Sure is. I don't know that we'll find anything, but I'm hoping we do. It may have some clues from an old accident-turned-murder case that was never processed correctly."

Jerry leaned back against the counter behind him and rubbed his chin with his hand. After a few long seconds, he asked, "That wouldn't be that wreck from back in the '90s...I can't remember their name. Wait. Young couple. Grant. Grange. No. Gann. That's it. Gann. I was just a young'un back then, but I remember that was a bad accident."

"That's the one. The forensics team should be here shortly."

"Speakin' of the devil," Jerry said, pointing at the parking lot through the window.

They waited until the team of three forensic guys walked into the office.

"George. Paul. Donny. You know Jerry?"

All three men nodded. "Sure do. This isn't our first rodeo with checking junked cars. Though they're usually only a few weeks old, not years," George said.

"I'll show you where it is, guys, if you'll follow me," Jerry said as he gestured to a door at the rear of the office. "We can cut through here."

Jerry stepped out of the building, but instead of heading toward the fenced-in yard, he turned to the left toward a garage. He led them through it and to a large metal warehouse in the back. Rows of shelves that held car parts lined the walls. A sectioned-off area in the back held ten work bays. Two of them had old cars that were over thirty years old—one of them was the '69 Chevelle.

"You're fucking kidding me," Hank said under his breath.

Jerry turned and walked backward and grinned. "Nope. The kid who answered the phone didn't tell you they kept it in storage?"

"Sure didn't. He said it was probably pretty rusted."

"He may not have known. He's only been here a couple of months." Jerry held out his hand as if presenting a VIP at a black-tie ball.

Hank stepped up to the car and peered in the windows. "Damn. This is in good condition."

Jerry nodded. "It is. I'll leave y'uns to it, then."

The forensics team took a lot of pictures and picked pieces of hair and other matter they thought they could get some DNA out of from the interior of the vehicle, including the trunk. Hank stood back, watching. When they finished, the lead team member said, "We found a lot of stuff, but don't get your hopes up. There's no telling how many people have been in and out of this vehicle."

Hank nodded and followed them out, not saying a word. When they reached the office, the forensics team promised to be in touch.

"Thanks, guys. Let's hope we can solve this mystery once and for all for Josh."

Chapter 22

On their way out of the fundraiser meeting, Josh overheard whispers. He shook his head and ignored them as he followed Novah out. "Time to get wet again," he said.

"Yeah," said Novah.

They ran to his truck, and once they got inside, Josh started it and turned on the heat. "This will help dry our clothes and keep us warm until we can change. I can't believe they didn't cancel this meeting. This is a nasty storm."

"You're not kidding." Novah paused. *...Insurance money. ...Burned it himself.* She wanted to ask him about the whispering she heard. She wasn't sure if he heard what they were saying, but she did. She narrowed her eyes at the thought and let out a sigh.

Josh glanced at her and then back at the road. "What was that all about?"

"What?"

"The narrowed eyes and sigh."

Novah turned in her seat to face Josh as he pulled into his driveway. "Those people," she said, sharper than she meant to. "They're always whispering shit, but don't have the guts to say it to our faces."

Josh shut the truck off and turned to look at her. You don't have the guts to tell her you love her. Just like you won't deal with the rumors going around. Josh's head tilted just slightly as the thoughts ran through his mind. Deal. Grow up while you're at it.

He swallowed a sigh. "Let's go inside and get changed. I have some sweats that will fit you. We'll make some lunch and just hang out for a bit."

Novah nodded and opened her door. They both ran inside, though they wouldn't have been any more soaked if they had strolled onto his porch. *Well, I guess he doesn't want to talk about it. I shouldn't let it bother me, and it probably wouldn't if all this other shit wasn't going on.*

She followed Josh into his bedroom and took the T-shirt and sweats he handed her. “Do you mind if I take a quick shower?”

“Not at all. I was thinking the same.”

Novah grabbed his hand and pulled him into the master bath with her. She turned the water on to let it warm up, and they both peeled the wet clothes off. “This feels so good to get out of these wet things.”

Josh winked at her. “Something else is going to feel so good, too.”

He stepped into the shower, leading her in after him and turning her so she was under the water. “You first,” he said. Once her hair was wet, he poured shampoo into his hand and rubbed it through her hair, piling it on top of her head.

The simple, familiar motion gave his hands something to do besides clench around the knot in his chest, and for a few precious seconds, it was easier to focus on slippery strands than on the article and the whispers about insurance money.

Novah leaned into him and moaned, “Damn, that feels so good,” as his fingers massaged her skull.

The sound loosened something tight inside him. If he kept her relaxed and smiling, maybe he could hold back the questions about who he really was for a bit longer. Turning her, Josh helped rinse her hair and then repeated the process with conditioner. “It doesn’t smell as nice as yours, but it still smells good,” he said, sniffing the conditioner, clinging to the harmless banter because talking about scent was safer than talking about parents who weren’t his.

Once he finished her hair, he grabbed a bottle of lavender body wash he’d bought for her and poured some on a loofah. He soaped her body, moaning as she turned to rinse. “Look at what you’ve done to me.”

Focusing on the ache in his body was easier than thinking about the way the town looked at him now, like they weren’t sure if he was a victim or a villain.

Novah grinned and reached for the shampoo. “First, we need to get you cleaned up before we run out of hot water.” She washed his hair and conditioned it, and then held up the body wash.

Josh nodded. “I don’t mind smelling like lavender since we’re not going anywhere in this storm.”

As she scrubbed him with the body wash, Josh reached down and gently pulled on her nipple with his lips. “Let me finish, Josh,” she groaned as her nipple hardened in his mouth and her muscles clenched with need.

He shook his head and then gave the other nipple the same attention.

Novah moaned as his tongue flicked back and forth over it. She hurried to rinse him as his fingers entered her and pressed against her walls. “Fuck, Josh,” she moaned.

She hung the loofah on the faucet handle and reached for his throbbing cock.

It jumped as soon as she wrapped her hand around it, and he ground out hoarsely, “Novah,” trailing off her name at the emotions from the day and the moment collided as his fingers pressed firmly inside of her pussy, sliding in and out.

When he felt the trembling inside her, Josh pulled her against him and moved his fingers faster. “Open your eyes, baby. Let me see it. I want to watch your eyes when you come all over my hand,” he choked out past the tightness in his throat.

His words were her undoing. Novah arched her back and screamed his name as she shattered around his fingers.

Josh lifted his hand and moaned as he sucked her juices from his fingers. Moaning, he grabbed the base of his cock. “Fuck. I need you now. I can’t wait. Turn around, baby.”

Novah turned and put her hands on the shower wall, bending enough to give him access. “Now, Josh. Fast and hard." Her legs quivered with anticipation as his hands wrapped around her hips, pulling them closer.

"Fuck," Josh muttered as he spread her thighs and lined himself up to her entrance. Without any warning, he shoved his cock into her as hard as he could, causing both of them to moan.

Novah's hips jerked into him as he stilled inside of her. "I need you, Josh."

"I know, baby. Give me a second, or I'm not going to last."

Novah spread her legs a little more, giving him better access, and reached between her thighs. "Josh, fuck me. I need to come again. I need to feel you..." She trailed off as Josh pulled almost all the way out and slammed into her.

"Yes," she moaned. "Harder."

Josh grabbed her hips with both hands and pounded into her over and over as her finger worked her clit in time with his pounding. He fought through her gripping muscles and shouted as he stilled in her, hot ribbons of cum pouring out of him.

"Water's getting cold," Novah huffed breathlessly as she turned it off.

Keeping his arms wrapped around her, Josh turned and pulled her down onto the built-in seat, keeping himself inside of her. He leaned his head against the shower wall, breathing heavily.

Novah leaned back against him, just as breathless. "So…Good. I… needed that. Need… you."

Josh's eyes closed as he shook his head. I can't love her, but I needed that as much as she did. I can't lose her, but I know I will if I can't get my head on straight. His arms involuntarily tightened around her, as if he thought she moved, she'd leave forever.

You don't need anything his subconscious yelled at him. Yes. Yes, I do. I need her.

Their breathing slowed, and Novah ground her hips against him when she felt Josh's cock stirring inside of her, pulling him out of his thoughts. She adjusted her legs for better balance and slowly rode him into oblivion.

Novah found some thawed pork chops in the fridge. She peeled back the plastic wrap and sprinkled them with salt, pepper and a dash of garlic powder. The cool meat was slick under her fingers as she flipped it to season the other side and rubbed it in.

Setting the chops aside, she reached for the potatoes and onions. The knife thudded a steady rhythm against the cutting board as she worked. Thin slices fell in neat piles as the sharp bite of the onion stung her eyes and mingled with the smell of earthy potatoes.

Josh grabbed two frying pans and the jar of bacon fat. He put them on the stove with a dollop of grease in each one and turned the burners on. The pale lumps melted into pools that smelled like Sunday breakfast as they heated. Grease popped, sending tiny flecks against the side of the pans.

Novah tipped the sliced potatoes into one pan, the vegetables hitting the hot fat with a loud sizzle. In the other, she laid the pork chops one at a time. The meat seared immediately, the edges turning opaque as the kitchen filled with the savory scent of pork.

"That smells so good. I worked up an appetite," Josh said, his voice low at her ear as he wrapped his arms around her waist. His chest was solid and warm against her back as she tended the potatoes.

"Me, too," Novah murmured. She flipped the potatoes with the flick of her wrist. The slices flew into the air and back into the pan, and then she leaned her head back on Josh's shoulder. Her hands settled over his, where they rested on her stomach. Her eyes closed when he brushed a slow kiss against the side of her head.

The scrape of his beard and the press of his lips sent a shiver down her neck. "Josh—"

"Shh," he said, his breath warm against her skin. Don't say it. I know she's gonna say it. I can't tell her I love her. She's gonna be hurt if I don't say it.

Novah pulled away from him and flipped the potatoes and the chops, watching the browned edges instead of looking at him. *He did hear me the other day. He won't say it back. Why?* Her jaw tightened as she stared at the pan, pretending to focus on getting the potatoes crisp.

"These are about done if you want to set the table," Novah said quietly.

He crossed to the cabinet and took out plates. The clack of the ceramic was louder in the sudden silence. *Damn. Now she's pissed. Of course she* is. He opened the silverware drawer, rattling the metal utensils as he grabbed forks and knives, and then set the table with more care than necessary.

After a beat, he reached into the fridge for two beers, the chill from the bottles biting into his fingers as he tried not to look at the tension in her shoulders.

Chapter 23

The only sounds at the table were the clink of forks against plates and the low rumble of the storm pressing against the windows. Wind rattled the panes every so often, a hollow shudder that seemed to echo in the quiet kitchen.

Novah cut into her pork chop, the knife sliding through the browned crust, and took a bite she barely tasted. The potatoes were crisp on the edges, soft in the middle, exactly how she liked them, but they might as well have been cardboard. The silence between them felt heavier than the rain-soaked clouds outside.

"So." Her voice came out too bright, too forced. She cleared her throat and tried again. "At least the fundraiser meeting went…okay? Once everyone stopped checking the weather every five minutes."

Josh nodded without looking up. "Yeah."

Not exactly a conversation. She picked at a corner of her chop. "If the storm keeps up, the lake's going to be high for a week. Might help the tourism numbers if the weather clears in time. People love the way it looks when it's full."

"Guess so." He stabbed a potato, jaw working.

She let the topic die. Every neutral subject she reached for slid out of her fingers, and underneath all of it, that moment at the stove looped in her head. His arms around her, his mouth at her temple, the way her chest had tightened as the word hovered on her tongue.

Josh—
Shh.

He'd known exactly what she was going to say. He'd cut her off before she could say it again.

Novah swallowed a too-big bite of potato that scratched on the way down. Maybe she should never have said it the first time. Maybe she'd shoved too much at a man who'd just watched his life burn down and then handed him an article that suggested his entire past might be a lie.

Her eyes slid up, just for a second, catching Josh's hunched shoulders. His attention was on his plate as if it had personally offended him. The folder she'd brought sat on the side table by the doorway where she'd set it earlier. Even closed, it felt like the frayed edges from handling it too much were staring at them.

Maybe I should have waited. Maybe I should never have brought it at all.

The scrape of her fork against the plate sounded loud in the quiet kitchen.

Josh speared another potato and chewed without tasting it, the texture turning pasty in his mouth. The quiet pressed in on him from all sides, thick as the steam fogging the window over the sink. He'd always liked silence when he worked, just the spin of the wheel, the whisper of clay under his hands, but this was different.

This silence left too much room in his head.

Every time he lifted his eyes, his gaze snagged on the folder on the side table. It sat there like a brick of dynamite someone had forgotten to disarm. He didn't have to open it. He saw the article anyway, the grainy black-and-white photo of twisted metal, the caption about a wreck on a two-lane road, the small note tucked into the corner about a little boy who survived and couldn't tell anyone his name.

No ID. No last name. Just "approximately three years old."

He pressed his molars together until his jaw ached.

Gann.

He'd written that name on every paper through school, signed it on checks, on contracts, on the deed to the studio. He'd spent years building a business around it, building a life around it. And all the while, the people who he thought were his parents weren't. It wasn't even his so-called mother's maiden name, like they'd told him.

He didn't know which possibility felt worse. That they'd known the whole story and lied, or that they'd never thought he deserved to hear it.

Rain slashed against the window, harder this time, a staccato rattle like handfuls of gravel thrown at the glass. In his mind, it blurred into the hiss of whispered voices at the fundraiser:

"Insurance money."

"Convenient timing, isn't it?"

"Wouldn't be the first time someone torched their own place."

He'd spent his entire life trying to be the opposite of the rumors his father drew, working himself half to death to be solid, dependable, the guy who opened his shop early and stayed late and never stiffed anyone on an order. Now, on top of finding out he might not even be who he thought he was, the town was already halfway to deciding he was a liar and a criminal.

Not really a Granger. Not really one of them.

He set his fork down a little harder than he meant to. The clatter made Novah flinch. Her eyes flicked up to his, then skated away, landing on the side table. On the folder.

Her shoulders tightened.

His gaze followed hers, locking onto the manila edge. The sight of it sitting there in his kitchen—a stranger's story that might be his—snapped something in him.

"How long have you had that?" The words came out sharper than he'd intended, cutting through the patter of rain.

Novah's head jerked back to him. "What?"

He pointed with his chin toward the folder. "*That.* The article. How long has it been sitting in your house while you and your friends talked about my life like it was—" He broke off, his hand curling into a fist on the table. "Like it was research for your next book."

Color drained from her face. "Josh, that's not—"

"How much did you know?" The questions tumbled out, hard and fast now that the dam had cracked. "Did your parents know all this time? Have they been sitting on this since I moved here? Since *before*?" He heard his voice rising and didn't pull it back. "Did anyone else see it before you decided to show it to me?"

Her fork clinked against her plate as she set it down with trembling fingers. "No. Josh, no. It's not like that." She took a breath, visibly forcing herself to slow down. "My parents weren't…sitting on some big secret about you. I found it. There was a subplot I was working on, and I asked them to help me dig through old local news from that county. When I mentioned it, they said they knew the family."

She gestured loosely, as if the motion could encompass all of it. The stacks of clippings, the countless small-town tragedies.

"I found that article by accident," she said. "At first, it was just…sad. Some little boy losing his family in a crash. But then I noticed the year, and the age they guessed he was. It stuck with me."

Josh stared at her, chest tight. "And you didn't think that was the kind of thing I should know right away?"

Her throat worked as she swallowed. "I didn't even *know* it had anything to do with you, Josh. There are a lot of kids who've been through hell in this world. I only suspected the dates lined up when I showed it to you three days after I found it. And even then…" She trailed off, eyes searching his face. "Even then, I wasn't sure. I was terrified of blowing up your life over a coincidence."

She reached toward him, then stopped halfway, her hand hovering over the table. "I only brought it up when it stopped feeling like some abstract and started feeling like something you deserved to see. Not to gossip about. Not for a book. For *you*."

"And you held it back 'for my own good.' Just like everyone else does. I'm a fucking grown man, for chrissakes."

Novah stood and moved behind his chair. Her hand hesitated as they reached for his shoulders. When they finally landed gently on his shirt, he flinched and then shrugged her off.

"No, Josh. You're not pushing me away again. And if you remember, you were drunk one of those nights." She wrapped her arms around his arms and upper body, as if she were restraining him, and spoke softly in his ear, trying to keep the quiver out of her voice. "Hank's investigation into the arsonist looked as though it had something to do with your past. It felt more likely to be real, but that made it *harder* to tell you what I found. Not easier. I really wanted to wait for a good time to tell you, but there is no good time."

He shrugged her arms off his shoulders and stood abruptly. "I can't do this right now," he snapped as he stomped down the hall, refusing to meet her eyes. She heard a bedroom door slam, but didn't know where he went.

Novah padded down the hall, the cool hardwood sighing under her bare feet. Josh's bedroom door was open, the bed a dark, rumpled shape in the gray light, but down the corridor a thin bar of yellow leaked from beneath the door of the room he'd turned into a makeshift studio.

She gathered her things with careful, quiet movements—phone, keys, bag strap sliding over her shoulder—and slipped out into the storm, the front door's latch clicking softly behind her. The night met her with a slap of cool, wet air. The rain drummed on the porch roof and spattered her cheeks, wind shoving at her as she stepped into it. *Why did he wait for three weeks to blow up?* Novah shrugged. *I hope I don't catch my death of cold walking in this mess.*

By the time she reached her own place, her jeans clung to her legs as if they were a second skin, and her jacket had gone from damp to useless. The water seeped through her shirt and trickled down her spine. The storm had eased to a steady, needling drizzle by the time she stepped onto her porch, but the street still glittered with puddles under the streetlights.

Rain still slicked down Novah's skin by the time she shoved the front door shut with her hip, the hollow thud echoing in the quiet house. Cool air rushed over her damp clothes, raising a shiver that had nothing to do with the temperature. She dropped her bag on the floor. Her fingers fumbled at the zipper of her jacket, the fabric sticking where it clung to her shirt, and she yanked it off, flinging it over the back of a chair without looking to see where it landed.

Chapter 24

Novah headed to her bedroom to get warm, dry clothes. Bringing them into the bathroom, she turned on the shower and let the water heat up. The harsh overhead light made the shadows under her eyes look like bruises as she peeled her wet jeans from her legs. Her knees ached faintly from the long walk back, and the faint, metallic tang of lake water clung to her skin beneath the sharper bite of Josh's cologne still ghosting her shirt.

She stripped it off with a jerk and tossed everything in a heap on the floor, and then stepped into the shower. As she finally started to get warm again, she thought, "I had to tell him, even if it costs our relationship. It would have been much worse if he had found out later that I knew."

Stepping out, she wrapped herself in a towel, rubbing hard until her skin flushed pink and the chill finally let go. A soft cotton T-shirt and worn flannel pants slid over her still-damp skin, the familiar fabric grounding her in a way her thoughts refused to.

She padded into the living room, bare feet whispering against the hardwood, and stopped in front of the big picture window. Outside, the storm dragged itself across the lake in slow, sullen waves, the sky a low ceiling of bruised gray. Raindrops pattered against the glass in uneven bursts, each soft tap a counterpoint to the sharper echo of the meaning of Josh's words in her head. *Just like the others who lied.*

The phrase hit again, a dull punch low in her gut. Her arms crossed over her chest and tightened, folding her in on herself as if she could hold the hurt in place before it leaked out.

I told him the truth, she reminded herself, jaw working as she stared at the blurred line where the water met the far shore. Her throat burned, a thick, hot knot sitting just behind her sternum, half made of guilt, half made of anger.

I'm the one who handed him the article. I'm the one who stood there while his whole history tilted sideways.

I did the right thing. I know I did. That doesn't mean it didn't hurt him.

Another memory slid in behind the first. The way his voice had sharpened, that raw edge when he'd asked how long she'd known, like every second she'd kept quiet, was another betrayal stacked on top of the rest.

She turned away from the window so fast the hem of her shirt flared, and paced a short path between the sofa and the coffee table. The house smelled faintly of the musk of damp wool from the blanket still tossed over the back of the couch. His scent clung stubbornly to it and threaded through the air as if he'd just stepped out of the room.

Her stomach rolled. "If he thinks I'm going to go running back to him this time, he's got another thing coming," she muttered under her breath, the words sounding small in the open room compared to the roar of them in her head.

"I can't believe he even had the gall to think I'm like those others who lied to him." The last word came out sharper than she intended, breaking on the edge of a bitter laugh.

Her phone buzzed on the coffee table. The screen lit the room with a pale blue glow as a notification popped up from some group thread she didn't care about. For a long moment, she only stared at it, the hollow space in her chest expanding.

You could call him.

The thought slid in, tempting and dangerous. She pictured herself grabbing her keys, marching back out into the rain, hammering on his door until he answered so she could shake him and demand he look at her—really look at her—and see the difference between her and every other person who'd walked away.

Her hand hovered over the phone, fingers trembling slightly, then curled into a fist instead. "No," she whispered, closing her eyes for a heartbeat. Chasing him down now, while his temper was still riding high and his past was bleeding all over the present, would only throw more fuel on a fire already out of control.

He needed room to breathe, to let the shock of the article wear off. She needed room, too, to remember that loving him didn't mean letting him swing at her with every old wound he carried.

She sank onto the sofa, the cushion sighing under her weight, and pulled her legs up, wrapping her arms around her knees until she was a tight ball of flannel and bare skin. The blanket bearing his scent beckoned from the arm of the chair, but she left it where it was. She didn't trust herself not to bury her face in it and fall apart. Instead, she grabbed her phone and unlocked it, thumbs hovering over the blank message screen for Josh's contact.

The words came in a rush, faster than she could censor them.

Josh, she typed, the tiny letters blurring once before she blinked hard and kept going.

You don't get to throw me in with the people who lied to you. Her thumbs flew, each tap of the glass a sharp little release. I found that article because I was doing my job—because I dig for stories, even the ugly ones. I told you about it because you deserved to know the truth, even though I knew it might blow up everything between us.

Her chest squeezed as she typed the next line, the truth sitting there like a weight.

That is what loving you looks like for me. I tell you the hard things. I stand next to you when they hurt. I do not smile and pretend they don't exist.

She swallowed, the taste of salt at the back of her tongue, and let the rest spill out, the parts of the conversation she hadn't gotten to have.

I am not Laura. I am not your parents. I am not anyone who walked away instead of staying long enough to see you fall apart. You don't get to use their lies to measure my honesty. I know you're hurting. I know this ripped open something old and deep. I won't be your punching bag every time it does.

Her thumbs slowed for the last paragraph. The anger in her chest softened just enough to make room for the ache underneath.

I love you, Josh. That doesn't mean I'll let you treat me like I'm temporary or expendable. When you're ready to talk to me, not at me, I'll be here. But I'm not chasing you tonight. We both deserve better than a conversation we'll regret in the morning.

Her fingertip hovered over the Send arrow, the tiny blue triangle blinking back at her like a dare. The urge to tap it, to force the words into his world and make him carry them, too, surged up hot and strong. For a long breath, the only sound in the room was the rain and the faint ticking of the kitchen clock.

Then she exhaled, a shaky, releasing breath, and moved her finger instead to the three dots in the corner. *Save as draft.* The option glowed for a second under her touch, and when she clicked it, the message vanished from the screen, tucked away where only she could see it.

The silence that followed wasn't exactly peaceful, but it was steadier. Novah set the phone facedown on the table and leaned her forehead against her knees, letting the storm outside and the thump of her own heartbeat fill the space where his voice had been. She had said what she needed to say, even if only to herself for now. Tonight, that had to be enough.

Novah tapped the brew button, and the old coffee maker sputtered to life with a wet cough, followed by the steady drip-drip of dark liquid into the carafe. She leaned her hip against the counter and let her gaze wander, only to snag on the blanket draped over the back of her desk chair.

Her shoulders dipped, the tension sliding out of them in a slow sag as the image of Josh sprawled on that same blanket flashed behind her eyes. His laugh. The way Alexis had waggled her brows and called it the "evidence blanket," teasing until Novah's cheeks burned.

Heat pricked the back of her eyes now, and she shook her head once, as if she could shake the memories loose. The coffee maker clicked off with a soft, final hiss. She poured herself a mug and carried it to her desk.

The blanket rested there, smelling faintly of lake water and Josh's cologne, and just for a second, she almost gave in. Almost pulled it to her face to breathe him in and let herself fall apart.

Instead, she folded the fabric in brisk, efficient thirds. Her fingers smoothed the edges until the wool lay in a neat rectangle. She slid it in on the top shelf in the small linen closet next to the bathroom. Out of sight, out of mind. Right. Tell her mind that.

Back at the desk, she set the mug down, the faint clink loud in the hush of the room, and hit the power button on her computer. The screen flared to life in a wash of cold blue light. She opened her manuscript and the research file side by side, scrolling through columns of text and highlighted notes.

Words blurred together into gray lines. She read a paragraph, reached the end, and realized she couldn't recall a single sentence. Her eyes skimmed the same lines again, the cursor blinking an impatient beat at the edge of the page. After the third pass, frustration tightened her jaw. *This won't do.*

She grabbed her phone, the smooth case cool against her palm, and thumbed out a quick text. *Taking the day off. Want to go out in the canoe with me?* Before the guilt over her word count could sink its teeth in, she shut the laptop down and listened to the whir of the fan fade into silence.

Unlocking the glass door on the far side of the main deck, she stepped out into air that smelled of wet wood and the faint mineral tang of the lake pushing up against the pilings. The boards under her bare feet were cool and faintly damp, the grain pressing lightly into her skin.

She descended to the lower deck, where the floor hovered only a few inches above the waterline, the lake lapping lazily against the support posts. The narrow storage bay's door stuck, as usual. She put her shoulder into it until it gave with a soft scrape, revealing the snug space just big enough for the long canoe and two stubby kayaks.

She reached for the nearest kayak, fingers curling around the faded plastic handle, when her phone chirped, Alexis's bright, two-note tone cutting through the quiet. Novah thumbed the screen awake.

ALEXIS*: 15 minutes*

NOVAH*: Make it a fast 15.*

Her lips twitched despite herself as she slid the phone back into her pocket. Instead of dragging the kayak out, she wrapped both hands around the smooth gunwale of the canoe. The fiberglass was cool and slick under her palms as she inched it along the deck, the nose whispering over the damp boards. At the edge, she braced her feet and gave one last shove, lining the canoe up with the shimmer of dark water below, the lake's quiet breath lifting to meet her.

She tied it off, waiting for Alexis. By the time she spotted Alexis's bright kayak cutting across the sun-dappled surface, the clench in her chest had loosened a fraction. Alexis raised her paddle in a lazy salute, sunglasses flashing as she paddled up next to the deck.

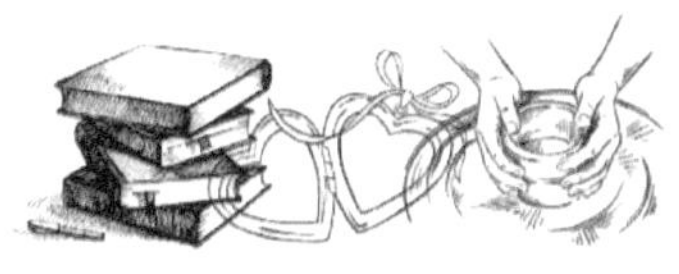

Chapter 25

"'Bout time," Novah said as Alexis climbed onto the deck and pulled her kayak out of the water. Novah helped her tie it to the piling.

Alexis snorted and said, "Details." The corner of her mouth tipped up. "So. We paddling in circles, or are we actually going somewhere?"

"Out," Novah said, jerking her chin toward the deeper water, where the lake opened up into a wide, glittering expanse. "Anywhere that isn't my own head."

They climbed into the canoe, facing each other, and each picked up a paddle. They worked together, paddling away from shore before turning to follow it. They fell into an easy rhythm, their paddles dipping and rising in an unspoken cadence, the only sounds the splash of water and the distant hum of a boat engine somewhere farther down the shore.

A pair of ducks skimmed low across the surface, wings skittering on the water before they lifted off again. The morning sun had already burned off most of the fog, leaving the air warm but soft, with just enough breeze to carry the earthy scent of wet leaves from the far bank.

It wasn't until they drifted into a quiet cove, ringed by trees and sheltered from the rest of the lake, that Alexis rested her paddle across her lap. "All right," she said. "You don't drag me out here when you're on deadline unless something is very, very wrong. Talk."

Novah lifted her own paddle into her lap, the canoe gliding to a stop on the small beach. She stared down at the water, watching sunlight fracture on the ripples. Her throat felt suddenly too tight.

"I told him," she said finally. Her voice sounded thin in the open air. "About the article."

Alexis pushed her sunglasses up onto her head, eyes sharpening. "The one about his parents?"

Novah nodded. "Yeah. That one." The words scraped coming out. "I thought—" She broke off and shook her head. "No. I didn't think he'd like it. I knew it was going to hurt. I just thought…he deserved the truth. Even if it came from me."

"How did he take it?" Alexis asked, though her wince said she already knew the answer.

"Like I'd shoved a knife between his ribs," Novah said, the image flaring behind her eyes again. Josh's face shuttering, his voice going from stunned to sharp in a single breath.

"He wanted to know how long I'd known. Why I hadn't told him the second I saw it. He looked at me like—" Her voice cracked, and Novah swallowed hard. "Like I was just one more person keeping things from him. Just like everyone else."

The silence stretched between them, broken only by the gentle slap of water against fiberglass. Alexis let out a slow breath. "And what did you say?"

"I tried to explain," Novah said. Her fingers tightened around the paddle shaft until her knuckles paled. "I told him I needed to be sure before I blew up his entire life. That I was scared of being wrong. That I was scared of being *right*." She huffed out a humorless laugh. "Didn't matter. All he heard was that I waited. That I didn't trust him with the worst of it from the start."

“And you?” Alexis asked. “What did you hear?”

“I heard him lump me in with his parents. With the women who walked away.” The admission landed heavily in the small boat, making the canoe feel suddenly too narrow. Novah blinked hard, but a hot tear still slipped free and slid down her cheek. She swiped it away with the back of her wrist. “I know he’s hurting. I *also* know I did the right thing. He needed to know. And who else was going to tell him?”

“So say it,” Alexis said softly. “Out loud.”
Novah’s gaze flicked up. “Say what?”
“That you did the right thing. And that you love him.”

The word hung there, wobbling between them like a loose paddle. Novah’s stomach fluttered. She looked away, out at the darker band of water where the cove opened back into the main lake. “Alexis—”

“Uh-uh,” Alexis cut in, her tone gentle but firm. “You already said it to me in a hundred sideways ways. You mooned over his damn *scent* for three chapters, Quinney. Own it.” She tipped her head. “Do you love him?”

The answer sat right there, a solid, undeniable weight in her chest. It had for days. Weeks. Maybe longer. Novah’s fingers loosened on the paddle. The breeze lifted a strand of hair and brushed it across her cheek.

"Yes," she said, the word barely more than air at first. She swallowed and tried again. "Yes. I love him." Admitting it to someone other than herself and Josh felt like stepping off a cliff and finding something holding her up instead of nothing at all. "And I still think I did the right thing by telling him. Even if he hates me for it right now. He deserved the truth. And…and…" Novah stopped and then finally whispered, "I told him."

"That you love him? Really?!" Alexis squealed and then noticed the crestfallen look on her best friend's face.

Relief and pain tangled together in her chest, sharp and sweet. Alexis's shoulders eased, and she nodded once, as if they'd just set something important in place. "Good," she said. "Now we're dealing with the actual problem, not the version you write in your head."

Novah let out a shaky breath that turned into a laugh halfway through. "That's not the actual problem?"

"Oh, it's *a* problem," Alexis said. "But it's not the only one. Josh has enough baggage to fill a charter bus, sure. But so do you, babe. He's not the only one dragging old crap into this."

Novah bristled on instinct. "I didn't accuse him of anything."

"No," Alexis said. "You accused *yourself.* You do it every time. 'I'm not his usual type.' 'I'm not that pretty.' 'I'm too soft here, not enough there.'" She mimed quotation marks with her fingers, paddle balanced across her knees. "You act like you're lucky he looked at you twice, and like any minute he's going to realize he made a mistake and bolt. That's trauma talking, too."

The protest died on Novah's tongue because it was too close to what she'd been thinking the night before, curled up on the couch with Josh's phantom scent wrapped around her. Her heartbeat picked up, thudding against the inside of her ribs. "I just…don't want to wake up one day and find out I was a phase," she muttered. "He has a history. I've seen the women he dates. They're all legs and cheekbones. I'm—" She gestured vaguely at herself. "Not that."

"Jesus, Novah." Alexis shook her head, water beading and rolling off the blade of her paddle as she lifted it and let it rest again. "You are not a consolation prize. And if you keep acting like you are, you're going to teach him that's all he has to give you. That he can hand you whatever scraps of trust he feels like, and you'll make do."

Novah's chest constricted. The words landed like stones, not because they were cruel, but because they were mercilessly accurate.

"So what?" she asked quietly. "I'm supposed to just…tell him what I need? While he's in the middle of having his whole life rewired?"

"Yes," Alexis said, shrugging. "Eventually. Not this second, while he's still bleeding from that article, but when you talk again? You don't just show up with casseroles and sex and unconditional understanding."

She leaned forward slightly, causing the canoe to rock under the shift of her weight. "You tell him, 'I need you not to take your parents' lies out on me. I need you to talk to me instead of shutting down or lashing out. I need to know you see me as a partner, not a placeholder.'"

The idea made Novah's stomach swoop. "He just lost the story of who he thought he was," she said. "What if asking for anything on top of that is too much?"

"What if it's the only way this doesn't eat you alive?" Alexis countered. "You don't have to scream it at him while he's in freefall. But you *do* have to say it. Because right now, you're letting his trauma set all the rules. And yours?" She tipped her head. "Yours is quietly telling you to keep your head down, take whatever he gives, and be grateful you got chosen at all."

The truth of that sank into Novah's bones, heavy and cold. A breeze rippled across the cove, lifting small waves that rocked the boat like a heartbeat.

"I'm scared," Novah admitted. The words came out small, stripped of the defensive edge she usually wrapped around them. "If I lay all that out, he could decide it's too much. That I'm too much."

"Or," Alexis said gently, "he could finally understand what it actually takes to be with you. Not the fantasy version. The real you. The woman who dug up the truth, handed it to him knowing it might blow up everything, and stayed anyway."

Novah stared at her, throat tight. The lake shimmered around them, bright and indifferent.

"You're allowed to need things from him, Novah," Alexis went on. "Love doesn't mean you swallow every hurt and call it devotion. If you want this to work, he has to learn your triggers the way you're learning his. That's what trust looks like both ways."

"When I tell him that I love him, he tells me he can't. Or ignores me and changes the subject. Twice, I've told him, and twice he's done that." Novah's words came out as a mere whisper.

"Tell him again. Shout it out to the world. Don't let him do that to you. The way that man looks at you, there's no way he doesn't love you, no matter what he says." Alexis shook her head. "Fuckin' baggage. It always gets in the way."

Novah's grip on the paddle eased. Her shoulders slowly unknotted, the muscles along her neck loosening one by one. "So I tell him," she said, more to the water than to Alexis. "I love you. I did the right thing. And if you want me in your life, you can't keep swinging that old pain at my head every time it flares up."

Alexis's smile was small but fierce. "Now you're getting it." She dipped her paddle back into the water, sending a fan of droplets sparkling into the air. "Come on. Let's paddle a bit more before we get into the 'how exactly you're going to phrase that without making him run for the hills' portion of today's program."

Novah let out a breath that felt like it had been trapped in her lungs since last night and pushed her paddle into the water. The canoe slid forward, the lake parting around the bow. For the first time since the article, the heaviness in her chest didn't feel like it was pressing her under. It felt like something she might—eventually—be able to carry and put down where both of them could see it.

Chapter 26

Josh dug his thumbs into the soft center of the clay until it fought back against his hands. The wheel hummed under his foot, a steady whir that should have soothed him, but the sound only seemed to grind his nerves thinner. Wet slip spattered his forearms in pale freckles. He leaned closer as the lump rose between his palms, letting the cool, slick texture pull him into the familiar tunnel of focus.

The article still sat on the workbench to his left, a crumpled, sweat-softened ball of newsprint half-flattened beside his tools. He'd thrown it away twice, and dug it out of the trash twice. Headlines and phrases flashed behind his eyes in jerky cuts every time his gaze brushed that direction: *Adams Mill Couple Killed... orphaned infant son Joshua... investigation stalled.* The baby photo with the red-circled face in his memory looked nothing like him, and exactly like him.

Not really a Granger. Not really one of them. The thought slipped in, quiet as smoke, and settled under his ribs.

He pressed harder, fingers shaping the spinning cylinder into a tall vase, and the clay buckled with a wet sigh. The upper wall thinned too fast, wobbling, and collapsed in on itself. The ruined form slumped sideways, the top flinging a cold slap of mud across his T-shirt. Josh swore under his breath and slammed the pedal to a stop. Silence crashed in, loud after the wheel's constant drone.

From the corner of his tiny temporary studio, the portable radio muttered on low, the newscaster's voice giving way to a local events blurb. "Don't forget the upcoming fundraiser for the Watauga Lake Volunteer Fire Department…" The word *fundraiser* made his jaw clench. He could still hear the whispers that had slithered through the last meeting, slick as oil. *Insurance money. Convenient timing, isn't it? Wouldn't be the first time somebody torched their own place.*

His throat went dry. He grabbed his mug, found only cold coffee at the bottom, and set it down hard enough that the ceramic clicked against the wooden work table. The sound echoed in the cramped space.

He wiped his hands on the towel at his hip, the coarse cotton rasping over his skin, and slapped a fresh hunk of clay onto the wheel. This one he attacked from the start, palms bearing down with more force than finesse, forcing it into the center.

The wheel's vibration traveled up his arms, into his shoulders, into the tight band at the base of his skull. If he could just get the form right—if he could throw enough bowls, plates, anything—maybe he could outrun the images of his parents' car wrapped around a tree, the Butler file Hank had dug out of some warehouse, the way people at Rowan's had stopped talking when he walked in.

Whole town thinks you burned your own shop, the anonymous caller had sneered, the words still carrying a faint tinny echo in his ears. *Pyro.*

His fingers slipped, digging a groove too sharp into the rising wall. The clay distorted again, wobbling crazily, and he tried to save it, pinching and coaxing with quick, practiced adjustments. His foot, tense on the pedal, pressed down instead of easing off. The wheel sped faster.

The lurch in speed dragged his hands, jerking his fingers wider. The misshapen pot flared in a sudden, ugly bulge and then flew apart, a heavy chunk of clay ripping free and slinging across the studio. It hit the side of the kiln with a dull *thunk*, splattering gray sludge across the metal casing and the thermostat dial.

"Fuck." Josh slapped the pedal up, heart punching hard against his ribs. For a second, he just stood there, chest heaving, hands dripping clay, as the wheel wound down in a whining decrescendo.

A smear of mud slowly slid down the kiln's control panel, beading at the edge of the temperature knob. Josh crossed the room in three strides, grabbed the knob, and checked the setting, even though he knew damn well he hadn't fired anything today. The metal was cool under his fingers, but the thought of that clay chunk hitting the wiring, shorting something, igniting in the middle of the night, made his pulse spike.

They already think you did it once.

He stepped back too fast, heel catching on the edge of a crate. His ankle rolled, sending a sharp jolt up his leg, and he windmilled for balance, one clay-slick hand banging against the wall hard enough to sting. Pain snapped bright at the base of his thumb.

For a moment, dizziness pressed in at the edges of his vision. The small room seemed to tilt, the shelves crammed with bisque-fired pieces and glaze jars closing in like a narrowing throat. The humid, earthy smell of wet clay, usually grounding, felt thick as smoke.

He braced his palms on his knees and sucked in a breath. The sound of the wheel finally stilled behind him, the last squeak fading.

Grangers don't burn things down. His adoptive father's voice surfaced from somewhere deep, an old memory of a lecture about fireworks and dry grass. *We work hard. We do right. We keep our heads down and our noses clean.*

Except maybe he wasn't a Granger. Maybe he had never been. Just some orphaned kid in a newspaper story, scooped up because somebody needed a baby to dress up their idea of a family.

"Not really one of them," he muttered, straightening slowly. His reflection caught in the dark kiln glass. Clay-streaked. Eyes shadowed. Jaw tight. "Not really one of anybody."

He turned back to the wheel, muscles already coiling as his hand reached for another lump of clay. The urge to sit down, to keep throwing, to fill every inch of shelf space with proof that he was more than a burned-out storefront and a maybe-fake last name, roared up hard. If he kept his hands moving, maybe the rest of it couldn't catch him.

His thumb throbbed where it had smacked the wall, a small, insistent pulse of pain under the skin. He flexed it once, twice, feeling the ache flare. He ignored it, grabbed the next block of clay from the bag, and slammed it down onto the spinning wheel with more force than necessary. The impact jolted up his arms.

"Work," he told the clay, his voice rough in the empty room. "Just work."

The wheel began to hum again, louder this time.

Two days after her conversation with Alexis, Novah still hadn't called Josh, and he hadn't called her. The silence between them had settled into something dense and heavy, like the fog that was currently pressed low over the lake. She tried to write, wanted to lose herself in the familiar rhythm of dialogue and description, but every time she reached for her characters, her mind slid sideways to Josh's face when he'd read the article, the way his jaw had clenched around questions he barely choked out.

The late afternoon sun finally burned the fog off the lake, but not out of her mind. It slanted through the office windows, striping her desk in gold. Her phone buzzed across the wood with a jittery little hop. "Unknown Number" flashed on the screen, but the local area code caught her eye. She almost let it go to voicemail, then sighed and swiped. "Novah Quinney."

"Hey, Novah. It's Hank." His voice carried the familiar gravelly warmth, but there was a thread of something tighter woven through it.

Her spine straightened. "What's wrong? Is Josh okay?" The question shot out before she could stop it, her pulse bumping hard in her throat.

"No one's hurt," Hank said quickly. Papers rustled on his end, a low rasp against the receiver. "Nothing like that. I just…needed to loop you in on something, and I'd rather you heard it from me than from a rumor getting away from us."

The chill that skated down her back had nothing to do with the air conditioning. "Okay," she said slowly. "Loop me in on what?"

"It's about Eric," Hank said. The name dropped into the silence like a pebble into deep water. "And Josh. And that file you asked me to pull in Butler."

Her fingers tightened around the phone. The cursor on her screen blinked on an empty line, waiting. "I thought you said you didn't have anything solid yet," she said.

"Still don't have enough to slap cuffs on him," Hank replied. "But the state lab and the feds helped us go through the mess we pulled out of his camper again. This time, we weren't just looking for fire stuff." A chair creaked faintly as if he'd leaned back. "We found something new."

The office seemed to narrow around her, the walls inching closer. "What kind of something?"

"Half a dozen old newspaper clippings tacked up behind a storage bin," Hank said. "Looked like he'd tried to hide them behind some shelves. Butler paper. Same article you found on Josh's birth parents—and a couple of shorter follow-ups from '97."

Novah's stomach dropped. She pushed back from the desk, the chair wheels squeaking as she stood and paced to the window. "You're sure it's the same article?"

"Positive," Hank said. "Your boy's picture, tiny little baby face and all, circled in red marker in one of 'em." His voice hardened. "We also found what looks like copies of partial adoption paperwork. Not originals—photocopies, bad ones—but enough to make us nervous. Josh's name. His date of birth. Some personal details that damn sure shouldn't be hanging in some whack-job's camper."

The hand holding the phone went numb, a faint buzzing filling her ears. "How would he even get that?" she whispered. "That stuff's sealed, isn't it?"

"That's what we're trying to figure out," Hank said. "Could be he sweet-talked the wrong clerk. Could be he dug in places he shouldn't have. Could be he's been following this story longer than any of us realized." A pen tapped quietly against something hard on his end, a fast, nervous rhythm. "Point is, Eric's fixation isn't just on you anymore. It's tangled up with Josh's past."

Novah pressed her free hand flat against the cool glass, staring out at the water as if she could see all the way across to Josh's place. "So what are you telling me, exactly?"

"That we're now working under the assumption that the fire, the stalker crap, and that old homicide are all sitting in the same ugly stew," Hank said bluntly. "And that Eric's been collecting Josh's life on his walls for God knows how long."

A prickle crawled over her skin. That room she'd only imagined before—the camper Hank had described with its wallpaper of her face—rearranged itself in her mind. Not just her, but Josh as a baby, his parents' names, the words *orphaned son Joshua* highlighted in some stranger's cramped handwriting.

"Josh doesn't know," she said, the certainty dropping into her gut like a stone. "Does he?"

Hank exhaled, a slow, rough sound. "Not yet. I wanted to have more before I walked into that conversation. Right now, it's a whole lot of creepy and not enough court-worthy." There was a brief pause, then, quieter, "That's why I'm calling you. I need you to sit tight on this until I can talk to him."

The words hit a raw nerve. Her fingers curled against the glass. "You're asking me not to tell him," she said, keeping her tone even by sheer force.

"I'm asking you not to blindside him with half-formed shit that we can't act on yet," Hank said. "Last time he got new information about his past, it damn near broke him in half. I don't want to light that fuse again without something solid to hand him."

Novah closed her eyes. The memory of Josh at his kitchen table, the article crumpled in his fist, his voice cracking as he demanded to know how long she'd known—it all crashed over her in a hot, suffocating wave. Her throat tightened.

"Hank, I get that," she said, each word careful. "I do. But you're asking me to hold *more* of his history in my hands and not tell him. Again. You know how that went last time."

"I do," Hank said quietly. "And I'm not saying keep him in the dark forever. I'm saying give me a day or two to nail down how far this goes. To make sure Eric's not about to try something stupider than he already has. Once I've got that, I'll sit Josh down myself. I'll need you there, if he lets you."

The idea of sitting across from Josh while Hank laid all this out made her stomach twist, but underneath the fear was something steadier. The certainty that she *would* be there if Josh wanted her.

She chewed the inside of her cheek. "So if you find out Eric's been closer than we thought," she said slowly, "or if there's anything that puts Josh in immediate danger, I'm not keeping that from him."

A beat of silence hummed on the line. "That's fair," Hank said. "If we get wind of anything like that, he'll hear it from me or from you, fast. I'm not playing games with his safety."

"And mine?" she asked, because the image of those walls full of her face wasn't loosening its grip.

"And yours," he said, no hesitation. "We still have someone on him. He doesn't fart without us knowing which direction the wind's blowing. You keep doing what you're doing. Lock your doors. Watch the trails. Call if anything even *feels* off. I just…needed you to know we're not chasing shadows anymore. There's a line from Josh's past straight to this guy. And I want to bring Josh in on it right."

Her pulse had settled into a hard, steady thud under her skin. She looked out over the lake, imagining the path through the woods, the ridge above their houses, the camper tucked somewhere up there like a rotten tooth.

"Okay," she said at last. "You get your day or two. But if I find out that man has been anywhere near Josh when you thought he was safely on a leash, I'm calling Josh myself before your next breath, and you can yell at me later."

Hank huffed out a short, humorless laugh. "Wouldn't expect anything less out of you, Novah."

They said their goodbyes, and the line went dead. Novah lowered the phone slowly, staring at the dark screen as if it might offer different news if she looked long enough. The office felt too small, the air too thin.

She set the phone on the desk and pressed both palms flat beside it, bowing her head between her shoulders. "I am not doing this the same way," she whispered into the quiet. "Not again."

This time, if the information in her hands became the difference between blindsiding Josh and him being safe, she'd choose him, every time. Even if it meant going toe-to-toe with the sheriff. Even if it risked blowing up whatever fragile thing still existed between them.

Chapter 27

What the fuck time is it?

Josh's first coherent thought dragged itself up through sleep as his phone rang. He reached for it on his nightstand, but his hand met air. A sharp ache knifed through the side of his neck when he tried to roll over. The worn sofa cushion dipped under his hip, springs complaining in a low squeak as he pushed himself upright. His feet hit the cool hardwood with a dull thud.

The phone went silent. Josh scrubbed a hand over his face, the sandpaper stubble rasping against his palm, and squinted toward the dim blur of the TV screen.

Before he could stretch the kink out of his spine, the phone started up again, ringing insistently on the coffee table.

"What the hell is so important this early?" he muttered, reaching for it. The screen's sudden white glare made his eyes water. *Hank* flashed across the top. It stopped ringing.

"God damn it, Josh, pick up the phone," Hank growled into the empty air a few miles away, pacing in his cramped office with the handset pressed tight to his ear. The oversized wall clock above his filing cabinet ticked toward eight a.m., each second a soft, accusing click. "You should be up by now," he muttered, lowering the phone just long enough to glare at the screen.

His desk was a chaos of paper. Typed reports, scribbled notes, and maps with circles and arrows. Hank shoved a fresh stack of printouts into a manila folder labeled *GANN, JOSHUA* and hesitated, then crossed out the name with a hard, ink-heavy line. He wrote *ERIC M.?* underneath, the question mark digging into the cardstock. The pen left a faint groove his thumb could feel when he brushed over it.

A cold ring of coffee stained the edge of one page. He lifted the chipped Watauga Lake Sheriff's Office mug, took a swallow of lukewarm brew, and felt the bitter bite scrape down his throat. Novah's voice from the night before threaded through his thoughts: *You're asking me to hold more of his history in my hands and not tell him. Again.* The memory sat heavily on his chest.

"Should've told him sooner," Hank muttered into the quiet, pulse ticking a notch faster as Josh's line kept ringing. "Before half the damn town started speculating." Word had already seeped through the local grapevine that Josh and Novah weren't speaking again. He'd heard Jaxxon and Skylar murmuring about it by the bakery door earlier this morning, their voices dropping when he walked up.

The call flipped to voicemail. Hank jabbed "End" with more force than necessary, then immediately redialed, the plastic buttons clicking under his thumb. "Come on, son," he said under his breath as the tone buzzed in his ear. Outside the small window, the morning light was already bright, throwing sharp rectangles across the scuffed linoleum floor. "Answer the damn phone so I can stop making this worse for everybody."

He drained the rest of his coffee in one swallow, grimacing at the bitterness, and set the mug down with a soft ceramic thud. "I wish Novah had said something before it got this far," he added, not sure whether he was talking about the case or the article, and knowing it was neither, but the raw, frayed string between Josh and

Novah that seemed to run straight through his office now.

He stepped toward the coffee pot, but saw only dregs at the bottom. “Damn it. I wish whoever took the last cup would make another one.” His lips tightened, and he walked out to his truck with the empty mug. He’d stop at Rowan’s and get a fresh cup.

Josh went into the bathroom and splashed water on his face. He stumbled back to the living room and picked up his phone. “This is Josh Gann. Hank was trying to call. Is he available?”

The dispatcher said, “No, he left on a call. I can leave him a message.”

“No, that’s okay. I’ll catch up to him sooner or later. Well. Wait. Yeah, if he comes back before we catch up, just tell him I was calling him back.”

“Will do. Y’all have a nice day, now.”

Josh mumbled his thanks and ended the call, the words scraping out of a throat gone dry. For a moment, he just listened to the dead silence on the line, too wrung out to move, then let the phone slip from his fingers so it skidded across the coffee table and bumped a crooked stack of bills.

He sank onto the sofa, shoulders caving in, and cradled his face in his hands, dragging his palms up and down over stubble and hot, gritty eyelids as if he could rub the heaviness out of his soul.

He didn't know how long he'd sat there like that when the pounding on his front door jolted through the quiet. The sharp thuds shot straight through his chest. His heart lurched, stuttering hard enough that it left a faint ache in its wake. He pushed himself up too fast, knees protesting, and crossed the room in long, uneven strides, his bare feet slapping the wooden floor as the banging came again.

"Hold your fucking horses," he mumbled as he unlocked and opened the door. "Hank." Josh stepped aside to let him in. "This can't be good if you're showing up on my doorstep."

"Well, if you'd have answered the phone, I wouldn't have to show up on your doorstep. You look like hell, son. Lose your razor?"

"Fuck off, Hank. What's so important that you woke me up?"

"Hell, Josh, it's after ten. You been pulling all-nighters again?"

Josh snorted softly. "You drove all the way over here to lecture me about my sleep schedule?"

He padded into the kitchen and filled the coffee maker with fresh coffee and water before turning it on.

Hank followed him into the kitchen and parked his ass at the table. "Josh. Speak to me."

"Nothin' to say, Hank."

Josh filled his mug and held the coffee pot out to Hank.

"I could use more."

Josh topped his coffee off and plopped down into a chair across from Hank. "So, what's so important that you didn't wait five minutes for me to call you back?"

Hank ignored the jab. He wrapped both hands around the mug and watched the steam curl up, buying himself a few seconds. "I'm here because this goes beyond you being mad at Novah or the damn town," he said. "We've got more on Eric."

Josh's fingers tightened around his coffee. "Eric? Did you ever figure out who this guy is?"

"The same son of a bitch who had your studio plastered on his walls." Hank's voice lost all softness. "Novah's pictures, your pictures, your shop front from every angle. We pulled photos from inside the studio too, stuff that he—or someone—hadn't taken through a window. He's been in your space, Josh."

The floor seemed to tilt a fraction under Josh's bare feet. "Inside?" His voice came out rough.

Hank nodded once. "We found the apartment he dumped in a hurry. Place was a shrine to both of you. Shots of the ridge trail where you and Novah hike, printouts of that article she found, and more that she didn't find. They all had annotations in the margins. Same handwriting as the anonymous note that showed up at your studio."

"The note..." Josh pictured the tight, slanted letters. The way his name had looked on that paper was almost intimate. "You're saying that's him?"

"That's him." Hank leaned forward, forearms braced on the table. "We've got partial prints that match the ones lifted from your back door and from a gas can left out by the tree line near your shop after the fire."

Hank's jaw bunched. "The lab came back with accelerant traces in the soil behind the building. Whoever did it knew enough to keep it small and hurried; it would look as though you burned your own studio."

Silence, less for the distant tick of the living room clock, settled between them. Josh stared at the knotted grain of the table, the way one curl of wood looked like a thumbprint.

"So this guy—Eric—torches my place and pins us on his walls for months, and nobody thought to mention that part sooner?"

"Don't you start." Hank's voice snapped sharper than the ceramic clink when he set his mug down. "We've been piecing this together as it comes in. I'm telling you now because the pattern's clear. He's not just fixated on your studio. He's fixated on you. And Novah."

Josh flinched at her name, then masked it with another swallow of coffee. It burned all the way down. "She already did enough damage."

"Bullshit." Hank's chair scraped as he shoved it back an inch. "Whatever's going on between you and her, that is not the problem on the table right now. This man followed her work. He followed your work. He knows your routines. He knew where to stand on that ridge to see you without being seen."

Images flickered through Josh's mind. The narrow trail as it switchbacked along the ridge. The places the brush opened up just enough to frame the town below. The studio's big front windows, glowing like a lantern after dark.

"He could have pushed you clean off that trail, and no one would've found you till morning," Hank went on. "Instead, he watched. Collected. Escalated. That note? That was him knocking."

Josh's throat felt too tight to speak. He set his mug down before his hand shook enough for Hank to notice.

"I need you to work with us," Hank said. "No more ignoring calls, no more locking yourself in this house pretending it'll blow over. You have to tell me if you remember anything. Strange cars. Faces in the crowd. Customers who hung around too long. Anything."

"And if I don't?"

"Then you're making his job easier." Hank held his gaze, steady and unflinching. "And you're making mine harder. You understand me?"

Josh stared back, the air between them thick with the stale scent of coffee and the faint trace of yesterday's paint still clinging to his skin. Finally, he flicked his eyes away. "Yeah. I understand."

"Good. Because I'm not just saying this as your sheriff." Hank's voice dropped. "I'm saying it as the man who watched you almost drown in this town once already. I am not doing that again while this guy circles you and Novah both."

"She can take care of herself," Josh muttered, but the words rang hollow even to his own ears.

"Maybe. Maybe not. Either way, the two of you freezing each other out is the exact thing a man like Eric counts on." Hank stood, the chair legs scraping on the floor. "You make it easier to isolate you. To move without either of you comparing notes."

Josh's pulse thudded in his ears. "So what, you want me to just… call her up and pretend that article didn't blow up my life?"

"No." Hank picked up his hat from the empty chair, thumb smoothing along the worn brim. "I want you to stop acting like she threw you to the wolves for fun. You don't have to forgive her today. But you damn sure have to stop shutting her out while someone with a box full of pictures and gasoline is thinking about both of you."

Josh's jaw clenched until his teeth ached. "You done?"

"Not yet." Hank paused at the doorway, turning back. "I'm gonna say this once. Just once, Josh. You can be mad, and you can be scared, but you do not get to be stupid. Work with us. And stop pretending you don't care what happens to her."

The words landed like small, controlled blows. Josh looked away, focusing on the thin crack in the linoleum near the fridge. "You finished now?"

Hank exhaled, long and tired. "For today." He tipped his hat toward Josh. "Lock your damn door when I leave. And answer your phone."

The front door shut behind him with a solid, final click. Josh sat there listening to Hank's truck rumble to life, then fade down the street until the house sank back into its thin, humming quiet.

Chapter 28

The coffee had gone lukewarm by the time Josh carried his mug back to the living room. He set it on the table beside the crooked stack of bills, staring at the phone where Hank's missed calls still lingered in the log. Beneath them, the headline of the article from 2017 glared up from where he'd left the printout on the couch.

He hesitated, then picked up the pages, the paper soft at the edges from how many times he'd crumpled and smoothed it. The black ink looked harsher in the thin daylight leaking around the curtains. He started reading from the top, even though he could have recited the opening paragraphs by now.

The first time he'd read it, all he'd seen was the exposure. The way it'd laid his history bare. The way the town had gobbled it up.

Now Hank's voice threaded between the lines, dragging his attention to the dates stamped under the photographs. She hadn't found his story because she'd gone digging for gossip. She'd tripped over it while chasing something else entirely: old case files, archived clippings, interviews with people whose names he didn't know. There it was in her author's note, the tiny handwriting in her neat script that was so clear that Stevie Wonder could see it. She'd been looking for patterns of missing kids across the region, not for him.

His mind snagged on a line about the night she'd told him. She could barely eat the dinner he'd made, as her hands started shaking. He remembered that part, at least. The shock on her face as he accused her of being like everyone else.

He swallowed, the memory rewinding and slowing down of its own accord. The tremor in her fingers when she'd passed him the photocopies. The way she'd hovered by the arm of the chair but hadn't touched him until his shoulders had tightened. Right before he blew a head gasket. How she'd watched his face instead of the pages, as if waiting for a blow that never came.

He'd been shaking too, though he hadn't realized it then. She'd made him tea he hadn't drunk, pushed a plate of food toward him and forgotten to eat her own. Later, when he'd finally lifted his head, she'd been right there beside him. She'd held that weight without flinching.

Other nights crowded in behind that one. Her standing in his doorway with takeout when he'd "forgotten" to cook. Her walking through sideways mountain rain because he couldn't handle his own demons and pushed her away.

He'd filed all of that under penance, he realized now. Things she owed him for the article, for the way she'd split him open by showing him that. By finding it. As if it were her fault. But the timeline on the printout didn't care what story he'd told himself.

And then the other memories came. The night they'd spent on the dyke after making love. The night they fell asleep in each other's arms on the floor in her office. The times they'd made love in the shower. The times he woke up with her in his arms.

She'd found the evidence first. She'd hesitated. She'd argued with herself about it—he could see it now in the care she took with her language, the way she'd separated the verifiable facts from the speculative thread about "one unidentified child who may have survived" when she showed him the article. She'd approached his life like something fragile and volatile, and still walked it over to his door.

His mind dragged over a sentence he'd hated since the first read. 'When faced with the choice between protecting a painful truth and protecting a loved one from it, most people choose silence.' Novah chose otherwise.

He'd read that as an accusation, proof that she'd chosen the story over him. Now, with Hank's warning still echoing in his ears and Eric's name scrawled across the inside of his skull, it rang differently.

She could have turned this into a clean narrative about a nameless survivor, left him out of it, pretended she never recognized the boy in the grainy photo. She could have kept her hands clean and her conscience quiet and never watched his face break as he pieced together his own childhood.

Instead, she'd walked through a storm to put the truth in his hands. Sat there while it tore him apart. Fed him when he forgot how. Showed up again the next morning, and the next, and the next.

His chest ached in a way that had nothing to do with being startled awake. The anger that had burned so hot for days—the tight, choking kind that made his vision go white around the edges whenever someone said her name—flickered and lost some of its oxygen. In its place, something heavier settled in. All the ways he'd punished her for doing the hardest thing.

He'd shoved her out of his home. Sent her calls straight to voicemail. Watched her cross the street to avoid his window and told himself that proved she didn't care enough to fight for him. All the while, she'd been the one person who had actually looked him in the eye and handed him the missing pieces of his own life.

Hank's words from earlier slid into that realization like the last puzzle piece: "You do not get to be stupid."

Josh set the article down on his knees, palms flat over the print as if he could hold it and everything it meant in place. The house buzzed quietly around him. The fridge cycling on. A car passing outside. The faint drip of the bathroom faucet he still hadn't fixed.

"I'm sorry," he said into the empty room, the words barely more than breath. They didn't fix anything. They didn't erase the hurt he'd thrown back at her. But for the first time since she found the article and showed it to him, he let himself admit that maybe she hadn't betrayed him. Maybe she'd chosen him in the one way that counted…By trusting him with the truth when silence would have been easier.

The realization sat in his chest, uncomfortable and solid. It didn't make calling her any less terrifying. It did make pretending she was the enemy feel suddenly, impossibly childish.

His phone lay on the coffee table where he'd dropped it earlier. He stared at it for a long, long moment, feeling the weight of his own choices settle on his shoulders. Not just what had been done to him, but what he'd done in response.

For the first time, he understood that if he wanted anything to change, if he wanted to keep himself and her safe from the shadow of a man like Eric, it wasn't going to be enough to brood on this sofa and wait for other people to fix it. At some point soon, maybe not today, he was going to have to pick up the phone and be the one who showed up at her door.

Josh stared at the phone for a long time before opening Novah's text. The last thing on the screen from him was a single, angry "Don't contact me again." He deleted it without letting himself reread it, thumbs hovering over the keyboard until his chest ached.

Can we talk? he typed. About the article. About…everything.

He stared at the blinking cursor, then added, I was wrong to yell at you. I owe you an apology. Can I come by later?

The words looked stiff and formal, like he'd stolen them from someone else's mouth, but he hit send before he could talk himself out of it. The message status flipped from "delivered" to "read" almost immediately. Then nothing.

He paced the narrow length of his living room, phone still in his hand, losing count of his own breaths somewhere after thirty. He'd just decided she wasn't going to answer when the phone buzzed. His hand shook as he swiped the screen.

The "1" showing at the top right of the text icon stared at him as if it were accusing him of…Something. Josh finally tapped her name.

> ***NOVAH****: If you're coming over to yell at me again, don't. I'm not doing that twice.*

Relief and shame collided in his chest. He sank back onto the sofa and typed, I'm not coming to yell. Just to apologize. You can tell me to leave whenever you want.

There was another pause. He watched the little dots appear, vanish, then reappear.

> ***NOVAH****: Okay. 4 pm. Front door will be unlocked. If you start in on how I "used" you again, I'm walking out of my own house.*

Wouldn't blame you, he answered, but she didn't respond to that. The read receipt sat there like a period at the end of a sentence.

He spent the rest of the afternoon in a fog of half-finished tasks. Washing a mug and leaving it on the counter to dry, pulling on a clean flannel shirt and then changing it twice because nothing felt right. At three forty-five, he gave up pretending he wasn't just clock-watching and drove toward her place, the truck's engine a low, familiar growl under his feet.

By the time he climbed her porch steps, his palms were damp. The front door really was unlocked and cracked open as if it were beckoning to him. He knocked anyway, a soft rap, and waited until her voice floated from inside.

"Come in."

He stepped into the small living room that had come to feel like a second home and then, abruptly, not his at all. Novah sat on the sofa, one leg tucked under her, laptop closed on the coffee table beside a spiral notebook. Her hair was in a messy knot, a pencil stabbed through it like a flagpole. The shadows under her eyes looked as if they'd been pressed there with her thumbs.

She didn't stand. She just watched him, arms folded loosely over her chest, like she was bracing for impact.

"I'm not sure if I'm ready for this," she said, before he could open his mouth. "But I'm here. So say what you came to say."

He shut the door behind him and stayed near it, hand resting for a second on the knob as if he might have to turn it again. "Okay," he said, voice rougher than he wanted. "I can do that."

He moved to the armchair across from her instead of his usual spot beside her on the couch. Putting space between them felt both wrong and necessary. The cushion sighed under his weight.

"I was an asshole," he said, without warming up to it. "The last time I was here."

Her eyebrows lifted a fraction. "That's…specific."

"I mean—" He exhaled hard. The script he'd rehearsed on the drive over tangled in his throat. "I yelled at you. I called you a vulture. Told you you'd used my life as research. That you were just like everybody else who wanted something from me."

His stomach twisted around the memory, the way her face had gone still and pale while he threw those words at her.

"That wasn't true," he said quietly. "Any of it."

She looked at him for a long beat, saying nothing. He forced himself to keep going.

"You told me something that ripped my world open," he said. "And I turned around and treated you like you'd hunted it down to sell books. I know now that's not what happened. You found it while you were chasing something else. You tried to tell me as gently as you knew how." His fingers tightened together, and he unclasped them deliberately. "And then I punished you for it."

Her mouth tightened, but she still didn't speak.

"I wasn't yelling at you," he admitted. "Not really. I mean, I was. But what I was really yelling at was being back in that house with my parents." The word tasted strange. *Parents.* "Them lying. Them deciding what I could handle. Them handing me half-truths and acting like that was kindness. When you told me the whole thing," Josh took a deep breath, "the parts that hurt, I lumped you in with them. I made you stand in for everything they did."

His voice went thin around the edges. He swallowed, forcing it steady. "You didn't earn that. You didn't deserve to be hit with all of that just because you were the one in front of me."

Her fingers flexed against her arms, then stilled again.

"I am sorry," he said, the words feeling inadequate and still the only ones he had. "For shouting. For accusing you of using me. For hanging up on you and shutting you out instead of…talking. You didn't betray me. I know that now. That doesn't magically fix what I did, but you should at least hear me say it. From my mouth, not…through Hank, or through the grapevine."

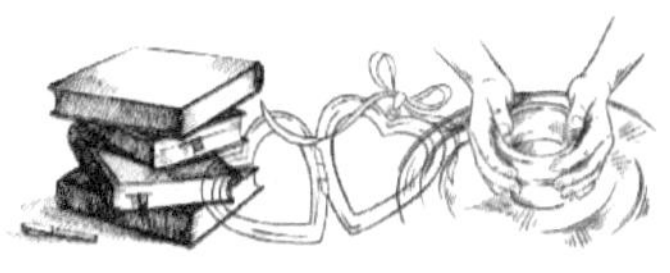

Chapter 29

Silence settled again, close and dense. Novah's gaze had gone distant halfway through his apology, like she was looking at some point just to the left of him. When she finally spoke, her voice was quiet, but there was nothing soft about it.

"Do you remember what you said?" she asked. "Word for word?"

He flinched. "Some of it."

"You told me I'd been taking notes on you since the day we met," she said, eyes snapping back to his. "That every meal, every kiss, every night on the sofa, every night in our beds, was just me gathering 'material.' That the only thing separating me from…from the people who hurt you was a byline."

He remembered now, with unpleasant clarity. The way his own voice had sounded, mean and wild and desperate.

"You looked straight at me in my own kitchen and said, 'You're no better than they are.'" Her throat worked around the quote. "I have been doing my level best not to think about that sentence every hour of the day."

He closed his eyes briefly. "I know."

"No, you don't," she said, heat flaring under the surface of the control that was quickly slipping. "You can't. Because for you, those words were you swinging at ghosts. For me, they were you taking me, the person who walked into a storm to bring you the truth, and shoving me into the same box as the people who left you there in the first place."

Her arms unfolded, and she braced her hands on her knees, leaning forward a little. "I get why you did it. I'm not ignorant. I know your trauma doesn't just sit in a neat little box on a shelf and wait for a convenient time to go off. But being able to name the reason doesn't make the impact disappear."

He opened his mouth, then shut it again.

"I love you," she said, the words hitting him like a slap and a balm at once. "And I am not interested in spending the rest of my life wondering when you're going to pick up your worst memories and hurl them at my head because we disagree about something."

"I—" His chest tightened. "I don't want to do that to you."

"Then you can't weaponize what happened to you every time you feel cornered," she said. "I'm not your parents. I'm not the social worker who looked the other way. I'm not the neighbor who pretended she didn't hear. I am not a stand-in for every person who failed you. If you can't start telling the difference when you're upset, then we don't have a relationship. We have…you reenacting the worst parts of your life with a different cast."

He stared at his hands, at the pale half-moons his nails had pressed into his skin.

"I hear you," he said quietly. "I don't know how to promise I'll never screw it up again. But I can promise I'll start catching myself sooner. That I'll get help figuring out how to be mad without…doing that."

"Good." Some of the tightness around her mouth eased, but not much. "Because the other option is that I leave. I won't stay in something where my choices get held hostage every time your fear wakes up."

He nodded, the movement jerky.

She exhaled, long and shaky. For a moment, the only sound was the faint hum of the fridge and the ticking of the cheap clock above her TV.

"There's another thing," she said finally, eyes dropping to her own hands. "And if we're going to try to do this differently, it doesn't get to live in my head anymore."

"Okay," he said. "Whatever it is, I want to hear it."

She huffed out a humorless little breath. "You say that now."

"Try me."

She pressed her lips together, then let them part. "Do you know what the women you dated before me looked like?" she asked, still not quite looking at him.

He blinked. "I mean…I remember some of them, yeah."

"Tall," she said. "Leggy. The kind of women who post gym selfies without thinking about it. Not a soft spot in sight. Not…this." She gestured down the line of her own body, from shoulder to hip, as if outlining something he couldn't see.

His brows drew together. "Novah—"

"I know you're going to say you've never cared about that," she cut in, voice gaining speed like a rock rolling downhill. "And I believe you believe that. But I also know what I look like. And what I don't. Every time I walk past a mirror, every time I see you in a room with someone who fits that old pattern, there's this little voice that whispers, 'He settled. You were convenient. He'll wake up one morning and realize you're a…phase.'"

The last word came out with a bitter twist.
He stared at her, stunned. "I have never thought—"

"I didn't say you had," she said sharply. "I said I had. In my own head. For months. And then I found the article. Showed it to you, and you were suddenly raw and exposed and furious, and I watched that anger swing toward me. All those fears I'd been fighting—the ones about not being your 'type', about you deciding I'm too much or not enough in all the ways that matter—they all lined up and said, 'See? We were right. He just needed a reason.'"

Her eyes shone, but she blinked the tears back, jaw set.

"So when you call me a vulture, when you tell me I used you, when you put me in the same sentence with the people who hurt you the worst, it doesn't just hurt because you're wrong," she said. "It hurts because it confirms every ugly thing I've ever been afraid you might secretly think. About my body. About my motives. About whether I'm someone you actually choose, or someone you just…got stuck with because I happened to be the one who found the file."

He swallowed hard, throat burning. "I choose you," he said, the words rough. "I have always chosen you. None of those women…None of that…Compares to—"

"I need more than words," she interrupted, though a fissure had opened in her expression. "I need you to show me, over time, that when you're scared or angry, you don't default to treating me like I'm temporary. Or disposable. Or the enemy."

He nodded slowly. "Okay. That's fair." It felt inadequate to say that, but anything more would have been a promise he didn't know how to keep.

She leaned back against the sofa, rubbing the heel of her hand briefly over her sternum like she was smoothing out a wrinkle. "So. You apologized. I said some things I needed to say. That does not mean we go back to how we were last month."

He let out a humorless laugh. "Last month, we thought setting the kitchen timer was the peak of our emotional maturity."

"Exactly." A faint ghost of a smile tugged at her mouth. "We can't just…pick up where we left off, pick a wall, and christen it again. That's not a reset. That's a distraction."

He thought of the way their bodies had found each other even when their words knotted, of how easy it would be to fall into that again, to use heat and skin and the familiar path of her mouth to avoid this sharp, difficult thing between them. His body ached for it. His chest knew better.

"What do you need?" he asked. "Right now. From me. Realistically."

She studied him, as if weighing whether he meant it. "I need time," she said. "And I need proof that we can do the hard talking without you either shutting down or detonating."

He nodded once.

"So here's what I'm thinking," she went on. "For the next week—seven days, not forever—we put a pause on sex. On anything that looks like a shortcut to intimacy. Kissing is fine. Touch is fine. But we don't use sex as a way to paper over this." Her fingers traced the seam of the cushion. "We focus on actually talking. On you going to that intake appointment Hank gave you the number for. On me…maybe talking to someone who isn't you about my own mess."

His throat tightened at the mention of therapy, but no part of him could argue with her logic. "I can do a week," he said, almost gently.

"This isn't a test you pass so we can go back to normal," she said. "It's a boundary. If at any point I feel like you're pushing it because you're uncomfortable, I will walk it back. If at any point you feel like you're climbing the walls and resenting me for it, we talk about that too. No martyrdom. No silent scoring."

"Okay," he said again, and this time it landed in his body like a choice, not a concession. "A week. We focus on…this. Talking. Not…that."

Color rose in her cheeks, but she nodded.

He hesitated, then cleared his throat. "There's something else I wanted to ask you," he said. "And you can say no."

"That's a promising preface," she murmured, but some of the tension had bled out of her shoulders.

"I've read your stuff," he said. "The column you do. The book chapters you left on my table that one time, 'by accident.' Your blog." One corner of her mouth twitched. "I know you work at the boathouse, but I've never…seen you work. And I realized that I've spent a lot of time wanting you to 'get' what I do, to understand how much the studio means to me, without giving you the same respect back."

She frowned slightly, curiosity edging out wariness.

"Hank said your writing is part of what put this puzzle together," he added. "That your attention to detail, the way you chase a thread, is why we even know Eric exists. I'd like to see that. If you'll let me. Not to…hover. Or critique. Just to be there. To see how your brain works when you're doing the thing you love."

Her eyebrows rose. "You want to come to the boathouse. While I'm writing."

"Yes." He leaned forward a little, forearms resting on his knees. "I'll stay out of your way. I won't read over your shoulder. You can stick me in a corner with my sketchbook and pretend I'm a potted plant. I just—" He searched for the words. "I want to start showing up for your work the way you've shown up for mine. Even when I didn't deserve it."

She was quiet for a long moment, studying him with a look that felt like it might peel him open. Finally, she exhaled.

"Okay," she said. "On conditions."
"Of course, there are conditions."

"One," she said, holding up a finger. "You don't hover. That means no exasperated sighs, no 'helpful' suggestions, no asking what page I'm on every twenty minutes."

He huffed a laugh. "Deal."

“Two.” A second finger joined the first. “You don’t make jokes about how long it takes me to write a paragraph. Or about deadlines. Or about true crime groupies. That’s a low blow right now.”

“Noted,” he said. “Muzzle engaged.”

“Three.” She let her hand drop. “If I ask you to leave because my brain won’t settle with you in the room, you leave. No sulking. No making it about you.”

He swallowed the instinctive flare of defensiveness and nodded. “I can do that.”

She watched him for another beat, then nodded back, as if committing herself to the decision. “Then you can come,” she said. “Tomorrow afternoon. I’ll text you the time.”

Somewhere under the ache and the nerves, something small and tentative uncurlled in his chest. Not forgiveness. Not yet. But a door nudged open.

“Okay,” he said. “I’ll be there.”

They sat in the quiet that followed, not touching, the air between them thick with everything still unresolved. It wasn’t fixed. The hurt was still there, sharp at the edges. But for the first time in days, they were at least facing the same direction—toward whatever came next, instead of away from each other.

Chapter 30

The town hall smelled like coffee and lemon-scented floor cleaner that never quite killed the damp underneath. Folding chairs clacked and scraped as people settled in rows, and paper programs crackled in their restless hands. Josh hovered near the back wall by the coat rack, fingers hooked through the strap of his messenger bag, trying to convince himself he was just there to approve a flyer design and not to run a gauntlet.

Up front, the whiteboard still bore the faded ghosts of last week's numbers: GOAL: $25,000, big looping letters now half-erased. The new totals gleamed in fresh dry-erase marker, a hopeful $13,472 circled three times.

Voices rose and fell around him in that particular small-town blend of cheer and complaint.

"...well, if the fire had happened closer to the gala date, we'd have hit goal already," someone said in a stage whisper near the refreshments table. "Nothing like a little tragedy to loosen wallets."

A few people chuckled. Josh's shoulders went tight. He stared at the back of the chair in front of him until the plastic blurred.

"I'm just saying," another voice chimed in, sly and bright. "It is awfully convenient timing. New insurance policy in March, fire in June, anonymous benefactor sponsoring half the rebuild? And now all this...mysterious past business." Paper rustled, and Josh could feel them gesturing with a copy of the article Novah found. "Makes you wonder what else he hasn't told us."

The word mysterious slid over his skin like oil. Josh's mouth went dry. He kept his gaze fixed on the front, where Jaxxon was fussing with a stack of pledge forms. It didn't help that his cheeks were already pink from climbing the steps with two boxes of decorations.

"Y'all, come on," someone else said, a low male voice. "You really think he'd burn down his own studio? He practically lived there."

"I think people do strange things when there's money and…trauma involved," the woman replied, lowering her voice on the last word but not enough. "The article said he doesn't even remember half of it. Maybe it's all mixed up for him. Maybe he doesn't know if he did it or not."

The room tilted for a second, the hum of conversation flattening into a high, thin whine in Josh's ears. Heat crawled up his neck. He shifted his weight, the metal legs of his chair squeaking against the floor, and a couple of heads turned, eyes flicking toward him before darting away like they'd brushed a hot stove.

He was still debating whether to walk out or stay long enough to avoid feeding the rumor mill when another voice cut through, clear and sharp.

"Did you seriously just say that?"

The words dropped into the room like a stone into shallow water. Conversations stuttered and broke. Josh turned his head despite himself.

Novah stood halfway down the aisle, canvas tote bag slung over her shoulder, her long hair shoved under a beanie that had slipped askew. She'd come in late, apparently, and caught just enough. Her cheeks were flushed, and it wasn't the bashful kind. It was the kind that came from anger held tightly in place.

Every head nearby had swiveled toward her. The woman by the cookies—Pam, one of the library volunteers—blinked, napkin halfway to her mouth. “I…excuse me?”

“You heard me,” Novah said. Her voice didn’t rise, but it carried. “You just implied that Josh would set fire to his own studio and not even know he did it. Because of ‘trauma.’” She lifted two fingers in air quotes so crisp they might have cut skin. “Do you have any idea how messed up that is?”

A murmur rippled through the room. Jaxxon froze at the front, eyes wide.

Pam’s mouth pursed. “I was just repeating what that article said. About his…gaps.”

“*That* article said he survived something horrific, and that memory is complicated,” Novah replied. “It did not say he’s wandering around town in some kind of fugue state, lighting matches for fun. And *that* article is years old. Why are you bringing it up all of a sudden? Who set you on it, because it sure as fuck wasn’t me.”

A few people looked down at their laps. Josh stayed still, breath held, heartbeat thudding in his throat.

Pam gave a little sniff. “People are talking, that’s all. When something like that happens, with that kind of payout—”

“Right,” Novah cut in. “And when the bakery had that grease fire three years ago, did you all stand around wondering if Jaxxon had poured oil on the burners to get a new oven? Or did you line up around the block to buy donuts and tell him how glad you were they caught it in time?”

Someone near the front coughed. Jaxxon, stacking paper plates by the coffee urn, froze mid-reach.

“That’s different,” Pam said quickly. “He’s from here. We know him.”

The words hung there, ugly and naked.

A cold little spark lit in Josh’s chest. He watched Novah take a slow breath, shoulders rising and falling under her thrift-store denim jacket.

“Josh is from here, too,” she said. “He’s lived in this county longer than some of you have. He’s the one who paints your kids’ backdrops for the school play for free. He donates frames to every retirement-home craft fair and never puts his name on the flyer. But because he didn’t grow up in the right house, with the right last name, you see one article that mentions foster care and adoption, and suddenly he’s a suspect instead of a neighbor.”

Pam’s eyes narrowed. “You’re awfully defensive today.”

"Neutrality isn't pretending all opinions are the same," Novah said. "It's telling the truth. And the truth is, the fire marshal's report is public record. Anyone in this room can pull it. It says evidence of accelerant and arson. It does not say 'local artist sets own studio on fire for fun and profit.'"

A few people shifted uncomfortably. Josh saw one of the older council members, a white-haired man who'd taught him shop class in middle school, give a slight nod.

"And as for his 'mysterious past'?" Novah added, her gaze sweeping the room. "If you read the whole thing and not just the headline, you know that Josh had something taken from him as a kid and has spent his whole adult life building something honest out of the wreckage. The way some of you talk about it, you'd think he wrote his own case file as a marketing campaign."

That got a short, strangled laugh from somewhere in the back. The tension in the room shifted, not gone, but cracked.

Pam's cheeks had gone blotchy. "I didn't mean—"

"Then don't say it," Novah replied. "If you've got questions, ask them to his face. Or better yet, ask Hank, whose actual job it is to investigate fires. But stop treating Josh like he's a character in a story you get to dissect while you're in line for coffee."

Silence stretched, thick and humming. Novah's hands were shaking; Josh could see it from where he sat, the tremor travelling from her fingers up through her wrists. She shoved them into the pockets of her coat.

Jaxxon cleared his throat at the front. "Okay," he said. "Let's…get started, y'all. We've got a lot to cover if we're going to hit the goal before the gala."

Chairs creaked. People turned their attention to the whiteboard with the frantic eagerness of those grateful for any excuse to look anywhere else. Novah slid into an empty seat near the middle, not glancing back.

Josh let out a breath he hadn't realized he'd been holding. His pulse was still high, but something else threaded through the adrenaline. A low, astonished warmth. She hadn't just defended his character. She'd put herself between him and the town's curiosity like a shield.

For the first time since she'd found that old article, he didn't feel like he was standing alone under a spotlight. He felt…chosen, in a room where it would've been easier for her to look away.

Hank's call came an hour after the meeting ended, just as Josh was leaving the hardware store with a packet of replacement bulbs he didn't remember picking up.

The truck's cab was hot from sitting in the afternoon sun, and the steering wheel burned his palms when he climbed in.

He thumbed the phone on, tucking it between his ear and shoulder. "Hey."

"You at home?" Hank's voice sounded rough around the edges, more gravel than usual.

"Not yet. Just leaving town. What's up?"

"Don't head there alone," Hank said. Paper rustled on his end, a chair scraping. "Swing by the station. You and Novah both. I've been calling her; she's not picking up."

Josh's skin went cold. "She was at the meeting. I'll grab her."

"Do it," Hank said. "And Josh?"

"Yeah?"

"Take the main road. Daylight and people. No scenic route up the ridge, you hear me?"

Josh tightened his grip on the wheel. "You're freaking me out, Hank."

"Good," Hank muttered. "Maybe that'll keep you alive." The line clicked dead.

Josh sat there for a beat, heart thudding, the truck's engine idling under him. Then he reversed out of his spot too fast, tires crunching on loose gravel, and pointed the nose toward the town hall.

He found Novah coming down the steps, tote bag bumping against her hip. The wind had picked up, blowing a strand of hair across her mouth. She swiped at it with the back of her hand. When she saw his truck pull up to the curb, her eyebrows narrowed.

"Everything okay?" she called as he rolled down the window.

"Not sure," he said. "Hank wants us both at the station. Now. He tried calling you."

She dug her phone out of her pocket, winced at the three missed calls, and swore under her breath. "My ringer's still off from the meeting." She looked back at the building, then at him. "Okay. I'll ride with you."

She climbed in, the scent of her—coffee, rain, a hint of the bergamot soap she liked—folding into the stale air of the cab and making it feel less empty. She snapped her seat belt and braced her hand on the dashboard as he pulled out.

"What did he say?" she asked.

"Something about not going home alone," Josh said. "And taking the main road."

Novah's fingers tightened on the edge of the seat. "That's…comforting."

They drove in tense silence, the truck's tires humming over asphalt, past clapboard houses with wind chimes clinking and kids' bikes abandoned on lawns. When they pulled into the station lot, Hank was already waiting by the side door, sleeves rolled up, tie askew, expression grim.

"Inside," he said, jerking his head toward the door. "Both of you."

The fluorescent lights in the squad room buzzed faintly, casting everything in a tired yellow. The coffee pot sat empty, the burned smell of old grounds hanging in the air. Hank guided them toward the back, away from the front windows, into a cramped conference room that smelled of dry-erase marker and dust.

On the table lay a thick manila envelope. The name ERIC MORROW was scrawled across the front in Hank's blocky handwriting.

"Sit," Hank said.

Josh and Novah did. The metal chairs were cool through Josh's jeans.

"What happened?" Novah asked. Her voice was steady, but her hands were white-knuckled around the tote strap.

"We went out to Eric's camper this morning to serve the warrant for his electronics," Hank said. His gaze flicked from one to the other, assessing. "Place was empty. Bed made, cabinets open. Door locked from the outside with a padlock we didn't put there."

Josh's stomach dropped. "So he took off."

"Looks that way." Hank's jaw flexed. "But he left us a little…parting gift."

Chapter 31

He opened the envelope and tipped it. A fan of glossy photographs slid out across the table, some overlapping, some face down. The top one showed the outside of Josh's studio before the fire, front windows blazing with light, Josh himself visible behind the glass, rearranging sculptures on the shelves.

Another showed him and Novah at the farmer's market, heads bent together over a crate of tomatoes. He recognized the shirt he was wearing. That blue plaid he'd only bought a couple of months ago. Novah had her hair in a high ponytail, and she was laughing at something. The shot was from a distance, taken over the tops of strangers' heads.

Novah reached out with slow fingers and flipped another photo. The two of them again, this time on the ridge trail, their backs to the camera. His hand hovered a fraction of an inch from hers in the picture, as if he'd been about to take it and then thought better of it. The trees framed them, branches bare, sky a flat gray. Winter hike. That was February.

"These are…recent," she said, voice dropping.

"Last six months, far as we can tell," Hank said. "Some of 'em have timestamps still in the metadata. The earliest is March. The latest is from last week."

Josh's skin crawled. "Last week we went up to the overlook after dinner," he said slowly. "Just to get out of town for an hour."

"Yeah," Hank said quietly. He pushed another photo toward them. It was the overlook, zoomed in tight on their profiles as they leaned on the guardrail, faces lit by the glow of Josh's phone as he'd shown her something. Behind them, out of focus but still unmistakable, the faint line of the trailhead parking lot.

"You said he'd left town," Novah whispered.

"I said we hadn't seen movement in a few days," Hank corrected. "I was wrong. Or he was smarter than I gave him credit for."

Josh's heart hammered against his ribs, too fast. The room felt smaller suddenly, the air thinner.

"There was more," Hank went on. He reached back into the envelope and pulled out a folded sheet of paper encased in a clear evidence sleeve. The familiar slanting handwriting leered up through the plastic.

You keep showing up, the note read. I like that. It means you're ready.

Novah's breath hitched. "Is that…?"

"Same hand as the note that showed up at your studio," Hank said. "This one was taped inside the camper door. On the back of the door, facing in. So he'd see it on his way out."

Josh swallowed bile. "So he's out there, watching us, leaving himself pep talks."

"Looks that way." Hank's voice had gone flat, the way it did when he was corralling his temper. "Which is why I called you in, instead of letting you go about your business this afternoon like nothing's changed."

Novah dragged a hand over her face, eyes closing briefly. "What do we do?"

"For starters, we up your security," Hank said. He grabbed a legal pad and clicked his pen. "New deadbolts on both your places. I'll have a deputy swing by with a list of camera systems that actually work up here and don't just give you grainy blobs. You'll install them this week."

Josh nodded. The idea of Eric's unseen gaze sliding over his windows made his skin prickle.

"And second," Hank continued, "you don't stay in your houses alone. Not until we find him."

Josh frowned. "We're not…kids, Hank. We can't just—"

"This isn't about your pride," Hank snapped. "This man has been escalating for months. He broke into your studio. He's been thirty feet from you in the woods with a camera while you thought you were alone. I am not taking chances that he'll decide his little photo project needs a more…dramatic ending."

Silence fell. The overhead light hummed.

"Are you suggesting one of us moves into the station?" Novah asked, attempting a weak joke that fell flat.

"I'm suggesting you pick a house and both stay there." Hank's gaze settled on Josh. "Yours has the fewer ground-level windows. Fewer entry points. Closer to town. Less tree cover."

Novah glanced at Josh, then looked away. "You want us to…what, play house until you catch him?"

"I want you to be alive," Hank said. Some of the heat bled out of his tone. "I can't put a deputy on you two twenty-four hours a day. I don't have the manpower. But I can damn well make sure you're not sleeping in separate places, giving him twice the opportunity."

Josh stared at the photographs on the table—the frozen version of himself at the market, on the trail, at the overlook. He imagined Eric somewhere off-frame, breath clouding in the cold, finger on the shutter.

"I'm not letting her stay alone with that out there," he said quietly. "So if the choice is my place or hers, it's mine. I've got the locks; I know the creaks. I'll get the cameras this afternoon."

Novah didn't immediately argue. Her hand had strayed to her throat, fingers pressing lightly against her skin like she was checking for her own pulse.

"And if we say no?" she asked Hank, not quite defiantly, more like she needed to hear it out loud.

"Then I call your mama," Hank said to her. Then to Josh, "And I call Jaxxon. And I tell them both exactly what we found, and I let them have a say in how much risk you take. I'd rather you hate me for being overcautious than have to knock on another door with my hat in my hands."

Josh blew out a breath through his nose. "Okay," he said. "We'll figure it out."

Hank nodded sharply. "Good. I'll have a patrol swing by your place more often. But don't let that make you sloppy. You keep your blinds drawn twenty-four-seven. You don't go walking alone at night. And if either of you sees anything—any car you don't recognize idling, any shadow that doesn't look right—you call, you don't investigate."

Novah's fingers curled into fists in her lap. "Got it."

Hank gathered the photos back into the envelope, leaving one behind almost by accident. It was a shot through the big front windows of the studio, months before the fire, Novah inside with her back against a wall, knees pulled up, laughing at something. His own blurred profile was at the edge of the frame, hand moving mid-gesture.

Josh remembered that day. He'd been behind the register. Novah was laughing at Alexis being silly. He'd kept to himself because he and Novah weren't exactly friends back then. She'd stayed against the wall while Alexis paid for her purchase.

Novah's duffel looked smaller than Josh expected when she swung it through his front door, thudding softly against the entryway rug. The late-afternoon light slanted in through the narrow front windows, painting pale stripes across the scuffed hardwood and the sofa where he'd woken up that morning with his neck at a bad angle.

"Didn't realize 'stay a few nights' translated to 'move your entire life,'" he said, trying for light and missing.

She huffed out a breath that was almost a laugh. "This is my entire life," she said. "Laptop, underwear, and a hoodie. I don't mind sacrificing to your washing machine. Everything else can fend for itself."

He shut the door, sliding the new deadbolt home with a solid, satisfying clunk. The metal was still shiny. He'd installed it an hour after leaving the station, his hands steadying only once the screws bit into wood.

"You can have the bedroom," he said. "I'll take the couch."

She glanced past him toward the bedroom door, then back at the sofa with its permanently indented cushions. "We'll share," she said. "We're both grown-ups. And we already decided this isn't about avoiding each other."

His pulse did a little stutter. "We also decided—"

"That we're not using sex as a coping mechanism," she finished. "I remember. Still valid."

She set the duffel down by the hall and brushed her hands off on her jeans. The house smelled faintly of the coffee he'd made when they got back, overlaid now with the clean, sharp scent of the new plastic from the camera packaging. A small pile of tools sat on the coffee table, next to an open box.

"Did you get them up?" she asked, nodding toward the cameras.

"Yeah," he said. "One over the front door, one at the back, one watching the driveway. Hank'll get the feed hooked into his system tomorrow." He rubbed his thumb along a phantom smear on his palm where the drill had vibrated. "Feels overkill and not enough at the same time."

"That's how you know we're doing it right," she said dryly. "Maximum inconvenience, minimum certainty."

They moved around each other in a careful dance the rest of the evening, her at the stove stirring pasta while he chopped vegetables at the counter, the click and scrape of his knife and the low boil of water filling the spaces where their conversation lagged. The normal domestic sounds took on a new weight. The squeak of the cabinet door, the hiss of the faucet, the muted creak of floorboards as they crossed paths.

By the time they turned off the lights and brushed their teeth in the cramped bathroom, the house felt different. Not safer, exactly. But less empty. The knowledge that another heartbeat was moving through the same rooms grounded him in a way that surprised him.

In the bedroom, the single lamp on the nightstand cast a pool of warm light on the rumpled quilt. Josh stood on his side, feeling suddenly aware of his own body in a way that had nothing to do with sex and everything to do with proximity. The worn softness of his T-shirt against his skin and the way the air felt cooler on the strip of bare stomach where it had ridden up.

Novah sat on the edge of the mattress, toes flexing against the rug. Her hair was down now, falling in loose waves well past her shoulders. She glanced at him, then slid under the covers, pulling them up to her chest like armor.

He switched off the lamp. The room dropped into a dim blue from streetlight seeping through the curtains. He found his way around the bed by memory, careful not to bump her, and eased onto his side.

They lay on their backs at first, shoulders parallel but not touching, the space between their arms a narrow strip of cool sheet.

"You ever realize how loud a house is when you're trying to hear if someone's outside?" she murmured after a moment.

The fridge kicked on in the next room, a low mechanical sigh.

"Yeah," he said. "Every creak sounds like a footstep."

They listened for a while, letting the familiar sounds declare themselves. The settling pop of the old wooden frame. The faint whoosh of a car passing on the road. Somewhere outside, a dog barked twice, then stopped.

"It's weird," she said quietly. "Last week, if you'd told me we'd end up here, I would've pictured…a very different kind of tension."

"Same," he admitted, mouth twisting. He stared up at the shadowed ceiling. "You still okay with the…boundary?"

"Yes," she said, without hesitation. "Are you?"

His body answered one way, but his better self answered another. "Yeah," he said. "I think if we didn't have it, I'd be tempted to…fast-forward. Pretend the scary parts aren't happening."

"The scary parts are happening," she said.

"Yeah." He swallowed. "They are."

Chapter 32

Silence settled again, not quite comfortable, not sharp. He stared into the dimness and felt something in him loosen. He'd promised her honesty. It seemed as good a time as any to pay up.

"You asked me the other day about my parents," he said. "About how they lied."

He felt more than saw her turn her head on the pillow, looking toward him in the dark. "I remember."

"I don't talk about them much," he said. "Too easy for people to turn them into villains in a story and pat themselves on the back for not being like them."

"Okay," she said softly. "Then don't talk about them. Talk about you."

He let out a slow breath. The sheet rustled as his chest rose and fell.

"When I was a kid," he began, "I learned really early that the safest way to exist was to be exactly what people wanted. Quiet when they were tired. Funny when they were bored. Useful when they were angry." He picked at a loose thread on the blanket, not quite feeling it. "If I could anticipate what they needed, maybe they'd forget to…do the things that hurt."

Novah shifted, blanket whispering. "So you turned yourself into a mirror."

"Yeah." He let the word sit there. "And then when things went to hell, the story that got told was that I was…resilient. That I was 'so well-adjusted, considering.'" He could hear the social worker's voice, bright and brittle. "Nobody asked if I was actually…me, under all the adjustment."

He felt the mattress dip as she rolled onto her side, facing him. "Who were you, under it?" she asked.

He stared into the darkness where he thought her eyes might be. "A scared kid who loved messing with clay because it was the only place I could put things exactly where I wanted them and they'd stay," he said slowly. "Who kept his backpack packed in case he had to leave in the middle of the night. Who knew the sound of every car in the neighborhood by heart because surprises were never good."

Her hand moved, then stopped halfway, hovering in the space between them. "Do you still keep a bag packed?" she asked.

He almost laughed. "There's one in the closet," he admitted. "With a change of clothes, some cash and a copy of my ID. In case everything goes sideways and I have to run again."

Her breath caught, small and sharp. "Josh."

"It's stupid," he said quickly. "I know that. Rationally. But every time I think about unpacking it, my chest does this…clench. Like I'm daring the universe to prove me wrong."

"It's not stupid," she said. "It's a strategy that kept you alive. It's just maybe…outlived its usefulness."

"Tell that to the guy leaving us love notes in the woods," he muttered.

She was quiet for a beat. "Fair point."

He turned his head toward her, making out the faint line of her profile against the lighter strip of the curtain.

"What about you?" he asked. "You grew up in the house where people dropped off casseroles when your mom sneezed too loudly. What strategies do you still use that don't fit anymore?"

She let out a slow, humorless chuckle. "I learned to disappear," she said. "In plain sight."

"How?"

"By being the good girl," she said. "The one who got straight A's and never drank before she was legal and always volunteered to help clean up after potlucks. If I were helpful enough, small enough, agreeable enough, maybe nobody would notice that I was…lonely. Or angry. Or that I wanted things that didn't fit the picture they had in their heads."

"Did it work?"

"Depends." The mattress rustled as she shifted her hand, letting it settle, finally, between them on the sheet. Not touching, but close. "It worked so well that half the town still thinks of me as 'Erin's sweet girl who writes those cute little books.' It worked so well that when I started writing about the uglier stuff in them, missing kids and systemic failures, people got whiplash. They didn't want to see that from me, even if it was fiction. I based a lot of it on truth. It messed with their narrative."

He thought of Pam's face in the meeting, and the way she'd said, *You're awfully defensive for a writer, as if it were an insult.*

"That's why this book terrifies you," he realized. "Not just because of the research for it would do to me. Because of what it would do to you. To your…mask."

"Yeah," she said quietly. "If I write it, I can't un-write it. I can't go back to being…palatable. I can't go back to people assuming my work was harmless."

"And you did it anyway," he said.

"I did. Well, I'm trying. I'm still on deadline, but I'm keeping up." The words had a tremor in them. "Because victims need to know the truth. And because there's more than one kid out there somewhere whose file looks like yours did, and I thought…maybe if we told this story, someone would see them sooner."

His throat tightened. "Do you regret it?"

"Some days," she said honestly. "When I see your face in the grocery store, and you won't look at me. When my mom asks me in that soft, disappointed voice if I 'had to be so graphic.' When I read comments on local groups at two in the morning and convince myself I've ruined your life and mine."

She paused. "And on other days? No. On days when someone emails me to say, 'I think my cousin is in that category you're writing about, what do I do?' Or when I see you reading your own history with your back straight instead of curled in on itself. Or when Hank tells me it gave him leverage to get a warrant he wouldn't have had otherwise."

"But how do people know what's in your book if you haven't finished it yet?"

"I keep a blog that talks about the research I'm doing. It helps keep me grounded and helps others who might be in the same situation, without giving away the story's plot."

He swallowed around the lump in his chest. "I don't regret you," he blurted.

The quiet stretched. "You don't have to say that," Novah whispered.

"I'm not saying it for your sake," he replied. "I'm saying it because if I don't start saying true things out loud, I'm going to drown in the ones I've never questioned." He shifted, the sheet whispering under him. "I regret how I reacted. I regret the words I threw at you. I regret not paying attention to your notes before deciding what you finding the article meant. But I don't regret you. Or us."

The air between them felt charged, even without touch. Josh could feel the heat of Novah's body along the inches of space between their arms.

"Ask me something," he said. "Anything you've wanted to know and were too polite to ask."

She was quiet long enough that he wondered if she'd fallen asleep. Then: "What's the first happy memory you can recall without it being followed immediately by a bad one?"

He blinked into the dark. "That's…specific."

"I spend a lot of time thinking about memory for work," she said. "Humor me."

He sifted through the murky catalogue in his brain, surprised at how quickly one surfaced.

"There was this one foster home," he said slowly. "I was maybe…four? They weren't saints or anything; they were just…normal. The man worked at a mechanic's shop. The woman taught third grade. They had a dog that shed everywhere and a fridge covered in magnets."

He could almost smell the peanut butter, the constant tang of motor oil on the man's jacket.

"Every Friday, she'd make grilled cheese and tomato soup," he said. "And we'd eat it on those TV trays in the living room, watching whatever movie they'd rented. No yelling. No…tension. Just crumbs and cheesy fingers and bad commercials."

He waited for the familiar second half of the memory to crash in—the one where the good moment curdled. It…didn't.

"And?" Novah prompted gently.

"And nothing," he said, surprised. "That's it. Nobody hit me after. Nobody slammed a door. The dog didn't die the next day. It was just…a nice night. And then another one the next week."

She hummed softly. "Sounds like heaven."

"At the time, it felt…fake," he admitted. "Like if I let myself relax into it, I'd get punished. Took me years to realize that's what normal is supposed to feel like. Not perfect. Just…safe enough that grilled cheese doesn't come with a side of fear."

The bed shifted as she scooted half an inch closer, the distance between their shoulders closing until they were almost, but not quite, touching. "You know we can make our own Friday nights now, right?" she said. "Different circumstances, same level of…unremarkable comfort."

He smiled into the dark, the expression small and unfamiliar on his face. "Grilled cheese and true crime?" he asked. "Very on-brand."

"I was thinking grilled cheese and whatever artsy foreign film you pretend not to cry at," she said. "But sure. We can take turns."

"What about you?" he asked. "Your first happy memory without fallout."

She exhaled, thinking. "My dad taught me how to drive the boat," she said. "Not the first time on the water. There were a million of those, all tangled up with fights about sunscreen and who left the cooler on the dock. But the first time he handed me the wheel and sat back and just…let me steer. No commentary. No micro-managing."

He could almost see it. The glint of sun on water, her hands on the worn wheel, hair whipping in the wind.

"He trusted you," he said.

"Yeah," she said. "For those fifteen minutes, he wasn't the former golden boy of the county showing me how to 'do it right.' He was just…my dad. Letting me make tiny, wobbly mistakes with the throttle without snatching it back." She swallowed. "I think that's why the boathouse is both my favorite place and the one that scares me the most. It's the closest thing I have to a symbol of both freedom and expectation."

"Let me come see it tomorrow," he said, surprising himself with the urgency in his voice. "Not as…security detail. As…your person. Even if I sit there and draw the whole time and don't say a word."

"You just want to judge my posture while I type," she murmured, but there was a softness in it.

"I want to see where you learned to steer," he said. "And not snatch the wheel."

The silence that followed felt different. Not empty. Full.

"Okay," she said at last. "Tomorrow."

He let out a breath he hadn't realized he'd been holding. The house creaked, adjusting to the night. Outside, the wind picked up, rustling through the trees.

They lay there, still not touching, two shapes in the dark with their histories spread out between them like maps. The danger was still out there; the cameras blinked silently at the edges of his property; Eric was still a shadow they couldn't see. Nothing about the external pressure eased.

But inside the small, dim room, something had shifted. They were no longer standing on opposite sides of their own pain, shouting across a distance. They were in the same bed, in the same house, listening to the same sounds and choosing, inch by inch, not to hide from each other.

Sleep came slowly, when it came at all. When Josh finally drifted under, the last thing he felt was the steady rise and fall of the mattress beside him and the faint warmth radiating through the thin strip of space between their shoulders.

Chapter 33

Josh slid into the hard plastic chair across from Hank's desk, the same one he'd occupied countless times over parking tickets, festival permits, and the occasional beer-fueled altercation. Today, the room felt smaller, the air thicker, like the walls had leaned in while he wasn't looking.

Hank closed the door all the way, the latch clicking with a small finality that tightened something between Josh's ribs. A thick manila folder sat in the middle of the desk, its edges softened with age. Someone had written BUTLER–GANN in block letters along the tab, then scratched GANN out so hard they tore the cardboard.

Josh stared at the crossed-out name until the letters blurred. “So that’s it,” he said, his voice rough. “That’s the file you went to Butler for.”

“Part of it,” Hank said. His voice had that careful, measured calm Josh had only heard a handful of times, right before he delivered truly bad news. “Some of what I need to tell you is from this.” He tapped the folder. “Some of it’s from what we pulled out of Eric’s place. And some is from people I talked to after.”

Josh’s fingers tightened on his knees. “Just say it, Hank. I’m done waiting for the other shoe to drop.”

Hank opened the folder. The old paper smell, faintly sweet and dusty, drifted across the desk. “You already know the basics,” he began. “Single-vehicle crash on a rural road outside Butler. Your parents dead at the scene. You, hurt but alive. File went into a box and sat in storage for years.”

“Sat and collected dust,” Josh muttered. “No one looked at it. No one cared.”

“That’s the part I needed to check,” Hank said quietly. “Because that’s how it looked on the surface.” He slid a thin, yellowed sheet free and turned it so the writing faced Josh. “But there’s more in here than the summaries from 2017 hinted.”

Josh leaned forward despite himself. The page was a photocopy of a handwritten note clipped to the front of the original report, the ink faded to a tired gray.

Butler PD –
Per call from CPS intake, keep case file intact.
Do not destroy at statute expiration.
Family member continues to inquire about missing minor (male, approx. 3 yrs).
Ongoing placement/adoption questions unresolved.

The signature at the bottom was illegible, just a scrawl and a badge number.

Josh's heartbeat stumbled. "Family member?" His voice came out thin. "What family member?"

"That's where it gets interesting," Hank said. "Back when the wreck happened, you had more than just your parents. You had at least one aunt on your father's side. Younger sister."

Josh swallowed, his throat suddenly dry. "He never talked about a sister."

"Her name back then was Lila Gann," Hank continued. "She lived two counties over. When she got the call about the crash, she drove in that night. She saw the car. She went to the hospital. But by the time she got there, you were already gone out of the ICU and into the state systems process."

"Gone where?" Josh demanded. His hands were shaking. He curled them into fists to hide it. "I was three. I don't just vanish."

"According to the case notes, CPS fast-tracked you and sealed the adoption records," Hank said. "It should have been easy enough to find you once you got your license, since your name hasn't changed, but…" Hank shrugged. "Sloppy police work, probably on purpose. You were a healthy toddler with no immediate relatives in-county, and your mother's side had a history that made them nervous." He grimaced. "That's written down in some pretty shitty language I'd rather not repeat."

Josh's jaw clenched. "Say it."

Hank exhaled through his nose. "They called them unstable. Poor. Trauma-prone. A lot of assumptions based on zip code and old arrest records." He flipped to another page, this one a typewritten summary with a crooked, stamped date. "Instead of placing you in emergency kinship care while they sorted it out, they moved you into foster placement with an eye toward adoption."

"And my aunt?" Josh forced the words out. "This Lila. She just… gave up?"

"That's the part that contradicts the story they fed you," Hank said. "She didn't give up. She called. She wrote. She showed up in person at least twice in the first year after the wreck."

He slid another photocopy across the desk. This one was a printout of a scanned letter, the edges dark where the copier had caught the shadow of the original.

To whom it may concern,
I am writing again about my nephew Joshua. I have called your office many times, and no one will tell me where you've placed him. I can take him. I have a room ready. I am not perfect, but I am his blood, and he deserves to know he is loved by his family. Please call me back.

"There's a note stapled to this one from the caseworker," Hank said, tapping the margin. "Says they left her a voicemail telling her you were stable in placement and that they were 'moving toward permanency.' CPS talk for adoption."

"Permanency," Josh repeated, the word tasting like ash. "You mean they were already shopping me around."

"They were trying to close the file," Hank said. "Too many kids. Not enough workers. You know the drill from the stories you've read."

A blog Novah had written some time ago about systemic failures flickered, unbidden, at the edge of Josh's mind, lines he'd skimmed once and dismissed as distant, not-him problems. Now they pressed in with ugly clarity.

"What happened to her?" he asked. "To Lila."

Hank reached for another sheet, this one a more recent printout. "That's the other thing that kept this file from being destroyed. She didn't stop asking. She kept calling Butler PD every couple of years, trying to see if anything had changed, if they had more information. That note up front? That was the department telling themselves not to shred the file because they knew she would raise hell if they did."

Josh stared at the paper until the letters doubled. "So all this time," he said slowly, "I thought nobody looked for me. That my parents were it, and once they were gone, I was just… leftover." He swallowed hard. "But she was there. She tried."

"Yes," Hank said. "You had someone in your corner from day one who did not walk away. The system failed both of you."

Something sharp and hot pricked behind Josh's eyes. He blinked hard, but the burn only intensified. "Why didn't my adoptive parents know?" he snapped. "Why didn't they tell me someone wanted me?"

"That's where it ties into the adoption records," Hank said. "Some of those copies we pulled from Eric's camper? They match what's referenced in here." He tapped the Butler file. “The adoption agency that handled your case filed for termination of parental rights and cut off all contact with biological relatives. They didn’t pass along that an aunt was fighting.”

Josh’s stomach rolled. “So you’re telling me the people who raised me might never have known there was someone else.”

“Maybe,” Hank said. “Some agencies kept it vague to make placements go smoother. You were a little kid. They wanted a clean slate. No ‘complications.’” The bitterness in his voice was unmistakable. “What matters for you now is this: You were not unwanted. They “mishandled” you.”

Josh let out a shaky laugh that wasn’t really a laugh. “Great. So instead of being the kid nobody wanted, I’m the kid everybody lost.”

“That’s one way to spin it,” Hank said. He leaned forward, his elbows creaking on the desk. “Here’s another: You are the kid somebody loved enough to keep knocking on locked doors for years. That’s different from the story you’ve been living.”

The words landed with a weight Josh wasn’t ready for. His chest felt too tight, as if the room didn’t have enough air. “Is she still alive?” he asked. “Lila.”

Hank hesitated just long enough for Josh to notice. “Far as the records show, yes. She changed her name when she married. Moved out of state for a while. Came back a few years ago. I've got a current address. I didn't knock on her door. That's not my choice to make."

Josh's hand drifted toward the folder, then stopped halfway. "So I could find her."

"You could," Hank said. "On your timeline. When you're ready." He paused. "And preferably not alone, given the other half of this mess."

Josh's gaze snapped up. "Eric."

"Eric," Hank confirmed. "The reason this file was reopened in '17? Somebody phoned in an anonymous tip suggesting the '97 crash might not have been an accident. That tip came from a cell triangulated to less than a mile from where a thirteen-year-old kid named Eric Morrow lived at the time."

Josh felt as if the floor dropped half an inch. "You think he called it in himself."

"We know he's obsessively tracked your case for years," Hank said. "We know he had clippings, maps, and those partial adoption forms in his camper. We know he's related to you—a second cousin on your mom's side, from what we can tell—and that his parents were abusive as hell while he watched your parents give you the life he thought he deserved."

Josh's skin crawled. "So he knew about the crash. Knew about me. And he's been orbiting my life ever since."

"Looks that way," Hank said. "The investigators in '97 opened the file, sniffed around, then shut it down without doing half of what they should have. No interviews with your extended family. No follow-up on that payphone call. No look at Eric's home life."

"Why keep the file if they weren't going to do anything?" Josh asked. "Why hold onto it past the statute if they weren't going to bother?"

Hank's jaw tightened. "Two reasons. One, the aunt I told you about kept asking questions. Her pressure is the only reason that the 'do not destroy' note exists. Two, somewhere in their gut, someone in Butler PD knew they'd half-assed the follow-up." He tapped the folder again. "You don't keep a file you consider fully closed. You keep the ones that bother you."

Josh stared down at the scattered photocopies, at his life turned into single-spaced paragraphs and margin notes in a stranger's handwriting. For the first time since Novah had handed him the newspaper article, the story of his life felt less like a void and more like a map—messy, water-damaged, but still legible.

"There was an aunt," he said quietly. "She fought for me. Someone wanted me."

“Yes,” Hank said. “That’s the headline you need to walk out of here with.”

Josh’s throat clenched. “And Eric?”

“We’re still piecing all of that together,” Hank said. “You already know he’s tied to the fire and to the stalking. Now we know he’s tied to your past, too. But this,” he nudged the page with Lilas letter, “is bigger than him. He doesn’t get to be the main character in your origin story.”

Josh sat back, the chair creaking under his weight. The panic that had been buzzing in his veins for days shifted, just a fraction, into something else. Not calm, exactly. But not freefall either.

“If I go see her,” he said slowly, “I’m not going alone.”

Hank’s mouth twitched. “That’s the smartest thing you’ve said all week. But...Wait until we catch up with Eric. I don’t want him following you—you leading him to her.”

Josh hesitated only a heartbeat before the next words came. “I need to talk to Novah.”

Chapter 34

Josh grabbed Novah's hand as he walked through the waiting room after leaving Hank's office. "We need to talk." He silently led her to his truck. When they pulled up to her house, he grabbed her arm before she could open the door. "We'll go through the house, but I want to sit by your inside lake."

Novah nodded. "Okay." They both slid out of the truck at the same time, meeting in front of it. Josh put his arm around her waist as they walked onto her porch.

He paused at the edge of her deck, hand on the railing. The last time he'd stood here with his chest tight and his past clawing at him, he'd chosen the easy path—silence and distance until she couldn't stand it and walked away in the rain. The memory hit like a slap.

Not this time.

Once in the lower level of her office, she turned to him. "Josh." Her knuckles tightened on the edge of the deck. "Is everything okay? Did something happen?"

"Yeah, something happened. But I'm here because I chose to be, not because the sky is falling."

The hard line of her shoulders loosened a fraction. She stepped back and opened the door wider. "Okay. Tell me."

He put his feet in the lake and swung them back and forth, breathing in the familiar mix of coffee, lake water, and the faint echo of his own cologne clinging to the throw blanket that Novah had refused to use for days. It was folded neatly now on the back of the chair, like a truce offering she wasn't quite ready to hand over.

"Do you want coffee?" she asked, defaulting to ritual. "I can make some."

He shook his head. "No. If I sit at a table, I'm gonna start pacing and knock something over."

She hesitated, then nodded. Novah waited while he gathered his thoughts. The difference this time was that the space between them felt chosen, not imposed.

Josh rubbed his palms on his jeans, then forced himself to look at her. "Hank found more in the Butler file," he said. "And in what they pulled from Eric's place. It answers some of the questions that have been eating my brain."

Novah's face tightened. "Is this something you're supposed to keep quiet about?"

"That's the thing," he said. "Last time, you were the one holding information because you thought it would crush me. And I punished you for it." He shook his head. "I'm not doing that again. Hank asked me to be smart about what I share while they build a case. But he also made it damn clear that shutting you out is the dumbest move I could make."

Her eyes flickered, a flash of hurt and hope both. "Hank said that?"

"More or less, with extra cussing." The corner of his mouth twitched. "Point is, I want you to hear what I'm allowed to share. From me. Not as gossip. Not as research. As my person."

Her breath caught. She sat very still. "Okay," she said quietly. "Tell me."

He told her.

He told her about the "do not destroy" note, about the aunt he had never known existed, who had driven in the night of the crash and kept calling for years. He told her about the letter begging to take him, the caseworker's cold summary, the way the adoption agency had chased a clean slate instead of a messy truth.

As he spoke, her hand rose to cover her mouth, eyes shining.

"So all this time," he finished, his voice raw, "I thought nobody came for me. And the truth is… someone did. She just never made it past the gatekeepers."

Novah dropped her hand to her lap, fingers shaking. "Josh," she whispered. "That's… huge."

He let out a short, disbelieving huff. "Yeah. Understatement of the year." He swallowed, his throat working. "I don't know what to do with it yet. Part of me wants to get in my truck right now and drive straight to her door. Part of me wants to stick this new truth in a box and pretend it doesn't change anything."

She nodded slowly. "Both of those reactions make sense."

"I keep trying to decide what it means about who I am," he said. "If I'm not the kid nobody wanted, then who the hell am I? The kid the system stole? The almost-nephew? The maybe–Granger, maybe-not?"

"Maybe you're all of those things," she said softly. "And maybe none of them alone has to define you."

He stared at her. "How do you do that?"

"Do what?"

"Talk like you're not trying to fix me but somehow still make it easier to breathe," he said. "I spent years in therapy with people who wanted to slap labels on everything. You just… ask questions and leave room."

She smiled, small and sad. "That's the job. And the choice. I don't want to fix you. I want to stand next to you while you figure out what to do with all of this. Even if that means watching you walk into something I can't control, like meeting your aunt. Even if it scares the crap out of me."

His chest tightened again, but this time it felt less like panic and more like pressure from something trying to expand.

"Hank also tied some of this to Eric," he said. "He thinks the 2017 tip that reopened the file probably came from him. That he's been circling my life since he was a pissed-off teenager with matches and a grudge."

Fear flickered across her face, mingling with anger. "So he's not just obsessed with you now. He's been obsessed with you—and your family—almost your entire life."

"Yeah," Josh said. "But Hank was clear about one thing: Eric doesn't get to be the main character in this story. Not the way it started. Not the way it ends."

Novah nodded once. "Then we make sure he's not."

"We," he repeated, tasting the word. "You're still in this with me?"

She blinked, incredulous. "Josh. You literally showed up to tell me the truth while it's still raw, instead of boiling in it alone for two weeks. That's all I've ever wanted from you." Her voice softened. "You choosing to share this with me is the opposite of what broke us the first time."

He exhaled, some of the tension in his shoulders loosening. "That's the point," he said. "I'm trying to learn from my own stupidity."

She scooted a little closer to him, slow enough to give him plenty of room to flinch away. He didn't.

"What do you need right now?" she asked. "Not in a big, life-plan way. In a tonight way. Do you want to sit here and rage? Do you want to look at the documents together? Do you want to not think about any of it for a few hours?"

The question landed with almost physical force. No one had ever asked him that directly without already deciding the answer.

He looked at her, really looked. The concern in her eyes, the steadiness under it, the way she made space without rushing into it.

"Honestly?" he said. "I need to feel like I'm still here. Not just ink on some case file or a name on a lab report. I need to be in my body instead of stuck in my head with three-year-old me."

Her cheeks flushed faintly, but she didn't look away. "Okay," she said quietly. "We can do that."

Josh's stomach rumbled again, betraying him louder this time, and he groaned, pressing a hand to his face to hide the warmth spreading from his collar to his cheeks. He could almost hear Novah's smile before she laughed. It was a sound that snagged something inside his chest, just like it had since the first time they'd made love.

She stood and extended her hand toward him. "Come on," she said, amused but kind. "You're not fooling anyone. I'm starving too."

Her fingers brushed his, soft and steady, and the simple contact made his pulse stumble. Passing by the bathroom, she stopped and grabbed a towel to dry their legs. Novah hung it on the rack and then locked the office behind them. For a moment, neither of them spoke. The hum of the building felt too loud, the air too close.

As they climbed the stairs, Novah's perfume floated between them. Josh let go of her hand near the top, pretending to adjust his sleeve, but the ghost of her touch stayed with him.

Outside, the evening air was cool, sharp with the scent of late evening lake water. A breeze carried her hair across her face, and she brushed it back quickly, eyes catching his. The look she gave him wasn't shy. It was searching, fearless in the way she always was. He wished he could match that. Wished he wasn't so tangled up inside.

They walked in silence into the kitchen. Josh sat at the table while Novah opened the fridge. "I took steaks out this morning. You want some fried potatoes, onions and peppers with it? I have leftover potato salad, too."

"The fried potatoes sound great. Want some help?"

"No, thanks. It'll only take me a minute to chop the potatoes and veggies, but you can make some coffee if you want."

Josh nodded. "I can do that." He reached into the cabinet for the coffee beans and the grinder. The whirr drowned out the thud of Novah's knife as she made short work of dicing potatoes and slicing the vegetables.

As he waited for the coffee to brew, Josh's mind kept circling back to her words from earlier. Her line in the sand. No more using sex to escape. He wanted to tell her he understood. That she was right. That he didn't just want her body, he wanted her time, her voice, her fire. But the thought of saying those things out loud made his throat tighten.

Novah put the potatoes and onion into the hot frying pan. "You're quiet," she said softly.
He shrugged. "Just thinking."
Her lips curved, tender but cautious. "Dangerous habit."

"Yeah," he said, finally meeting her eyes. "But maybe it's the one I should've picked up a long time ago."

Novah lifted the pan off the flame and flipped the potatoes and onion. She added salt, pepper and a little garlic powder and then flicked her wrist to mix everything in.

When the coffee finished dripping, he poured them each a cup and handed Novah hers. He hoped she didn't notice that his hands were shaking. When she took the mug, her fingertips skimmed his, a brief, warm contact that lit up his skin and sent a sharp jolt racing up his arm.

Seemingly unfazed, Novah sipped her coffee and then set the mug on the counter. She seasoned the steaks and plopped them in a pan hot enough to create the darkened crust that she loved on blue rare steaks, and then scoooped the green peppers off the cutting board, adding them to the potatoes.

Each time she glanced sideways at Josh, his eyes were already on her, the weight of his gaze warming the side of her face as the steaks sizzled in the pan, filling the kitchen with the rich smell of bacon grease and seared meat. The soft crackle of fat and the low hum of the vent fan faded a little every time she caught him, like the whole room was stepping back to give them space.

She turned to slide the steaks from the skillet to their plates, a puff of savory steam rising to brush her cheeks as she shifted her weight from one hip to the other. When she looked up, she found his gaze glued to the slow sway of her hips, his expression dazed and unguarded, elbow resting forgotten on the table beside his untouched drink.

He didn't even flinch when her head started to turn, still lost in watching the curve of her body as she moved. A slow, wicked smile curled at her lips. She gave her hips an extra, playful wiggle, the fabric of her pants whispering over her skin, just to see what he would do.

Josh's eyes widened, color flooding his face as if someone had flipped a switch. A startled laugh burst out of him, a little too loud for the small kitchen, and he ducked his head, scrubbing a hand over his mouth as if he could hide the grin stretching across it.

"Busted," he said, shaking his head.

Novah placed a plate of steak and potatoes in front of him and leaned down to kiss his temple. "Yeah," she said softly. "Busted."

Chapter 35

Josh's life cycled through his mind at lightning speed, the images slamming into each other. His aunt's laugh from a memory that was so old, he wasn't sure it was his. The sense of not belonging anywhere his whole life. The fresh blur of phone calls and dead ends from last week. Every time he imagined finding his aunt, his chest cinched, and his breath snagged on the thought of her eyes going flat and her mouth shaping his name like a stranger's. Or not at all.

Part of him leaned into the rush, planning the next step, the next call, anything to keep moving, while another part dug in its heels, whispering that once he knocked, there'd be no taking it back if she turned away.

The glow of the television cast a soft light across the darkened living room, fighting for attention from the low lamp in the opposite corner as Novah found a movie for them.

As much as they preferred to sit out on the porch on an evening as perfect as this—not too hot and not too cool—they didn't want to make themselves an open target for Eric.

Josh leaned back against the sofa with his legs crossed and his hands idle on his thighs. Every muscle in his body buzzed with restless energy, but he stayed very still. Novah sat leaning forward beside him, looking for a good movie. When she couldn't find anything, she settled for a chick flick.

She handed him the remote. "I can't find anything good. If you don't want to watch this, see if you can find something."

He flinched as the remote landing in his lap surprised him. "If that's all you can find, that'll have to do," he said, leaning over to put the remote on the end table. They sat silently, watching the movie, but not really watching it—each lost in their own thoughts.

"Novah," he said softly.

She didn't look up right away, just drew in a breath and let it out slowly. "Yeah?"

He turned his hand palm up between them, not touching, just offering. "Can I…hold your hand?"

Her mouth twitched, the smallest, tired ghost of a smile. "You're asking now?"

"Yeah," he said, a humorless huff of air leaving him. "I'm trying this whole 'not being a coward' thing."

That got a genuine, if fragile, smile. Novah placed her hand in his, fingers cool and a little stiff at first. He closed his around hers carefully, like he was afraid of squeezing too hard and sending her skittering away.

"Tell me if anything feels like too much," he murmured. "At any point. Even if it's just this."

She squeezed his fingers. "I will," she said. "Same goes for you."

He nodded, eyes dropping to their joined hands. The sight caused an odd but steady tightening and aching in his chest.

For a moment, they just sat like that. Novah's thumb began a slow, unconscious stroke over the back of his hand, tracing a line from his knuckles to his wrist. An insistent heat followed in its wake.

His mind flickered, unbidden, to the first time she'd had her hands in his hair in the shower, how she'd laughed at the soap in his eyes, then gone quiet when he'd leaned into her like a starving man. Back then, the hot water had been another excuse to blur things, to turn everything into steam and skin and nothing that had to be named.

The memory hit him differently. He remembered the careful way her fingers had worked through the tangles at the nape of his neck, the way she'd pressed her nails lightly against his scalp, not to excite but to soothe. He'd pretended he didn't need that.

"Hey," she said, drawing him back. "You're a million miles away."

"Just…remembering," he admitted.

Her brows lifted. "Good remembering or bad?"

He considered that, drawing in a breath that tasted faintly of her shampoo and the peppermint tea cooling on the nightstand. "Both," he said honestly. "Same scenes. Different…lens, I guess."

She waited, not pushing.

"You washing my hair," he said quietly. "In the shower. I thought I wanted you because it was easy. But I think I—" He broke off, jaw working. "I think I wanted that. The way you were careful with me. And I didn't know what to do with that, so I just…turned it into sex."

Her hand stilled in his. The pause stretched, but didn't snap.

"Josh," she said gently.

He shook his head, not in refusal, but as if he were shaking something loose. "I don't want to do that to you again. Or to me." He swallowed, throat tight. "If we…if anything happens tonight, I need it to be something that keeps me here. Not somewhere to hide."

She shifted closer, their knees brushing. "Then we go slow," she said. "And if at any point it feels like hiding, we stop."

He looked at her, really looked. The faint redness at the rims of her eyes, the way her hair had fallen out of its tie, the tiny worry line between her brows that hadn't quite eased. Want twisted in his gut, yes, but it came braided with something heavier, older. Relief, maybe, or the fierce, unfamiliar urge not to run.

"Okay," he said. "Slow."

He lifted their joined hands and, after a heartbeat's hesitation, brought her knuckles to his lips. The kiss was barely there, more breath than contact, but it sent a quiet shiver through her.

"Still okay?" he asked.

She nodded, then surprised him by scooting closer, close enough that he could see the faint freckles at the bridge of her nose. “Can I…?” She reached up, stopping short of his hairline.

His chest tightened at the familiarity of the gesture. He gave a small nod. “Yeah. Please.”

Her fingers slid into his hair, slow and deliberate. She started at the crown, nails grazing his scalp in gentle, circling motions, just like that first night—but there was no rush now, no frantic edge. Warmth spread from her touch down the back of his neck, loosening muscles he hadn’t realized were clenched.

His eyes fluttered shut on a low exhale he didn’t quite manage to disguise.

“Too much?” she asked.

He shook his head, leaning subtly into her hand. “No. Just…good.” His voice came out rougher than he meant it to. “Feels like my brain finally shut up for a second.”

Her laugh was soft, almost disbelieving. “Should’ve known it was your head that needed fixing.”

He cracked one eye open to look at her. “You’ve been fixing my head for a while,” he said. “I just kept dragging us back into my body so I didn’t have to notice.”

Color rose along her cheekbones, but she didn't look away. "Maybe tonight we let both exist," she said. "No either/or."

Her other hand found its way to his shoulder, thumb rubbing absent circles over the cotton of his shirt. Each small point of contact—her fingers in his hair, her palm on his shoulder, their still linked hands—felt like separate anchors, tying him to the sofa, to the room, to her.

A flash of another memory cut through: Her at the stove, steam curling around her face, his hands tight on her hips as he'd crowded her against the counter. The need then had been sharp, a blade pressed against a wound. Now, as his hand drifted, slowly, to rest at the curve of her waist, the same place he'd gripped hard before, his fingers settled instead of seized.

He brushed his thumb once over the soft cotton at her side. "Here okay?"

She glanced down at his hand, then back up, eyes clear. "Yeah," she said. "Here's good."

The words lodged somewhere under his breastbone. Good. Not "fine," not "whatever," not the brittle bravado they used to live in.

He let his hand rest there, not pulling her in, just holding. Feeling the subtle rise and fall of her breathing under his palm, the quiet strength of her body, he realized he wasn't waiting for the usual rush—he was waiting to see if she would come closer on her own.

After a beat, she did.

She shifted so that her thigh was tight against his, her head resting on his shoulder. The movement was unhurried, giving him every chance to back away. He didn't.

"Josh," she said, searching his face. "What's going on in there?"

He let out a shaky laugh. "You really want the play-by-play?"

"Yes," she said simply. "I do."

He swallowed, then forced himself not to look away. "I'm thinking about every time I grabbed you like you were a life raft and then pretended you were just…fun. I'm thinking about how that was unfair. To you. To me."

She listened, hand still moving through his hair in slow, comforting strokes.

"I'm thinking," he went on, "that I want you. A lot. But for the first time, that doesn't feel like the most dangerous part."

Her brows knit. "What does?"

He gave a crooked, vulnerable half smile. "Wanting you to stay after."

For a long moment, the only sound was the soft rustle of fabric as she shifted her weight. Then she brought her forehead to his, their noses almost brushing, breath mingling. The intimacy of it—no flash, no spectacle, just warm skin and shared air—hit him harder than any frantic kiss they'd ever shared.

"I'm not going anywhere," she murmured. "Not because of this. Not if we're honest. Not if we keep choosing each other on purpose."

His hand at her waist tightened just a fraction, not in possession, but in response.

"Can I kiss you?" he asked, the question almost reverent.

Her lips curved against his. "Yeah," she whispered. "Please."

He didn't rush it. He let the moment hang there—their foreheads touching, her hands in his hair, his palm steady at her side—so that when he finally closed the distance, it felt less like an escape and more like a decision.

Novah deepened the kiss as her hands slid under his shirt, fingertips skating over the heat of his skin and the tense line of his stomach. Her touch sent a low, spreading ache through him, and when she finally tore her mouth from his, her breath ghosted hot against his lips. *"Josh—"*

He shifted, hips jerking almost involuntarily as he tried to ease the throbbing pressure straining against the front of his jeans, denim suddenly too tight, too rough. His fingers flexed uselessly in the air before hovering at her waist, trembling, like he was afraid to grab on and equally scared to let her go.

Novah's voice wrapped around him, soft and breathless. "Touch me," she whispered.

His hands moved as if they belonged to someone else, hovering for a heartbeat before settling at her hips, fingers splaying against the warm curve there. Her other hand slipped into the hair at the nape of his neck, nails grazing his skin in slow, soothing strokes that sent a shiver down his spine. His grip tightened and relaxed in small, uncertain pulses as he kneaded her hips, trying to focus on the simple rhythm of his hands instead of the chaos in his chest.

Then the rush started. Scenes flickered through his mind in jagged flashes—hospital-white hallways, caseworkers' tight mouths, the grainy black-and-white of that old article, the hollow look in his own too-young eyes—spooling past so fast his stomach flipped. The room seemed to tilt, the present blurring at the edges as if someone had hit fast forward on his entire life.

Novah's eyes narrowed, the heat between them cooling into concern. "Are you okay, babe?"

Her voice sounded warped, distant, like it was traveling to him down a long, echoing tunnel. His chest squeezed, a sharp, clawing pressure, and a single thought pushed through the noise, bright and raw. *I exist now. I'm not just the kid in the article.*

Hands—hers—found his face, warm and steady, cupping his cheeks. Her thumbs brushed beneath his eyes, and only then did he feel the wetness on his skin, tears sliding hot and unchecked over the trembling line of his jaw as his breath hitched and finally broke.

"Josh?"

Her voice cut through the noise in his head, a low, steady note in the middle of all the static. His eyes snapped up to hers, pupils blown, chest heaving as if he'd just surfaced from deep water. The air felt thick in his lungs, heavy with her shampoo and the faint salt of his own tears. *I'm me. The real me.*

"Don't let go, Novah," he managed, the words rough and scraped raw on the way out. His fingers curled in the fabric of her shirt, knuckles whitening. "Please tell me you won't let go."

"I won't let go, Josh. I'm here." Her answer was immediate, solid. She drew him into her arms, guiding his head to her shoulder. The familiar curve of her collarbone pressed against his cheek, warm and real, her heartbeat a steady thud against his temple. Her hands moved in slow, soothing circles over his back, palms dragging lightly over the thin cotton of his shirt, grounding him with each pass.

His breathing gradually evened out, the sharp, hitching gasps softening into something closer to sighs. The room shrank to the slide of her hands, the quiet rustle of their clothes as she held him, the soft whoosh of air from the vent. She felt his weight settle more fully against her, his muscles loosening one by one, and for a moment she thought he'd drifted off.

Then he straightened, just enough to see her face, but he didn't let go. His hands stayed fisted at her waist, their foreheads nearly touching, breaths mingling in the small space between them. The heat that had burned hot and fast earlier had mellowed into something slower, deeper—a warmth that settled low in his chest rather than rushing straight to his skin.

"Can we just…stay like this?" he asked quietly, voice hoarse but steadier. "No more running. Just you and me. Tonight."

Her shoulders softened, relief and affection washing through her features. "Yeah," she whispered, brushing her thumb under his damp eye. "Just you and me."

She stood and held her hand to him. “Come to bed. Just to sleep. Just so I can hold you.” He reached for her hand and stood, looking lost.

“Come on, Josh. Let’s go to bed.” In her room, they stripped down to their underwear and slid under the covers. Novah wrapped her hand around his waist, pulling him closer. “Let me hold you, babe,” she whispered.

They lay back together, limbs tangled, the mattress dipping beneath their combined weight. Her fingers threaded lazily through his hair while Josh’s arm banded around her waist, holding her close, not with urgency, but with a quiet, desperate kind of certainty. In the dim light, with their breaths slowly syncing, the decision to simply hold on—to each other, to the moment—felt more intimate than anything else they could have done.

Chapter 36

Novah's hands never stopped moving over his back, palms tracing slow, steady circles, the heat seeping into his skin with each pass. His breathing had lost its ragged edge, settling into something more profound, but not yet the quiet, even rhythm of sleep.

"Josh," she whispered, her voice cracking on his name, the word brushing warm against his ear.

"Mmm," he mumbled, the low sound vibrating in his chest. Heat tightened low in his body at the way she said his name, a heavy ache pulsing between them as he shifted minutely, his cock throbbing between them. He prayed she couldn't feel how hard he was, even though some part of him knew the tension there was impossible to miss.

His hand lay warm and unmoving on her waist. He didn't dare drag his fingers even an inch, afraid of shattering the fragile, careful balance they'd found. The backs of her knuckles skimmed his cheek in a feather-light stroke, cool against the lingering heat there, and he lifted his gaze to meet hers. His breath hitched, catching hard in his throat at the depth in her eyes—wide, glistening, filled with a tenderness so fierce it made his chest ache.

Josh's eyes softened, and Novah saw something she'd only caught glimpses of before. Her hand moved to his hip, causing his cock to jump.

"Touch me," she moaned.

I'm me. I'm really my own person. His hand slowly skimmed up her side to the side of her breast.

"Please, Josh," she whispered hoarsely.

A moan escaped from his throat as his hand cupped her breast, his thumb rubbing her nipple through the lacy material of her bra.

Novah's back arched into his hand as a streak of heat rolled through her. Her hand bumped his as she reached between her breasts to unfasten the clasp holding her bra on. The warmth of his lips and tongue on her nipple went straight to her belly as her hips involuntarily rose.

"Jesus, Novah," he mumbled around a mouthful of her breast, his hand worrying the nipple on her other breast.

She couldn't wait any longer. Grabbing Josh's hand, she pushed it into the top of her panties, her fingers guiding his to her clit. Her fingers pressed his where she wanted them, and as soon as he touched her, her hips ground against his fingers. An involuntary scream that ended on a long moan left her throat as she spurted, soaking his fingers as she writhed next to him.

His cock throbbed, pre-cum leaking out of the tip, as he tried to pull her soaked underwear down. Giving up, he knelt between her legs and grabbed them in both hands, tearing them in one strong rip.

"Novah," he ground out, looking for explicit permission. He held his cock in his hand at her entrance, stroking it roughly.

She reached down and stilled his hands. "Inside," she ground out. "I need to feel you—" her words trailed off as he shoved himself inside of her in one hard thrust. She arched into him, tossing her head as her muscles instantly gripped and released his cock.

Josh fought through her spasms, barely holding on.

"Harder, Josh. I need more," Novah moaned breathlessly.

The last strings of his emotional barrier broke as his hips became more aggressive. He felt her building again as skin slapped skin, but he couldn't wait. Supporting himself with one hand, he reached between her legs and rubbed her clit. As soon as his hand touched the sensitive organ, Novah's hips bucked into him. His hand moved under her hips to hold her against him as he stiffened and shot his load deep into her.

He started to push up, muscles bunching as he braced on his elbows, but Novah's arms looped around his back and tightened, her palms spreading flat between his shoulder blades as she pulled him down until his weight settled fully into her.

For a heartbeat, he froze, chest pressed to hers, feeling the stutter of his own pulse slam against the steady thud of her heart, two frantic rhythms slowly finding the same beat. A rushing heat rose behind his eyes—not the sharp, panicked burn from earlier, but something warmer, flooding and strange—as the old instinct to pull away collided with the fierce new relief of having nowhere to run.

Novah exhaled shakily beneath him, her fingers curling into the hair at the back of his head as if anchoring herself there, too. The enormity of it crashed over her in waves. This man, who had spent years wrapped in armor, was choosing to sink his full weight into her, not as a shield or a distraction, but as himself, bare and breakable. Her throat tightened, a hot ache blooming in her chest as joy, protectiveness, and a wild, terrified love tangled together until she couldn't tell where one ended and the other began.

When their breathing had slowed, and sweat cooled on their skin, the room fell into that deep, humming quiet that only came after storms. The bedside lamp cast a small pool of light, turning Novah's hair into a dark halo against the pillow.

Josh rolled to his side, pulling her with him so he stayed inside of her. One arm moved her under her head, the other gripped her back, crushing her against him, as if to anchor himself to her. Her fingers traced idle patterns over his shoulders and the base of his neck.

"If you need to go back to your place tonight, I get it," she murmured. "I know this is a lot."

He shook his head, tightening his hold just enough that she stopped tracing. "No. I don't want to go anywhere."

"Okay," she said, voice soft. She resumed her patterns.
"Then we stay."
The simplicity of it almost undid him.
"Novah?" he said quietly.
"Mm?"

"Remember the boathouse?" he asked. "When you said those three words, and I pretended I didn't hear?"

Her fingers stilled. "Kind of hard to forget." A small, self-conscious laugh escaped her. "I've tried."

"I heard you," he said. "Every time. On the floor, in my kitchen, in that draft you never sent."

Her eyes widened. "You read—"

"No," he said quickly. "Hank told me you wrote it. You didn't send it. That's enough." He swallowed. "Point is, you've been saying those words in more ways than one for a long time. I've been the coward who choked on them."

"You're not a coward," she said automatically.

He huffed. "I've stared down a burning building and a man with gasoline in his veins, and I still couldn't look you in the eye and say three syllables. That's not bravery."

She shifted, turning onto her side so they were face to face. "It's fear," she said. "And you have reasons to be afraid. Every time you've let yourself believe you were permanent in someone's life, they either left or it turned out to be a lie."

He closed his eyes for a second. The file. The letter. The erased aunt. The parents who had been, at best, incomplete in their love.

"When I told you at the stove not to say it," he said, "I thought I was protecting both of us. If I didn't say it, you couldn't leave and prove me right." He opened his eyes again. "Turns out I was just proving myself right in advance by pushing you away."

Her throat worked as she swallowed. "So why are we talking about this now?"

Because Hank had sat at his kitchen table and called him out. Because Lila's letter existed. Because he was tired of letting fear write his lines.

"Because this afternoon, Hank handed me proof that my story isn't 'unwanted and discarded,'" he said slowly. "It's wanted and mishandled.' And if that's true—if I wasn't fundamentally unlovable as a kid—then maybe my heart isn't a ticking time bomb for anyone who gets close to it."

Her eyes shone. "Joshua."

He took a breath that felt like stepping off a cliff. "I love you."

The words hung there, heavy and bright and terrifying.

Her lips parted on a soft inhale, but she didn't rush to fill the silence. She only reached up and touched his cheek, thumb brushing lightly along the rough line of stubble.

He pushed on, because once he'd opened the door, the rest wouldn't stay back. "And that scares the shit out of me," he admitted. "I have never had anything permanent. Not parents, not a last name that didn't feel like it could be snatched away, not a house that wasn't somebody else's before me." He swallowed. "But you…You make this place feel like home in a way that has nothing to do with property lines."

Her thumb trembled against his skin.

"You're the person I picture when Hank says I shouldn't do this alone," he said. "You're the voice in my head when I'm about to be stupid. You're… the anchor I didn't know I was allowed to have."

Tears spilled over onto her cheeks, hot and sudden. She laughed through them, a wet, shaky sound. "You picked a hell of a way to say it," she whispered.

"Too much?" he asked, suddenly uncertain.

"No," she said, shaking her head. "Exactly enough." She leaned in and pressed her forehead to his. "I love you too. Still. Again. Always. But I'm not here to be your only anchor, Josh. I'm here to be one of many. You get to build the rest."

"Deal," he said, voice thick.

They lay there with their foreheads touching, breathing the same small pocket of air while his heart hammered and gradually, mercifully, began to slow.

Outside, the lake threw soft reflections against the ceiling, restless but contained.

"I might want to find her," he said after a long moment. "My aunt."

"Then we'll figure out how," she replied. "On your timeline. With whatever boundaries you need."

"We," he repeated, and this time the word settled in his chest like something that might last.

He pulled her closer, tucking her against him, and for the first time since the article, the file, the fire, the whispers, he let himself believe that love didn't have to mean an eventual exit. It could mean staying.

Chapter 37

Josh let go of Novah's hand to navigate the steep stairs to the boathouse. His boots tapped along the deck, echoed by the soft knock of lake water against the pilings. The air was thick with the green scent of algae and wet wood.

Behind him, Novah's laptop bag bumped gently against her hip as she walked, the nylon whispering against her jeans. She reached out once to trail her fingers along the railing, the almost-smooth composite wood shining in the early evening light, then let her hand drop to her side.

"Feels weird being here after the last couple of weeks at your house," she murmured.

"Yeah." Josh's voice came out low, the word disappearing into the slap of waves under the boards. "Least the wind's calm. Don't have to worry about the boat getting away from us."

Novah unlocked the office door so she could put her laptop on her desk and grab her purse before they headed out. The humidity caused the door to the outside storage where she stored her canoe and kayaks to stick. Josh pushed it open with his shoulder. The hinges complained in a long groan that set his teeth on edge. Inside, the dimness smelled like warm water, sun-baked wood, and the ghost of gasoline. Dust motes drifted in the slanted beams of light from the narrow windows, turning the air into slow-moving glitter.

He held the door for her. As she stepped past, her shoulder brushed his chest, a small, grounding contact. "You grab that end, and I'll grab this one."

They never made it that far.

The door slammed behind them with a sharp crack, harder than the breeze could manage. The vibration shivered through the floorboards under Josh's feet.

"What the—" he started, turning.

A man filled the doorway, one hand still on the knob. He was average height, wiry, his T-shirt hanging loose over jeans that had seen more parking asphalt than dirt. The thing that hit Josh first wasn't his build but his pale, washed-out blue eyes that didn't seem to settle on anything for long, skittering around the room like trapped flies. A camera strap hung crosswise over his chest, the plastic body of the camera resting against his hip like a holstered weapon.

"Door sticks," the man said, voice almost conversational. "You gotta put some muscle into it."

Novah's hand scraped against the edge of the table as she set her bag down slowly. The zipper pull clicked softly against the wood.

"Eric," she said. The name tasted like metal in her mouth.

Up close, he didn't look like a movie monster. He looked like the guy behind her at the grocery store, the one who never made eye contact. Slight sunburn on the bridge of his nose. A cowlick that refused to lie flat. A smudge of something—oil or charcoal—along the side of one thumb.

"Hey, Novah." His gaze flicked over her, then landed on Josh, pupils tightening. "Been wanting to meet like this for a while. Just us. Well. Plus the golden boy."

Josh's pulse jerked. His body wanted to move—forward, back, anywhere—but he forced his boots to stay planted shoulder-width apart, palms open and loose at his sides.

"You picked the wrong place just to drop by," he said. "Boathouse isn't open to the public."

Eric laughed, a short, breathless sound that didn't reach his eyes. "Oh, it's plenty public. People on this lake act like these docks are altars or something. All their big moments here." His gaze cut to Novah. "First time Daddy let you steer, right?"

The hair on the back of her neck prickled. "You've been watching us that long." Her voice came out steadier than she felt.

"Longer." He took a few unhurried steps into the room, letting the door drift almost closed behind him, leaving a thin blade of daylight at his back. The boards complained faintly under his boots. "You just didn't know to look."

Josh shifted his weight, casual, like he was adjusting his stance to lean against the post. It moved him half a foot closer to where an old boat hook leaned, handle worn smooth by years of hands.

"What do you want, Eric?" Josh asked, keeping his tone flat. "You didn't stalk a woman for months to comment on her family memories."

Eric's mouth twitched. "Straight to the point. That's what they wrote about you. Driven. Focused. Tunnel vision." He tipped his head, mocking thoughtfulness. "They left out 'ungrateful.' And 'stupid.'"

Novah's fingers, still resting on the table, found the edge of her purse. She curled them around the strap, drawing it closer by degrees.

"You've read his features," she said. "The articles. The profiles."

"Of course I have." Eric's voice warmed, a sudden flash of something like genuine enthusiasm. "Had a whole binder. Before Hank stole it." His eyes jittered to Josh. "You looked so shiny in those pictures. God's own potter. Poor orphaned boy makes good. People eat that shit up."

He took another step, angle shifting so that the wedge of light behind him fell across his face. It etched new lines into the hollows under his eyes, pulled hard years into the corners of his mouth.

"You know what nobody wrote?" he asked softly. "Nobody wrote about the kid who wasn't good enough. The one whose dad drank and swung and never gave him anything but bruises. The one who watched the nice couple in the blue Chevy take their perfect baby home from the grocery store, three Saturdays in a row."

Josh's stomach turned to stone. "Chevelle," he said before he could stop himself. "It was a Chevelle."

Eric's gaze snapped to him, hungry, as if he'd finally heard the note he'd been waiting for. "You do remember." He smiled, thin and sharp. "That's cute."

"I don't remember you," Josh said. He could feel Novah's eyes on his profile, the weight of her attention like a hand between his shoulder blades. "You were just another face. If you were even there."

"I was," Eric said. "At the store. At the gas station. At the stop sign, they always hesitated like they couldn't decide if they wanted to go left or right." His breath came a little faster. "And that night. Most important of all, that night."

The boathouse seemed to shrink. Outside, the gentle slap of water against the pilings went on, oblivious.

"Eric." Novah kept her voice low, deliberately non-threatening, the way she'd speak to a skittish panel interviewee. "Why don't you sit down? You're rambling. I can tell you have a lot to say. Might as well get comfortable."

His head jerked toward her, jaw tightening. For a second, Josh's muscles coiled, ready for something sharp and stupid.

Then Eric huffed, shoulders loosening a fraction. "You always did know how to talk on the page," he said. "Figured you'd know how to do it in person, too." He glanced at the folding chair and sneered. "I'll stand."

Josh slid his phone from his pocket with a slow, practiced movement, letting the denim drag along its case to mask the motion. The familiar weight settled against his palm, reassuring.

"You said 'that night,'" Josh said. "The night of the wreck." He stepped into the opening, giving Novah space to draw her bag all the way onto the table, the zipper just within reach of her thumb. "What about it?"

Eric's throat moved as he swallowed. His hand lifted unconsciously toward the camera at his side, fingers tapping along the lens in a restless rhythm.

"They're telling you now it wasn't an accident," he said. "Homicide. Cold case. All those fancy words." His mouth twisted. "Like they suddenly give a shit twenty-eight years too late."

Novah's heart thudded painfully against her ribs. She knew the article by heart. The phrases tasted too familiar to be a coincidence.

"You read the Butler piece," she said. "The one from 2017."

"Course I did." He took one more step, enough that Josh could see the fine tremor in his hands. "I was the anonymous tip. Thought if they reopened it, they'd finally see what happened. That somebody might look at those skid marks with actual eyes."

Josh's grip on his phone tightened, the edges biting into his palm. "You called it in?"

"I did more than call," Eric said, voice sharpening. "I made it happen."

The words dropped into the boathouse like a stone into still water. The air seemed to ripple around them.

Josh's hearing narrowed, the distant lap of the lake fading to a dull hum. "You're saying you caused the wreck."

Eric's gaze went distant for a heartbeat, like he was watching an old home movie, only he could see. "Their taillights were this soft, stupid red in the fog," he said. "They drove so slowly on that stretch. Always careful. Hands at ten and two. Signal every turn." His lip curled. "They'd stop at the shoulder sometimes and hand you crackers. Like you were some charity case. Like that made them saints."

Josh's stomach turned. He had faint, flickering images of hands passing him something salty and dry in crinkling plastic, of soft voices saying easy, buddy, we got you. He had always assumed those flashes belonged to foster parents, not his birth parents.

"They slowed in that curve that night, too," Eric went on. "Fog thick as milk. I was thirteen. I knew that road better than they did. Knew the curve. Knew the drop." His pale eyes focused again, drilling into Josh. "I rolled a log down the hill, just as they approached. He saw it at the last minute and swerved to miss it. The tire caught in that ditch, and he overcorrected. Steel and glass and screaming."

His shoulders rose and fell in a sharp breath that sounded too close to a laugh. "Your car hit that guardrail like it was paper. They never fixed the angle. Cops called it bad weather. Told me to go home."

Josh's knees felt suddenly unreliable. He locked them, forcing himself upright. The boathouse swam slightly, edges softening.

"You did it because… why?" he asked. His voice had gone hoarse. "Because they were nice to you?"

"Because they were my proof," Eric snapped. "Proof that the world was rigged. That some people got pretty little wives who made casseroles and dads who showed up for games. That some kids got bedtime stories and others got told they were a mistake." His jaw clenched, tendons standing out. "Your mom smiled at me once. At the store. My dad said, 'Figures she'd waste kindness on the wrong kid.'"

He spread his hands, fingers shaking. "So I made sure she didn't waste any more."

The raw, broken logic in his voice scraped something deep inside Novah. She had written characters like this. Men whose warped tenderness turned to violence when the world didn't match the storylines in their heads.

"You were a kid," she said quietly. "A hurt one. And then nobody caught it. Nobody helped. They just called it an accident and left you alone with what you'd done."

His eyes flicked to her, a flash of something like gratitude sparking under the anger before drowning again. "Don't you therapize me," he said, but it lacked teeth.

Josh forced a slow breath through his nose. "You've been following me since."

"Second cousin," Eric said abruptly. "That's what the paperwork calls it. Your mom's cousin and my dad were brothers." He snorted. "Small gene pool around here. You were the one who got out clean. Pricey adoption." His gaze wandered over Josh's shoulders, his hands, his jaw. "They gave you everything."

"They gave me a roof and rules," Josh said, bitterness slipping out before he could catch it. "They didn't give me them."

Eric's fingers curled into fists at his sides. "You still had more than I did. You had talent that people actually valued. People came to see your work. Wrote articles. Took pictures. Made you a hero on paper."

Josh's phone was warm against his palm. His thumb found the side button by touch, pressing until he felt the faint buzz of the screen waking. Six quick taps, no more pressure than the twitch of a muscle. The shared code he and Hank had set up the week after the anonymous call: 911 and leave the line open. He hesitated long enough for dispatch to pick up. He hoped.

"You burned the studio," Josh said. Saying it out loud steadied him, like hauling a pot onto the wheel and slamming it down. "You called me a pyro on the phone. You used paint thinner, not turpentine. You made sure the rumor was loud enough for the whole town to hear."

Eric gave him a thin, satisfied smile. "Somebody had to knock you back into reality. You were too comfortable. Too… loved." His gaze slid to Novah, lingering. "You get dangerous when you start believing you deserve that."

Novah's pulse thudded in her ears. "Dangerous to who?" she asked. "To you?"

"To women like you." His lip curled. "Sunshine girls who think they can save sad men with hot sex and casseroles. My mom was one of those. You know what she got for it? Split lip and a lifetime of apologizing for his bad days."

He pointed at Josh without looking away from her. "He's the same model. Just shinier. Left unattended, he'll burn everything you build together. So I accelerated the timeline. Cleared the board."

"You set his life on fire to 'protect' me." Novah let incredulity color the words, not mockery. She needed him talking, not lunging.

"I set his shrine on fire," Eric corrected. "So people would see what he really is. Insurance money, sympathy, the whole town chasing his pain. You know how many times I heard your name in the same breath? 'Poor Josh. Poor Novah.' Like you were some tragic power couple the county needed to rally around." His laugh came out ragged. "You two are one lightning strike away from a Lifetime movie."

Chapter 38

Josh cataloged exits and obstacles automatically, the way Hank had drilled into him. Door behind Eric—blocked. Two windows, one to the water, one to the trees. The water side had a boat still tied, rope looped twice around the cleat. If he could get Eric three steps farther in, he'd have a path past him to the dock.

"You think burning down my studio exposed me?" Josh asked. "What do you think this is doing? Walking into a locked boathouse with a stalker rap sheet a mile long and confessing to homicide."

Eric's smile thinned. "You won't tell. You're not built for that kind of fight. You fold when it gets too loud. I've seen it." He jerked his chin toward Novah again. "Besides, if you push this, she loses the boathouse. The aura. The story. You want to be the reason this place gets bullet points on a crime podcast?"

Novah's laugh was soft and disbelieving. "You really don't understand how stories work," she said. "People don't fall in love with shrines, Eric. They fall in love with the people who survive them."

"Survive?" His breathing sped, chest rising and falling faster. "You think this is survival? Walking around every day knowing he was the kid they picked while the rest of us rotted?

Her fingertips brushed the corner of her purse, feeling for the shape of her phone through the canvas. The weight of it was a small, square comfort.

"You know what I see when I look at you?" she asked quietly. "I see a man who has been rehearsing this speech in his head for years. Maybe decades. Every little injustice sharpened to a point. But you picked the wrong script."

Eric snarled, the sound sharp in the cramped space. "What the hell does that mean?"

"You keep casting Josh as your father," she said, voice steady. "Drunk. Violent. Careless with lives. You set fires and then blame him for the smoke. But that thirteen-year-old on the side of the road? That kid who shoved a log down a hill because he thought it might erase the unfairness?" She shook her head. "That's your father's son, not his."

For the first time, something like doubt flickered across Eric's face. His stance wavered, weight shifting from one foot to the other.

Josh seized the moment, his tone mild. "She's good at this," he said. "Reading people. Seeing what they're not saying. You've probably read her books. You know that."

Eric's shoulders jerked. "I read them," he muttered. "Every one. She writes the truth cloaked in bullshit. Women eat it up."

"Then you know how this scene ends," Novah said. "The guy who walks into the boathouse with a confession and a grudge does not get the girl. He gets handcuffs."

As she spoke, she slid her phone free under the cover of the table edge. The smooth glass was cool against her fingertips. She flicked it awake with a practiced motion, thumb dancing over the screen without looking: Hank, open chat, three quick words typed in a shorthand they'd joked about once and then agreed to for real—BOAT. HERE. NOW.

Her thumb hit send. You could barely hear the tiny whoosh of the app over the waves lapping below them.

Josh kept talking, voice calm, carrying over the subtle digital sound. “You said you were my second cousin,” he said. “You’ve had twenty-something years to decide what that means. You picked arson and anonymous calls. That’s on you. Not me. Not her. Not some thirteen-year-old version of you standing in the fog.”

“Don’t you dare pity me,” Eric snapped. The camera strap creaked as his fingers tightened around it.

“I don’t,” Josh said. “I just know this lake. I know what happens when people try to hold their breath and swim across with pockets full of rocks. They drown.” He tipped his head toward the water beyond the wall. “You are sinking in your own lies, man.”

“Lies?” Eric’s voice went shrill at the edges. “You want lies? How about the one where you tell her you can keep her safe when there’s cameras pointed at her from the trees? Or the one where you pretend you don’t like the way they talk about you like you’re some tragic hero?”

Josh took a slow step sideways, angling his body between Eric and Novah, moving closer to the wall with the window that faced the shore.

“You’re right about one thing,” he said. “I can’t promise to keep her safe from everything. Neither can you. But I can promise to stand between her and the man who lit my life on fire and called it a favor.”

He stopped, just under the window. From here, he could see the glint of Hank’s patrol truck through the dusty glass, parked half down the lane to the dock. Relief washed through him, sharp enough to sting.

A distant crunch of gravel carried faintly through the floorboards, followed by the subtle shift in the air pressure that came when another door at the far end of the dock opened.

Eric heard it too. His head whipped toward the boathouse door, muscles tensing. “You called him,” he hissed. “You—”

“Easy,” Josh said, lifting both hands in a pacifying gesture, palms out. “You walk out on your own feet, talk to Hank like a man, you get to tell your side. You bolt, it ends with you face-down in lake mud or worse.”

Eric’s gaze darted between them, between the door and the back window, calculating. The world narrowed down to the twitch of tendons in his throat, the flex of his fingers around the camera, the way his knees bent as if he might spring.

“Eric,” Novah said, a thread of steel under the softness now. “Look at me.

Against apparent instinct, he did.

"This is the part where you decide if you're the villain forever or if you're the guy who finally stops the cycle," she said. "You keep saying you did what you did to protect women like me from men like him. Her mouth quirked. "Well, I'm telling you. He's not your father. And you are not obligated to be his ghost."

Something in his expression cracked. His shoulders slumped, just slightly, like someone had cut the strings holding them taut.

Outside, boots thudded along the dock, the sound hollow and sure. Hank's voice, muffled by the door, called, "Josh. Novah. You in there?"

Josh didn't look away from Eric. "Yeah," he called back. "We're here. And so is he."

Eric let out a strangled sound, halfway between a sob and a scoff. "Traitors," he whispered. "Both of you."

"You walked in holding the matches," Josh said quietly. "We just took the lighter."

The doorknob rattled. Hank pushed the door open a foot, gun drawn but low, two deputies stacked behind him. Light knifed into the boathouse, catching the smear of sweat along Eric's temple, the ragged rise and fall of his chest.

"Eric Morrow," Hank said, voice gone flat and formal. "Hands where I can see them. Now."

Eric's throat bobbed. For a heartbeat, Josh thought he might reach for the camera, bring it up like a shield.

Then, slowly, Eric lifted both hands, fingers spread, the strap of the camera dragging against his shirt with a soft rasp.

"Good choice," Novah murmured.

Hank and his deputies moved in, efficient, the air suddenly full of the rustle of fabric, the clink of metal. Cold cuffs snapped around Eric's wrists with a decisive, echoing click.

"You're under arrest for arson, stalking, and on suspicion of homicide related to the Gann case out of Butler," Hank recited, voice steady. "You have the right to remain silent…"

As he spoke, Eric's gaze found Josh one last time over his shoulder. The hatred there was still burning, but under it something smaller and sad flickered—like a kid realizing the game was over and he'd lost.

"They'll still talk about you," Eric said, words slurred by emotion. "Even when I'm gone. You can't scrub smoke off a story."

Josh swallowed, forcing himself not to look away. "Maybe," he said. "But at least now they'll be talking about the truth."

Hank steered Eric toward the door, deputies flanking. The floorboards hummed under their combined weight as they stepped back out onto the dock.

The boathouse exhaled.

For a moment, Josh and Novah just stood there, listening to the receding footsteps, the murmur of radio chatter drifting in through the open door.

Then Josh realized his hands were still up, palms out. He let them drop, fingers tingling.

"You okay?" he asked, turning toward her.

Novah's knees chose that moment to stop pretending they were reliable. She sank onto the edge of the table, hands braced on either side, the wood cool under her palms.

"I will be," she said. Her voice shook once. "Are you?"

He took the two steps between them and sank to a crouch so they were eye level. Sweat had dampened the collar of his shirt, making it cling to the back of his neck. His heart still hammered, too fast and too hard.

"Ask me again after my hands stop buzzing," he said. "But yeah. Better than I would've been six months ago."

Footsteps returned, slower, heavier. Hank stepped back into the doorway alone this time, hat in hand, lines around his mouth deeper than when he'd left.

"You two did good," he said. "Kept him talking. Got him to hang himself with his own tongue. Dispatch has the recording from your phone, Josh. Every word he spat is on the line."

Josh blinked. "You stayed on the call."

"Soon as it pinged my phone with that code." Hank tapped his chest pocket where his cell sat. "You did exactly what we talked about. Proud of you."

He turned his attention to both of them, shoulders squaring. "Just so we're clear—and so I can say it out loud, in this place where he stood—you, Josh, are officially and completely cleared in the studio fire."

The words landed like a physical weight lifted. Josh's chest expanded on a breath that didn't hitch halfway for the first time in weeks.

"We matched Eric's prints to the paint thinner can we pulled from the rubble," Hank continued. "His DNA's on the rags we found in the alley dumpster. His phone has search histories that read like a how-to manual for amateur arsonists. With his confession today tied to the recorded call to your phone and the walls of his camper, there's not a jury in this county or the next that's going to buy the town gossip ever again."

Novah let out a watery laugh. "Can we get you to repeat that at the fundraiser?"

Hank's mouth twitched. "Funny you should say that." He sobered. "One step at a time. Today, we get him processed. Tomorrow, we start cleaning up the mess he left behind—legally and otherwise."

He hesitated, then added, "Also, Butler PD and the DA down there are pretty interested in that little speech he gave about your parents' wreck. Between what we pulled from the Chevelle and his oral diarrhea today, they've got enough to move that case from 'homicide, unknown suspect' to 'homicide with a name.' You might get another call from them. But if you do, you won't be going into that alone."

Josh nodded once, throat tight. "I know," he said. He glanced at Novah. "I have… backup now."

Hank followed his gaze and softened. "Damn right you do." He tipped his hat back on. "I'll let the two of you breathe. Got paperwork screaming my name. Y'all need anything, you call. No more playing phone tag with psychos."

When he left, the boathouse seemed to stretch back to its normal size. The lake sounds returned to full volume—the gentle slap of waves, the far-off buzz of a boat motor, a gull's indignant cry.

Josh pushed to his feet and offered Novah his hand. "Come on," he said quietly. "Let's get out of here. This place has seen enough ghosts for one day."

She slid her fingers into his. Her palm was damp, her grip firm. As she stood, her shoulder bumped his chest. She didn't step away.

Halfway to the door, she stopped and looked back once at the scuffed floor, the folding chairs, the fan still whirring uselessly in the corner.

"This was where I learned to steer," she said. "Fitting, it's where we finally got a clean line on who's been trying to run us off the road."

Josh squeezed her hand. "Yeah," he said. "But from now on, this place is about us. Not him."

They stepped out into the sunlight together, boots thudding in unison on the dock. The breeze off the water lifted the damp hair at the nape of Josh's neck and carried away the lingering scent of gasoline and old fear.

Novah leaned into his side, just enough that their hips brushed with each step. "You kept your promise," she said. "You didn't shut me out. You stood in front of me, but you never once tried to push me out of the scene."

He huffed a breath that was almost a laugh. “You kept your promise, too,” he said. “You didn’t fix me. You helped me fight.”

At the top of the dock, he stopped, tugging her gently until she faced him. The lake glittered behind her, broken light dancing on the surface.

“We literally just faced down the guy who burned my life to the ground,” he said. “And you’re still here.”

“Where else would I be?” she asked. The wind tugged a strand of hair loose from her knot, and he reached up without thinking to tuck it behind her ear. Her skin was warm under his fingers.

“Home,” he said, the word catching a little. “You’re home.”

Her eyes softened. “So are you.

He bent his head and kissed her, slow and sure, the taste of lake air and adrenaline and something steadier threading between them. For the first time since he’d watched flames chew through his old studio walls, the future didn’t look like a blank, charred space. It looked like a path—crooked, muddy, maybe—but one they were walking together.

Chapter 39

Folding chairs scraped against the scuffed town hall floor as people shifted, the low hum of conversation swelling and breaking like shallow waves. The smell of coffee, sheet cake, and damp denim hung in the air, threaded with a faint whiff of smoke from the firehouse bay where someone had opened a truck door too long.

Josh stood off to the side near the wall of framed black and white photos of past fire chiefs, the rough plaster cool against his shoulder. Beside him, Novah's arm brushed his every so often when someone squeezed past, each brief contact a steadying little bump.

Up front, Alexis finished rattling off raffle winners and bake sale totals, her voice bright over the microphone. "Last thing on the agenda before y'all bolt for the dessert table," she said, "Sheriff Hank's got a few words about the recent arson investigation."

The room tightened. Conversations stuttered and died. A few heads angled, instinctively tracking Josh where he stood.

Hank stepped up, the microphone squealing once as he adjusted it with a practiced flick of his fingers. His tan uniform looked more rumpled than usual, the lines around his eyes deeper, but his voice came out clear.

"Most of you know we've been working with the state and the feds on the fire at Josh's studio," he began. "You also know this town has had more rumors floating around than ducks on the lake." A few uneasy chuckles rippled through the room.

Josh's jaw flexed. Novah's hand slid down, fingers brushing his knuckles. He didn't look at her, but he took her hand in his.

"So let me be plain," Hank said, voice firming. "The fire was arson. The evidence—the lab work on the accelerant, the prints on the gas can, the camera from the ridge, and, most importantly, the confession we recorded—puts it squarely on one person's shoulders. Eric Morrow."

A buzz shot through the crowd, low and sharp. Someone muttered, "Knew it," under her breath. Someone else sucked air between their teeth.

"And just as important," Hank continued, raising his hand until the room quieted, "that same evidence clears Josh. Completely. His hands are clean. The paint thinner used wasn't even something he kept on site. We have Eric's prints at the scene and on the tools he used. We have his voice on a recorded call, bragging about it."

The words settled over Josh like warm water, heavy and easing at once. The knot that had lived under his sternum since the fire eased a notch.

Hank looked straight at him. "Josh has been cooperative with this investigation from day one," he said. "He let us tear apart what was left of his life, more than once. He worked with us every time we needed him, even when it meant reliving the worst day of his career and parts of his childhood that should've stayed buried." He let that hang a beat. "He deserves your respect. Not your suspicion."

A little heat prickled the backs of Josh's eyes. He blinked it away, swallowing.

Hank turned back to the room. "This fundraiser is for the volunteer fire department that fought that blaze and every other one in this county. It's about keeping each other safe. So if you got questions, you come to me. Not to the gossip mill." He tapped the mic lightly. "That's all."

Applause broke out—scattered at first, then gathering strength until it filled the hall in a rough, uneven wave. It wasn't a stadium roar, but it wasn't the pointed silence he'd gotten at the grocery store, either.

As people started moving toward the folding tables loaded with casseroles and pies, Josh stayed where he was, letting the flow of bodies eddy around him.

The man from Rowan's Hearth—compact, gray-haired, with a perpetual coffee stain on his shirt—hesitated a few feet away, then squared his shoulders and approached. The smell of fresh cinnamon rolls clung to his shirt.

"Josh," he said, voice gruff. "Got a second?"

Josh braced automatically, then forced his shoulders down. "Yeah."

The man cleared his throat, gaze snagging somewhere around Josh's chest instead of his eyes. "Couple months back, you came into the bakery. I gave you a look I had no business giving you." He shifted, the plastic plate in his hand creaking. "I listened to more talk than facts. That's on me. I'm sorry."

The apology landed with a dull, unexpected weight. Josh blew out a quiet breath. "Appreciate you saying that," he said. "Thought maybe I started making my coffee wrong."

The man huffed a short laugh, some tension loosening from his shoulders. "You come in tomorrow, your coffee and a cinnamon roll are on me. And if you don't, I'm leaving instructions with Jaxxon to charge me for it. Try and stop me."

Behind him, one of the women from the grocery store—one half of the gossiping pair he had overheard by the meat counter—hovered, hands wrapped tight around a Styrofoam cup. Her lipstick was brighter than he remembered; her expression, smaller.

"Josh?" she ventured when the baker stepped away. "I just…wanted to say I was wrong." Her fingers worried at the rim of the cup, squeaking faintly. "We all thought we knew what happened. I should've kept my mouth shut until we did." She swallowed. "I'm sorry for what I said. For how I looked at you."

He could still hear the hissed words. Insurance money. Burned it himself. The echo hurt less than it used to.

"Thanks," he said simply. "Words carry in a town this size."

Her face flushed. "I know," she said. "That's…kind of the problem." She glanced at Novah. "Loved your last book, by the way." Then she made a quick retreat toward the dessert line.

Novah let out a breath she hadn't realized she'd been holding. "That felt surreal," she murmured. "In a good way."

"Yeah." He watched Hank laugh at something Jaxxon said by the door. The sheriff's shoulders finally loosened a notch. "Feels like somebody turned the volume down on the static."

"Ready to get out of here before someone drags you into a selfie and hashtags it #LocalHero?" she asked, eyes glinting.

He snorted. "Please, no." He tipped his head toward the exit. "Come on. Wanna show you something."

The air near the lake carried a sharper chill, crisp with water and cut wood instead of recycled town hall breath. The new studio's skeleton rose out of the dirt like a promise—framing complete, plywood skin in place, windows still just empty rectangles looking out toward the water. The tang of fresh-cut lumber mixed with the faint, smoky ghost of the old fire, a contrast that sat oddly in Josh's nose.

He pushed the temporary door open and gestured her inside. "Watch your step. There's still a couple rogue nails."

Her boots thunked on the raw subfloor as they walked into what would become the gallery. Sunlight poured through the big front windows, turning dust motes into lazy constellations.

"Okay," he said, rubbing his palms on his jeans, suddenly more nervous than when he'd walked into the town hall. "Picture this with actual walls. Over here," he nodded toward the right wall, "shelving for the everyday stuff. Mugs, bowls, plates. Center of the room, pedestals for bigger pieces. Back there," he pointed toward the rear, "small bistro tables, coffee, snacks from Rowan's and Hensley's. People can sit, breathe, stare at clay until they remember their own pulse."

Her mouth curved, eyes tracking where he pointed. "It's going to be gorgeous," she said. "Open, but still cozy."

He exhaled, some of his tension bleeding away. "That's the idea." He led her toward the far left corner, where a shorter wall jutted, creating a nook by the window. A couple of two-by-fours still stuck out at odd angles, like unfinished thoughts.

"And this," he said, "is the part I didn't tell the foreman." He turned to face her. "Well, I told him about the shelves. Not the why."

She lifted a brow. “You keeping a secret library of smuggled whiskey in here?”

“Tempting,” he said. “But no.” He gestured to the blank wall. “This is the author’s corner. Local writers. Paperbacks, some signed hardcovers. Maybe a comfy chair if the fire marshal doesn’t yell at me. People can grab a book with their coffee, or pick something up after they look at the pottery.”

Her breath caught. “Author Corner,” she repeated slowly.

He nodded, suddenly aware of his own heartbeat. “You said once this town liked the idea of you more than the reality. That they wanted the cute stories, not the ones that poke at systems that fail kids.” He shrugged, the motion rough. “So I’m giving you a wall in a place they already come to feel good. They can pick up your books because they want something to read with their grinder, not because they’re braced for a lecture.”

Chapter 40

Novah stepped closer to the window, fingertips grazing the unfinished stud, the wood rough and splintery under her skin. Outside, the lake glittered through the empty frame, light winking on the surface.

"You're making room for my words alongside your work," she said. It wasn't a question.

"Your books are work," he said quietly. "Same as my clay. You don't get relegated to some back table afterthought." He cleared his throat. "And yeah, selfishly, it means I get to see your name on my wall every day."

Her eyes shone, but she blinked the wetness back before it spilled. "Josh…" The syllable came out on a breath. "You know what that feels like?"

He gave a half smile. "Like free inventory for you?"

"Like you're telling the town I belong here," she said. "Not just online. Not just in some article. Here. In this room."

He stepped into the nook, the two of them fitting in the small space with the easy brush of shoulders and the faint creak of the subfloor. "You do belong here," he said. "With me. With this lake. With everything that comes next."

She swallowed, then drew in a steadier breath. "About that." Her fingers toyed with the hem of her sleeve, twisting the fabric once before letting it go. "I've been working on something."

His brows rose. "On deadline, Novah, working on something? Should I be alarmed?"

"A little," she said, a wry tilt to her mouth. "It's a new project. Different tone. Closer to what my blog's turned into." She drew a small notebook from her bag—leather cover scuffed, edges soft from use—and flipped it open to a page marked with a sticky note.

He noticed the tremor in her hand as she held it out. "I wanted you to see this before my editor ever does. Before anyone does."

He took the notebook carefully. Her handwriting curved across the page in dark blue ink, a few sentences underlined, a couple of words scratched out.

A boy who grew up on paper instead of memory, it read. Case files and adoption decrees told him who he was supposed to be. The lake told him something else. So did the woman who put his story on the page, even when it hurt.

Underneath, another line: He was never research. He was the question the whole town should've been asking.

His throat tightened. The letters blurred for a second before sharpening again.

"This is…about me," he said slowly. "And not about me."

She nodded. "It's fiction. Names changed, places smudged. Some pieces will be you, some won't. But I wanted you to know up front that I'm drawing from us. From the fire, from the article, from you telling me the first happy memory you could remember. No surprises. No 'by the way, I wrote something that might sound familiar.'"

He traced a knuckle lightly under the line about research, not quite touching the page. "You're putting my mess into a story on purpose this time," he said. "With my eyes open."

"Yes." She held his gaze. "If you tell me you can't stand it, I'll scrap it. I mean that. I'll find another backbone for the book. But when I look at the kids I've been writing about—the ones who get lost in red tape—it feels wrong not to show one who crawled back out, even if his knees are still bloody."

He let out a slow breath, the smell of sawdust and lake air settling in his lungs. "You think I've crawled out?"

"Bloodied, yes," she said softly. "Standing, also yes."

He flipped the notebook closed and handed it back. "Then write him," he said. "Write the kid with the paper life and the lake and the woman who's too stubborn to let him drown."

Her shoulders dropped, tension draining like air from a balloon. "You're sure?"

"Long as you keep doing what you just did," he said. "Letting me in before the rest of the world reads it. No feeling like I'm finding out about my life in print with everybody else."

"Deal," she said. "Full informed consent." A small smile tugged at her lips. "Consider it a standing research contract."

"With fringe benefits," he said, leaning forward to brush a quick kiss against her mouth.

She laughed softly, the sound bouncing off the bare studs. “Obviously.”

They ended the tour on the back deck, where new boards overlooked the stretch of grass running down to the water. The lake lapped lazily at the shore, each ripple catching the late afternoon sun in flashes of silver. Farther along, the boathouse roof peeked through the trees on the slight curve of shoreline.

Josh leaned his forearms on the unfinished railing, the raw wood rough against his skin. Novah stood beside him, elbow brushing his. The air smelled of lake water, sap, and a faint trace of the burger smoke that seemed permanently embedded in his hoodie.

“Been thinking,” he said.
“Dangerous,” she murmured.

He huffed. “Smart ass.” He rolled a small splinter between thumb and forefinger, grounding himself before the words. “Hank gave me an address. For Lila.” Her name felt strange and new in his mouth. “My aunt.”

Novah’s gaze flicked to his face, then back out over the water. “Yeah?”

“Yeah.” He watched a pair of ducks cut a V across the surface. “Couple weeks ago, the idea of knocking on her door made me want to puke. Felt like picking at a scab that never healed right." He swallowed. "Now, it feels more like…finishing a sentence that's been hanging for thirty years."

She was quiet for a moment, the wind teasing a strand of hair loose to tickle her cheek. "What are you thinking?" she asked. "About her. About us."

He turned to face her fully, leaning back against the rail. "I'm thinking I don't want to do that alone," he said. "And I'm thinking there's no version of my life going forward where we keep living like we're just borrowing each other's houses."

Her brows lifted. "That's a lot of thinking," she said lightly, but her pulse fluttered at the base of her throat.

He reached into his pocket and pulled out a small key ring, the metal warm from his palm. A new brass key, edges still sharp, glinted beside his truck key.

He held it out on his open palm. "So," he said, "here's what I'm proposing. Two concrete things. One: We set a date. Two months from now. We drive to see Lila. Together. If I chicken out, you get to call me on it. If I want to bail halfway there, you get to pull into the diner parking lot and make me breathe through it."

Her fingers closed gently around the edge of the key ring, metal ticking softly against metal. "Okay," she said. "That's the first thing."

"Second," he said, curling his hand so the keys slid into hers, "you take this. Full-time. No more 'just in case' overnight bags. No more pretending you're just visiting when half your stuff lives in my drawers already."

Her thumb rubbed over the grooves of the new key, feeling the tiny ridges. "You're asking me to move in," she said, voice low.

"I'm asking us to move toward something on purpose," he said. "My place, your boathouse, the studio, they're all within shouting distance. We can figure out exactly where we sleep most nights. But this—" he tapped the key—"means you never have to ask if you're welcome. This means home isn't a question mark anymore."

She looked up at him, eyes bright, wind bringing a faint flush to her cheeks. "What about your go bag?" she asked softly. "Do you keep it packed?"

He let out a slow breath. "I was thinking the next time we go back to my house, we unpack it together," he said. "Maybe not trash the bag—I've been too attached to that ugly thing—but take the clothes out, put them in drawers like normal people. Leave the cash in the safe instead of the closet."

"Symbolic," she said.

"Concrete," he countered. "Even if my stomach flips while we do it."

She turned the keyring over once, twice, then closed her hand around it, the metal imprinting faint crescents into her palm. "Okay," she said. "Two months from now, we'll go see Lila. Together. And tonight, we unpack the go bag." Her mouth tipped into a crooked smile. "But I'm keeping a toothbrush in the boathouse. I'm not giving up my writing cave."

"Wouldn't dream of it," he said. "I like knowing where to find you when you're hiding from deadlines." He paused, and the corner of his mouth lifted. "Or me."

She slipped the keys into her front pocket, the small weight settling against her hip. Then she reached out, sliding both hands up his chest to loop around the back of his neck

"Feels like a big step," she murmured. "Without bells or fireworks."

He rested his hands on her waist, thumbs brushing the warm sliver of skin where her shirt had ridden up. "Fireworks are overrated," he said. "We've had enough explosions for one lifetime."

The lake murmured against the shore below, the sound steady and familiar. A fish jumped, the splash punctuating the moment like a small exclamation mark.

"Hey, Josh?" she said.

"Yeah?"

"This—" she tapped his chest lightly, over his heart—"this is home too. Even when it scares you.

He swallowed, the lump in his throat tightening and then loosening. "I know," he said. "You're the only person who ever made it feel that way."

He bent his head and kissed her, slow and grounded, nothing rushed or frantic. The taste of her—coffee from the meeting, a hint of sugar from a stolen cookie, and something entirely her own—settled on his tongue. The wind lifted around them, cool fingers ruffling his hair, carrying away the last faint trace of smoke from the old fire.

When they broke apart, foreheads resting together, the new studio behind them and the lake in front, the future no longer felt like running from something. It felt like walking toward it, keys in hand, together.

Epilogue

The bell over the Gann Studio & Gallery door chimed in a bright, familiar jangle as the lunchtime rush thinned to a lazy trickle. The air inside held the warm, comforting mix of espresso, clay dust, and roasted garlic from the panini press in the back. Sun poured through the front windows, spilling across shelves of colorful mugs and bowls and catching on the glossy curves of larger pieces arranged on pedestals

Josh wiped a damp ring off one of the bistro tables with the edge of a dish towel, the wood smooth and worn under his palm. A couple from out of town hovered near a display of lake blue vases, murmuring over which one would look better on their mantle. At the author corner, a teenager in a fire department hoodie flipped through a paperback with Novah's name in looping script across the cover.

The wall of books still made his chest tighten in a good way every time he looked at it. The shelves, stained a shade darker than the floor, held spines in every color—local histories, romance, mystery. Novah's series clustered together, the newest release at eye level, its cover glossy and pristine.

A small crowd had gathered around the register for the informal signing Alexis had bullied Novah into doing. The low buzz of conversation mixed with the soft whir of the espresso machine as Jaxxon Rowan's nephew pulled another shot behind the small coffee counter.

Novah sat on a high stool near the Author Corner, a stack of her books at her elbow and a blue gel pen between her fingers. Her hair was twisted up in a loose knot, a few strands escaping to brush her neck. A faint smudge of ink stained the side of her hand where it rested on the top book.

"Name?" she asked the woman in front of her.

"Beth," the woman said, cheeks flushed. "And, um, my sister? She couldn't make it. Kayla."

Novah smiled, dipping her head as she wrote. The quick, confident scratch of her pen carried faintly to where Josh stood.

To Beth and Kayla, she wrote. May you always know that home is a who, not a where.

She paused, then added a small heart and her signature.

When the line finally dwindled and Alexis called a break, Novah slid off the stool, flexing her cramped fingers. The cartilage in her knees popped softly as her feet hit the floor. She stepped around the table, the hem of her soft green dress brushing against Josh's jeans as she reached him.

"You survived your first in-store signing," he said, handing her a paper cup of water. Condensation had already beaded along the side, cool against his fingertips.

She took it, the cold shocking her pleasantly as she lifted it to her lips. "Barely," she said. "I forgot how much my hand hates my career." She wiggled her ink-stained fingers. "But the dedication looks good in print."

He glanced at the display copy propped on a stand, the dust jacket already showing the faintest hint of wear at the corners from being picked up so many times. Inside the front, in simple black font, the dedication read:

For the man who taught me home is a who, not a where.

Heat crept up his neck. "Crazy woman," he muttered, but there was no bite in it.

She bumped her shoulder lightly against his. "You started it," she said. "You gave me a wall."

He took a breath of clay-scented air and let it out slowly. Beyond the shelves, a little girl tugged on her dad's sleeve, pointing up at a collection of mugs with mismatched handles.

"The gallery looks good full," Novah said quietly, following his gaze. "Feels…right."

"It does," he agreed. The low hum of voices, the clink of ceramic against ceramic, the gentle hiss of the espresso machine—all the sounds he'd heard in his head when he first sketched the plans—wrapped around him like a well-worn hoodie.

His phone buzzed in his pocket with a reminder. He fished it out, thumb swiping the notification away. "Speaking of full," he said, "renters are moving into my place tomorrow. Hailey dropped the lease off this morning."

Her brows lifted. "So it's official official," she said. "No more 'we're just seeing how it goes' on the living arrangement."

He grinned, crooked and real. “Pretty sure the dozen boxes of your books in my hallway made it official,” he said. “But yeah. Paperwork helps. You ready to have me underfoot at your house permanently?”

“You? Underfoot?” She snorted softly. “You get up before God most days. The house barely knows you’re there before you leave for the studio.”

“Hey, I make my presence known,” he protested. “I leave coffee mugs in at least three rooms.”

Her mouth tilted. “Fair point,” she said. “Our house.” She tested the phrase, rolling it around like a new piece of dialogue. “Weird to say. Still fits.”

He reached out, brushing his knuckles along the inside of her wrist where a faint smear of blue ink trailed toward her pulse. Her skin was warm, the beat steady under his touch.

“Close up with me?” he asked. “I was thinking we could head down to the rocks before the sun drops.”

“The rocks, huh?” Her eyes glinted. “Bold choice, Gann.”

He felt his ears heat again, remembering slick stone and desperate hands and the sharp, breathless rush of that first time. “Less panic this round,” he said. “More…breathing.”

"Sold," she said. "Let me sign a last couple of books, then you can kick people out."

He watched her move back to the table, the easy way she slipped into conversation with a reader who asked about the new book. The anxiety she carried into the world with her last release—about being "too much," about losing her mask—was still there, but now it sat beside a new steadiness. She knew who would show up for her. So did he.

Twenty minutes later, the lights in the gallery glowed soft and low, bar lamps switching off one by one with satisfying clicks. Josh flipped the sign on the door to CLOSED, the painted letters reflecting faintly in the glass as the streetlamps outside winked on.

They walked out the back door, locking it behind them. The evening air wrapped around them in a cool, damp hug, smelling of water, fresh earth, and the faint tang of someone grilling a couple of streets over.

Grass dampened the soles of their shoes as they crossed the narrow strip of lawn and picked up the trail toward the rocks. Crickets had already started their chorus, a steady, high-pitched underpinning to the soft shush of the lake.

The rocky outcropping looked the same and different all at once. The lichen spotted stone still jutted out into the water like a blunt question mark, but Josh had laid a weathered blanket over the flatter part and wedged a lantern in a crack, its warm light pooling over the fabric.

Novah's bare toes curled as she slipped off her sandals, the rock cool and slightly rough under her feet. The lantern threw a halo around them, leaving the water beyond in gentle, shifting shadow.

"Look at you, planning ahead," she said. "No gravel digging into my ass this time."

"Growth," he said gravely. "I hear it's what adults do."

They sat, shoulders brushing, knees bent. The blanket had the faint scent of laundry detergent and lake air. Josh stretched his legs out, boots tapping lightly against the rock.

For a while, they just watched the water. Small waves lapped at the stone with soft, rhythmic slaps. Somewhere across the lake, a dog barked twice before being called in. Frogs added their low, throaty croaks to the cricket chorus.

"It feels…quieter," Novah said at last. "In my head."

Josh tipped his head toward her. The lantern light gilded the gentle line of her jaw, caught in the silver glint of the small hoop in her ear.

"Yeah," he said. "Less sirens. More…dishwasher hum."

She laughed softly. “That’s the most domestic metaphor I’ve ever heard from you.”

“Get used to it,” he said. “You married a potter with a mortgage and a favorite grocery aisle.”

She stilled, the word married hanging between them like a breath.

“You proposing to me with a dishwasher metaphor?” she asked. There was no panic in her voice, just amusement and something bright under it.

He rolled a small pebble between his fingers, feeling its smoothness. “Not today,” he said. “Not exactly. I’ve got ideas for that one.” His mouth quirked. “But I have been thinking.”

“That phrase should come with a warning label,” she said lightly. “Continue.”

“We did the big scary step,” he said. “Moving in. Renting my place. Closing the studio and opening it again. Calling my aunt.” The memory of Lila’s hug on her front porch, the way her perfume had smelled faintly of lavender and old paper, brushed his mind. “Now it feels like the next things don’t have to be so…all or nothing. They can be pieces.”

“Like?” She turned toward him, tucking one leg under the other, her knee pressing warm against his thigh.

"Like," he said slowly, "maybe talking to Lila about those photo albums she mentioned. Seeing if there are pictures of me before the crash that don't live in a case file. Like adding a kids' clay class twice a month in the studio and seeing which ones light up when their hands get dirty. Like making sure there's room in your office for a second desk when I inevitably start sketching in there instead of my studio."

She hummed, a pleased, low sound. "You want to invade my office?"

"I want to share the space where you make the words," he said. "Maybe eventually share…other things." He shrugged, a little self-conscious. "Rings. Names. Stuff." The last word came out softer.

Her breath hitched, then evened. "Okay," she said quietly. "Good to know that's rattling around in there." She tapped his temple lightly with one finger. "For the record, my brain has been shopping for kid-proof coffee tables for months. Even if those kids end up being nieces and nephews, or Hank's grandkids, or just the horde from your clay classes."

A warmth that wasn't whiskey or adrenaline spread through his chest. He could almost see it—small hands smearing clay on his work apron, crayons on the coffee table, a pair of little boots kicked off by Novah's front door.

"Guess we're both contaminated," he said, his voice roughening.

She leaned sideways until her shoulder rested against his bicep, the weight familiar. "The good kind of contamination," she said. "Like starter dough."

He laughed, low and surprised. "That's the most on-brand metaphor I've ever heard from you."

They fell quiet again, into the kind of silence that no longer needed filling. The lake breathed around them. The lantern flame flickered once, then steadied.

After a while, Novah slid her hand into his, fingers threading through easily, like they'd been made to fit. Her skin was cool on top, warm in the spaces between.

"You remember the first night out here?" she asked. "You were vibrating out of your skin. I was pretending I wasn't."

He winced fondly. "I remember being pretty sure I'd messed everything up beyond repair," he said. "And thinking if I just touched you enough, maybe the noise in my head would stop."

"Did it?" she asked.

"For about five minutes at a time," he said honestly. "Then it roared back." He turned his head, letting his temple rest briefly against hers. "Now it feels more like background radio than a fire alarm."

“Progress,” she murmured.
He squeezed her hand. “You?”

“Months ago, I was terrified I’d turned you into a character without your consent,” she said. “That I’d written us into a box we couldn’t get out of.” She huffed a small laugh. “Now the only thing that scares me is missing a deadline because I keep stopping to watch you sketch.”

“You like my sketching that much?” he asked, mock offended.

She turned her face up, lantern light catching her smile. “I like you that much,” she said simply.

The words settled on him with the same quiet certainty they’d carried the night he’d finally said them back.

He lifted their joined hands and pressed his mouth to her knuckles, the faint tang of ink and salt on her skin.

“Home is a who,” she said softly, echoing the line from her dedication.

He nodded, lips still against her hand. “And you,” he said. “You’re the ‘who.’”

She shifted, swinging one leg over so she straddled his lap, careful of the uneven stone. Her hands framed his face, thumbs brushing along his jaw where the evening stubble rasped under her touch.

“Then I guess we stay put,” she said. “In my too-big house that is now our too-big house, five minutes from your studio, with your renters breaking in the porch swing tomorrow.”

“And your boathouse full of half-finished manuscripts and my coffee mugs,” he added.

“And this rock,” she said, glancing down, the corner of her mouth curving. “Reserved indefinitely.”

He smiled up at her, the familiar combination of desire and something steadier sliding through him. The urgency that had lived in his muscles months ago—the compulsion to grab and hold before the world took things away—had been replaced by something that felt suspiciously like trust.

He pulled her down into a kiss that was slow, deep, and unhurried. The stone under them was solid. The water around them kept its gentle rhythm. Above, the first stars pricked through the darkening sky.

When they broke apart, foreheads touching, breaths mingling, the moment didn’t feel like an ending so much as a resting point on a road they’d decided to walk together.

“C’mon,” she whispered after a while. “Let’s go home. I want to see your face when you realize I reorganized your side of the closet.”

He groaned theatrically as he helped her stand, their fingers still linked. “Barely days in and you’re already messing with my hangers,” he said.

“Partnership, baby,” she replied, threading her arm through his as they picked their way back across the rocks. “We share the space. We share the mess. We share the future.”

The lantern light winked out behind them as they walked toward the path, leaving the rock to the lake and the stars. Ahead, the warm squares of their windows glowed through the trees, steady and sure, like beacons.

A Note from the Author

Thank you for joining me in the pages of *Reserved Indefinitely.*

This is for the readers who find a piece of themselves in the quiet spaces between these pages. *Reserved Indefinitely* is more than a title; it is a promise that certain places, people, and seasons of our lives stay held for us, even when everything else feels uncertain. The cabin on the lake, the unfinished conversations, the second chances we were sure we'd never get again—all of it lives here, waiting for you to return as many times as you need.

When this story began, it was only a question: What happens when someone who has given up on being chosen discovers that a place—and a person—have been quietly saving them a seat all along? That question grew into a grumpy-sunshine clash on a secluded shoreline, into neighbors who would rather argue than admit how much they care, and into a heroine who has spent so long surviving that she almost forgets how to want more.

If you have ever stayed too long in a situation that hurt, or walked away from one before it could, this book is for you. If you know what it is to crave both solitude and connection, to guard your heart and still hope someone might notice the way it beats, this book is for you, too.

Thank you for taking a chance on these characters and this world. Your time, your trust, and your willingness to feel alongside fictional strangers are gifts no author is ever owed and never takes for granted. May these pages remind you that nothing in your story is wasted, and that somewhere, something good is already being held, *Reserved Indefinitely*, with your name on it.

Rhea Morrigan

About the Author

Rhea Morrigan is a contemporary romance author whose stories blend Appalachian grit, heartfelt emotion, and the raw spirit of mountain living. From her home on the Cumberland Plateau in Tennessee, Rhea draws inspiration from misty mornings, soulful walks through the woods, and the warmth of small-town life, all brought to life in her much-loved Buck Hole Hollow Series and other steamy, deeply human romance novels.

A paralegal and content strategist by day, Rhea crafts stories at night that capture resilient heroines, flawed but redeemable heroes, and emotionally honest relationships facing real-world challenges. Whether weaving legal drama, blue-collar ingenuity, or second chances into her books, she writes with a commitment to authenticity and a deep love for the southern settings she calls home.

Rhea lives with her loyal German shepherd and her spirited umbrella cockatoo, and finds joy in crocheting, pyrography, and, most of all, sharing stories of hope, heartbreak, and the healing power of love. With every book, she invites readers into worlds where romance is as rugged and beautiful as the mountains themselves.

Other Books by Rhea Morrigan

Discover more heartfelt romance from Rhea Morrigan, where Appalachian grit, strong heroines, and swoon-worthy love stories come alive in every book. From the deeply emotional Buck Hole Hollow Series to stand-alone stories of redemption and second chances, Rhea crafts each book to sweep you away into small-town secrets, family bonds, legal drama, and unforgettable characters.

If you enjoyed this book, please consider leaving a review on your favorite retailer, social platform and/or Goodreads. Your reviews help authors reach new readers and keep the stories coming. Your support truly makes a difference!

Romance

The Buck Hole Hollow Series

Adley

Marley

Sarah

Shannon

Brynne

Jade

Stand Alone Novels

A Twisted Infinity Christmas

Short Stories

The Last Drink

The Watauga Lake Series

A 12-book steamy romance series that is in the works. You can find it here:

rheamorrigan.com/books/watauga-lake-series

You can find all of my books on Amazon in paperback and e-book formats.

Where to Find Rhea

Looking for new stories that stir your heart, fuel your imagination, and leave you craving more? Connect with Rhea Morrigan—the romance author whose emotionally rich books are winning over contemporary fiction fans everywhere. On this page, discover all the ways to follow Rhea, explore her series, and buy romance books that deliver unforgettable journeys, complex characters, and the right balance of passion and drama.

Rhea Morrigan's Website: RheaMorrigan.com

Good Reads Profile:
goodreads.com/author/show/8090471.Rhea_Morrigan

Rhea's Amazon Page: https://amzn.to/4pkWCPJ

www.ingramcontent.com/pod-product-compliance
Lightning Source LLC
LaVergne TN
LVHW050915080826
845145LV00001B/87

* 9 7 8 1 9 6 9 0 1 2 0 6 8 *